SILVERSTORM

Suzanne Cass

S C

STORM CLOUD
PRESS

Silverstorm

Storm Cloud Press, Perth Australia

Copyright © 2022 by Suzanne Cass

Edits by Evermore Editing

Cover by Vikncharlie

All rights reserved.

This is a work of fiction. Names, characters, places and incidents are products of the authors imagination or are used fictitiously. Any resemblance to actual events, locales, organisations, or persons, living or dead, is entirely coincidental.

To Rebecca, good friends forgive all typos.

CHAPTER ONE

Aria Cusack drove slowly down the main street, watching everything pass by through her open window. It all looked exactly the same. But why was she surprised? In the eight years she'd been away from Stevensville, nothing had changed. The sleepy little town, set in the foothills of the Bitterroot Mountains, Montana, was still a haven for the outdoorsman who liked hunting, fishing, or biking, as well as the rugged cowboys who lived and worked in the surrounding agricultural areas. And that was about where the attraction finished.

Main Street's historic storefronts with their pretty awnings and rows of potted flowers hadn't altered one bit. Trucks and SUVs lined the streets, parked in the angled bays along the curb. People ambled along the sidewalks, and cafe tables spilled out onto the street. It was all so *normal*. The rest of the suburban streets leading to semi-rural properties on the outskirts, and eventually graduating to ranches and agricultural farms as far as the eye could see, were all still much the same, too. Some might call it quaint and unique. Aria called it boring, cloying, claustrophobic. It was one of the many reasons she'd left; to get away from this dingy little backwater. There'd been other reasons, too—much darker reasons—but she brushed them aside, not wanting to dwell on her shitty life.

If only circumstances beyond her control hadn't brought her crawling back to her hometown. The picturesque town might like to flaunt its historic roots, but Aria's own history here was locked firmly in a carefully constructed box inside her head, where she could keep it safely hidden away and not think about it. Except, now that she was back, pushing those memories down was getting harder and harder to do.

Her long, dark hair swirled in the breeze, and she pulled it over her shoulder to stop it from getting in her eyes. Shivering, she wound up her window, the chilly air raising goose bumps on her skin beneath her thin sweater. It was only November, but the fall sunshine was weak. Winter always hit Stevensville earlier and harder than in other, less mountainous states. She'd need to get hold of a thick, winter jacket before long. Living in the coastal city of Portland for the past four years had made her soft. At least, that's what her father would say.

The storefronts lining Main Street thinned out as she entered the western end of town, replaced by warehouses and a mechanic shop. She cruised past the Montana Chocolate Company, her mouth watering at the thought of the delicacies she knew were inside. The best chocolate this side of the Rocky Mountains was their motto, and they may well be right. Aria had tasted a free sample the other day when she'd ventured inside, but there was no way her meagre funds would allow the purchase of such a luxury, so she'd slunk out again.

Soon the suburbs turned to open fields, and her mood improved. Changing up a gear, she put her foot down on the gas pedal as she came to the city limits. Her old, gray Subaru grumbled a little, then slowly built up speed.

Patting the steering wheel affectionately, she said, "Come

on, Gandalf, you can do it." The car was on its last legs, but she couldn't afford to replace it, and it'd got her from Portland to Stevensville in once piece, so she treated him gently and nursed him along. She'd purchased Gandalf four years ago, when she'd arrived in Portland, and the car had done a great job of getting her around. People laughed at her when they found out she'd given her car the name of the great wizard from the Tolkien books. But she shrugged off their hilarity. Her Subaru may be long in the tooth, but by some form of magic, it'd kept her safe for this long. Even offering her shelter when she needed it.

The road stretched out in front, and her chest expanded a little. While she hadn't missed the town itself, the Bitterroot Valley was definitely one of the most beautiful spots she'd ever seen. Green pine trees marched up to the imposing silhouette of St. Mary Peak, the highest mountain in the area, stark and barren, running parallel to the highway. Although she couldn't see it, the Bitterroot River would be winding its way through the foothills, hidden by a line of trees. She remembered swimming in the clear, pure water of the river as a child in the summer, listening to the musical burble as it rippled over the stones and around boulders.

Perhaps this place wasn't all bad.

Then Aria shivered again, but this time it wasn't from the cold. Her mind had switched back to her encounter with her father, Tango Cusack, three days ago. Much like the town of Stevensville, he hadn't changed, either. In fact, he'd probably gotten worse. Even more mistrustful, if that were possible. The way his eyes had screwed up, becoming tiny pinholes as he opened the front door a crack and spied her standing on the veranda. The way his gravelly voice had grated as he'd said, "What're you doing back in town? You were better off staying away. Now scram." The way he'd spat a glob of mucus through the opening of the door that landed at her feet, making her scramble backward so she nearly fell down the rickety stairs. And the way he'd slammed the door in her face with a bang of finality.

Aria tried to put her father out of her mind. She shouldn't have expected any more. Just because she hoped time would've softened him a little, she'd known deep down that wouldn't be true. But hope was a slippery thing. It filled you with ideas of forgiveness and the possibility of something better. She was stupid to have let hope in. But Aria had nowhere else to go. Her father and her sister were her only remaining family. She'd wished that by coming back to her hometown, she might find some redemption. Heal old wounds. Try and get past what'd happened. Aria was a realist, and she knew her kin wouldn't welcome her with open arms. But still… Even a roof over her head would be nice at this point. Because she was fast running out of money. And running out of options.

After her disastrous encounter with Tango, Aria had been putting off trying to locate Iliana, her sister. Iliana had married some local rancher and was living on a farm somewhere outside town. Aria had received a wedding invitation two years ago, but had put off replying. In the end, she'd left it too late. Or at least that's what she told herself. Now she regretted not attending the wedding. Regretted throwing away the invitation, so she no longer had her contact details. Regretted throwing away that tenuous connection Iliana had offered her. She wondered if their relationship could still be mended.

Part of the reason she'd gone to see Tango was to ask for an address for her sister. She knew the last name of the guy Iliana had married was Doncaster. But he must be relatively new in town, because she didn't remember anyone with that last name. Her visit to her father hadn't turned out like she'd planned, however, and so she'd have to resort to asking careful questions around town. But even after three days, she still hadn't worked up the courage to pose the question to any of the locals, preferring to keep a low profile, scared someone would recognize her. Which was kind of stupid, because someone *was* going to recognize her, sooner or later. This was her hometown, after all. She was just putting off the inevitable. Not wanting to see the pity enter their eyes when they remembered who she was; what'd happened to her family. Or see their condemnation when they found out about her *little problem*.

Shaking her head to clear it of all the painful memories, she grasped the steering wheel tighter. She needed to concentrate on where she was going. She had a job interview at Stargazer Ranch, a few miles out of town. And while she knew where it was, she'd never actually visited there before.

Stargazer Ranch was well known around town. Mostly, it had a good reputation, and the owners, Dean and Naomi, were well-liked by the locals. Aria had heard plenty of stories about the luxurious resort during her childhood. They attracted many rich clientele, and even their small share of celebrities, eager to experience the Montana mountains while staying in the lap of luxury.

This interview might be her only chance. A change in her fortune. The job was for a social media and marketing position. Aria had been studying graphic design with a minor in advertising at Portland State University, and had been halfway through her last year before she was forced to leave. She loved graphic design, had a knack for it, a real flair some of her professors had told her, and her grades had been excellent. She'd been using some of those skills at a part-time job at an ad agency, working in her spare time when she wasn't studying. The people she'd worked with had been young and motivated, pushing her to expand her ideas, think outside the box when it came to marketing. It was a bright and vibrant place to work. But there'd been a reshuffle of the staff a month ago, and the CEO of the company decided they needed someone to take up her position full time. Of course, she was offered that position, but she couldn't do both, not work full time and finish her university degree. So, with a heavy heart, she'd left the company. That'd been the start of her downward spiral, even though she hadn't known it at the time. She'd been confident of finding another part-time job fairly easily. And Beau had seemed understanding at the time, saying he didn't mind supporting her for a few weeks until she could find a new job. How wrong that sentiment had turned out to be. The bastard.

At least she had a glowing reference from her old job. It was the one thing in her favor. If she could get this position, she'd be able to earn some money. In a few weeks, she might even be able to afford a place to stay, and a proper meal, instead of existing on stolen candy bars and sleeping in her car. She *needed* somewhere safe to stay, and soon.

With a guilty glance, she looked down at the small pile of chocolate sitting on the passenger seat. The older woman tending the cashier in the milk bar hadn't even noticed when Aria walked past with five candy bars stuffed in her pockets. The place had been packed, and the woman looked run off her feet. The guilt almost made her confess her crime right there, but her rumbling stomach had forced her to keep on walking.

"See what you've reduced me to, Beau," she grumbled, but only Gandalf was listening. Beau was her stupid boyfriend. No, stupid ex-boyfriend, she had to keep reminding herself. He was part of the reason she was in this pickle in the first place.

A car appeared in her rearview mirror. She concentrated on the road ahead, slowing a little to allow the vehicle to overtake her. But the car didn't pass as she expected, instead, it hugged her rear bumper.

"Crap, go around me," she urged the driver behind her.

Suddenly, red and blue flashing lights lit up her rearview mirror.

Crap, crap, double crap. This was the last thing she needed. To be pulled over by the sheriff. Not that she was doing anything wrong. But she couldn't be late for the interview.

Aria pulled over to the side of the road when it was safe and watched the cruiser pull in behind her. An officer opened his door and began walking down the white line at the edge of the bitumen toward her, his hat pulled down low. She rolled down her window with a sigh of resignation. Right before he reached her window, she remembered the candy bars and knocked them into the footwell on the passenger side, hoping he wouldn't notice them down there.

"Good morning, ma'am," he said, standing next to the window and leaning down to stare at her from beneath the brim of his hat.

Not anymore, she thought sullenly, but turned to smile brightly at him.

"Morning, Deputy," she replied, noting the insignia on his uniform.

"I noticed you have a taillight out. And that rear tire of yours is bald," the young deputy continued.

Holy crap. Aria hardly heard the words as she stared at the man in shock. It was Jude Wilder. *The* Jude Wilder. The guy she'd had a crush on for most of her senior high school years. A crush so bad, she'd even written a poem on the back of the girls' toilet stall door as a teenage token of her love for him. But her love had been unrequited, because it seemed Jude hadn't even known she'd existed.

It'd been eight long years since she'd last seen him, but now she was glad that one thing in this town hadn't changed.

Those hazel eyes and full lips were just as delicious as they'd always been. Just as magnetic. But, oh my, he'd grown nicely from the gangly youth she'd once known. Now his shoulders were so broad, he filled out that brown uniform in all the right places. And biceps. Holy cow, did he have killer biceps beneath the fabric of his shirt. She shut her mouth with a click, hoping he hadn't noticed her staring. And drooling, just a little. He'd been gorgeous back then. But now he'd grown up to become devastating.

Jude didn't seem to have noticed her reaction, or even recognized her, thank God. "Can I see your driver's license please, ma'am," he asked, removing his hat and placing it on the roof of her car. His brown hair was curly and luxurious, cut short on the sides, but left a little longer on top.

She fumbled in her purse, trying to rid herself of the image of running her fingers through that hair. Handing it over, she discerned the exact moment he saw her name on the license, because he looked up to meet a gaze.

"Aria Cusack? Is that you? I remember you from school. You're Iliana's sister." So he had known she'd existed. Her heart beat a little faster with the knowledge.

"Ah… Yeah, that's me," she replied softly, not quite meeting his eyes. Her elation died a quick death, however, because she wasn't sure if it was a good thing he remembered her. She was skating on thin ice when it came to the law. The last thing she wanted was to draw attention to herself.

"You back in town, then?" He handed her driver's license back and leaned in a little farther, a wide smile creasing his face. His eyes met hers, and she watched as they widened, his gaze sweeping over her body and face. What did he see? Was he cataloguing her changes, too? Longer hair, maybe a few extra pounds. But it was on the inside where most of the changes had taken place, where he would never see them.

"Yeah, for a little while," she hedged, not returning his

smile. Which was harder than she thought, because, goddamnit, Jude Wilder was smiling at her. It seemed as if he expected more details, but she didn't know what to tell him, so she blurted, "I've come back to spend some time with Iliana. And maybe catch up with my dad." Lies and half-truths, all of them, but he wouldn't know that.

"Okay." He considered her for a second. "She married Craig Doncaster. He took over the old Skyridge Ranch. Nice guy. I was at their wedding a couple of years ago. I don't remember seeing you there." He tilted his head to the side, a bit like a curious puppy, the motion so endearing, she wanted to capture his face in a photo just so she could look at it later on.

"Ah… No, you're right. I couldn't make it to the wedding. I had a…a really important exam, and they wouldn't let me re-sit it later," she finished lamely. "That's why I'm back to visit her now."

"Hmm." He didn't sound like he believed her. "Are you staying with your sister, then?" he asked. But Aria didn't miss the deputy's astute glance at the piles of stuff crammed in the back of her car. Her two bags stuffed full of clothes, shoes thrown haphazardly on the floor, a picnic basket and some pots and pans she'd stolen from Beau's place before she left, and a pillow and a comforter. All the things she needed to start a new life, but with nowhere to stay, she had nowhere to store all her belongings.

She could see the cogs in his head turning. If she was staying with her sister, why was all this stuff still jammed in her car? She saw the exact second when he worked it out, in the hard line of his mouth as his eyes came back to hers. He knew she was sleeping in her car.

It shouldn't be surprising to her how close to landing back in the shit she was. She'd been balancing on a knife-edge for the past few years, just making ends meet, juggling a low-paying job and a university degree, living with her boyfriend in a run-down place where the rent was low, but still took most of her money. All it'd taken was one little wrong step, one *little problem* to bring her house of cards crashing down around her. And now she was forced to sleep in her car and steal candy bars to survive.

"I'm sorry," she said, "but I'm on my way to an interview, and I don't want to be late."

"What? Oh, sorry. Right." Jude seemed to recover his professional veneer. "Well, I won't issue you with a fine this time. But you need to get those tires replaced and that taillight mended as soon as you get back to town. Okay?"

"Yes. Yes, of course I will," she promised. More lies. She couldn't even afford to put a roof over her head, let alone buy new tires. At least he'd saved her from having to pay the fine, but now she was going to have to be extra careful and try to avoid him at all costs, so he didn't find out the depth of her deceit.

"Where's your interview?" he asked, retrieving his hat from the roof of the car.

"At Stargazer Ranch," she replied, hoping he would just get in his car and drive away.

But he didn't. Instead, he pursed his lips. "That's a great place to work. Nice people. I'm actually heading up there myself to see the owner, Dean."

Aria's heart sank. Crap.

"I'll follow you, if you like. Make sure you get there in one piece. Do you know the way?"

"Oh, you don't have to do that," she argued. "I'll be fine. And yes, I know the way." How could she convince him to just go about his business and leave her alone? But one look at the determined furrow between his brows and she knew he wasn't taking no for an answer. And she shouldn't be arguing with a deputy anyway. She should just keep her mouth shut.

Fine, she'd let him follow her up there, even though she'd be sweating bullets all the way, wondering if he was going to find something else wrong with her car, or decide to confront her on her lies about her living arrangements. "Whatever. No problems," she conceded with barely concealed frustration.

"You get going. I won't be far behind you," he said pleasantly enough and turned to walk back to his car. Even though she was cross with him and at herself for landing in this situation, she couldn't help but watch his nicely toned butt and long legs striding away from her in the side mirror. Was he sporting a slight limp? She watched him walk, and there was definitely a hitch in his stride. But it only made him more appealing; the fact he wasn't one hundred percent perfect. Why did the man have to be so good-looking and so annoying all at the same time? And why had the only man from this two-bit town to have left an indelible imprint on her soul, shown up in her life the minute she returned?

CHAPTER TWO

Jude followed the gray Subaru at a safe distance. But his mind was only half on the road as he turned over his short conversation with the woman in the car in front.

Aria Cusack. That name was a blast from the past. He hadn't recognized her at first, even though the familiar shape of her face and the long, dark hair had tickled something at the back of his memory. It wasn't until he'd read the name on the driver's license he'd connected the dots.

Aria had left town the day she'd turned eighteen, and he didn't really blame her. Her father was an overbearing prick who'd kept her and her sister isolated from the rest of the community. And then there was the thing that'd happened with their mother. Now the father lived practically as a hermit, with only his conspiracy theories and rantings about some sort of secret cult to keep him company. Jude remembered Aria as a quiet, shy girl, and when she'd left, no one really noticed she was gone, apart from perhaps her sister. But he also remembered that slightly ethereal quality Aria had about her. A willowy, fragile beauty that he'd noticed from afar. But she'd been two years younger than him, and outside the scope of his group of friends. He'd had his soccer mates, and his rowdy clique of sporty friends, followed around by the pretty girls always trying to get a date. The popular group, if you liked, although he hated the connotations of that word.

Aria still had that ethereal beauty. Long, dark hair that fell around her shoulders, and dark-brown eyes—so dark they were almost black—fringed with the longest lashes he'd ever seen that'd studied him warily. And that quick smile she'd flashed, wide mouth and full lips showing off a row of perfectly white teeth, had him catching his breath. But it wasn't the fine beauty of her face that he remembered now, but the cute way she wrinkled up her nose when she smiled. It made her both endearing and irresistible.

Her car had been crammed full of belongings, easy to assume that perhaps she hadn't unpacked when she'd got to her sisters. But he'd seen it before and he knew it for what it was. Aria was sleeping in her car. For whatever reason, she'd lied to him about staying with Iliana. Jude considered paying a visit out to the Doncaster Ranch. He and Craig had become acquaintances over the past few years after Craig moved to town and bought up the run-down ranch a few miles out past Stargazer. Craig had joined the same karate dojo as Jude, and they'd struck up a friendship of sorts. Plus, Jude had been in the same year as Iliana at high school, which was perhaps why he'd been invited to the wedding. But then, he decided it was probably none of his business. Not yet, at least. It wasn't against the law to sleep in your car. But he wondered at her circumstances to be reduced to sleeping rough.

The Subaru slowed in front as they crested a hill and the large stone wall marking the entrance to Stargazer Ranch appeared over the rise. Following her car onto the gravel road, Jude opened his window and drew in a deep breath of clean mountain air. He loved this place, and could see why resort customers came back year after year. Individual log cabins slipped past on either side of the road as they wound their way into the foothills. Dean had built twenty luxury cabins on the property, all completely secluded by the tall pine trees, just the way the guests liked it, and had recently added three more cabins for the staff. People came all year round to partake in the many activities the resort offered, like horseback riding or hiking in the summer, or skiing and dogsledding in the winter.

He drove his cruiser through a tunnel of overhanging branches and emerged into a huge, open area of rolling hills and fields. And there, nestled into a shallow valley, sat the main lodge. When Dean and Naomi had bought it seventeen years before, it had good bones, with soaring ceilings and lots of large windows to take in the views; it just needed some remodeling, and a whole lot of TLC. Now, it could almost be called a log mansion as it rambled across the hillside over three levels. There was a communal area, a huge, five-star restaurant and a vaulted foyer ceiling that opened up to large windows at the top to show off the big, never-ending sky, and ten luxury rooms for people who wanted the lodge experience but didn't need a whole cabin to themselves. The big kitchen out back was where the gourmet meals were created and was also where the staff often came together for communal meals. Jude joined them on the odd occasion when he wasn't working in a professional capacity. Dean and Naomi had private quarters nestled on the top level of the building.

It was now midmorning as he pulled into a marked spot in the large parking lot beside the battered Subaru. From here, he could see the undercover area at ground level, where a group of guests were playing ping-pong.

"Wow, this is...amazing," Aria said as she stepped out of her car, head tilted up to stare at the lodge.

"Is this your first time out here?" he asked.

She merely nodded, eyes wide as she swiveled her head,

trying to take everything in at once. Now that she was standing, he could see her hair almost reached down past her mid-back, and it blew in long strands around her face. His gaze roamed up her figure, taking in black, heeled boots, jeans and a light-green crop top that bared her midriff, showing off her lean hips and a slender waist. A gust of wind that might've come straight off the top of Canyon Peak whistled through the parking lot, and she wrapped her thin arms around her middle and shivered.

"I forgot how cold this place gets," she muttered. He had a sudden urge to offer her his uniform jacket, but she reached into the rear door of her car and emerged with a denim jacket, which she slung over her shoulders.

"How do I look?" she asked.

"What? Ah…"

"I mean, do I look okay? For the interview."

"Oh, right." He saw the fine tremor in her hands and suddenly understood that she was nervous. "Yes, you look fine. Naomi isn't one for fancy dresses or expensive shoes," he went on to assure her. "She'll love you," he gushed and then wished he'd stopped at *you look fine*. It wasn't like him to trip over his own tongue. And it wasn't like him to give out compliments like they were candy. But she clearly needed moral support, and it seemed like the chivalrous thing to do.

"Thanks. I really need this job." The last few words were muttered through gritted teeth.

"Follow me. I'll take you to Penny, she'll know where you should go for the interview," he said, ignoring the implied desperation in her words.

He led her up the stairs to the first floor, hoping his calf didn't choose this moment to cramp up. He was back on full duties, but his leg still twinged every now and then. They went in through the large, glass doors, where it was much warmer out of the wind. There was an open-plan reception area and lots of big and small sitting rooms scattered throughout the first floor for guests to gather in. A dozen people milled around the main reception area now, probably guests getting ready to check out. Jude waved at Penny, who was behind the reception desk, talking to an older couple. She beckoned him over, and he threaded his way through the crowd. But when he looked back to make sure Aria was following, he saw her gawping up at the huge vaulted ceiling and the enormous stone fireplace that took center stage. She was staring so hard, she stumbled into a guest and then apologized profusely and hurried after him. It was cute that she found this place so overawing, and he couldn't help grinning at her.

"Excuse me just a second," Penny said to the couple, and came around the desk to give Jude a hug. "Great to see you," she said, kissing his cheek lightly. "I was just saying to Clayton that we hadn't seen you for a few weeks. How's the leg coming along?" She let him go and returned to her position behind the counter, nodding at the couple to let them know she'd be with them in a second.

"The leg's good," he replied. "I finished rehab a month ago, and I got clearance to be back on full duties."

"That's fantastic." Penny beamed at him, shaking her long, blonde braid over her shoulder. Penny and Clayton had become good friends over the past few months. It was so great to see their love grow, especially after the hell they'd been through. A hell he'd also been a part of, helping to rescue them from a gunfight at an old fishing shack. He'd been wounded in the process, shot in the calf, but he'd do it all again, if he had to. He was serious about his job. Protect and serve weren't just words to Jude, they were his motto.

"I'm here to see Dean," he said, settling his face into a slightly serious frown. "He called me to come take a look at…" He didn't finish his sentence, aware that the older couple were now watching him with great interest.

"Dean's up in the machinery shed. Something about Cat throwing a hissy fit because she couldn't get the correct part to fix the old tractor."

"Right, I'll go up and find him in a minute." Jude turned and motioned Aria around to his side. She was still gawking at the grandeur all around.

"And this is Aria. She's here for an interview."

Penny's face brightened. "Ah ha, for the marketing job. Hi, nice to meet you. Naomi is meeting with another applicant right now, but she won't be long. If you take a seat over there," Penny pointed to a chair behind the reception, next to the door to Dean's office, "she'll be out in a moment."

"Thank you. Nice to meet you, as well." Aria gave Penny a wide smile, but clutched her bag to her side and stared around, as if not sure about all these people.

Aria looked a little like a fish out of water, and Jude, wanting to reassure her, took her by the elbow and led her to the chair, leaning down to whisper in her ear, "Just be yourself. Naomi much prefers people who are down to earth and trustworthy. She's not impressed by airs and graces." She tucked her long hair behind her ear and he caught a trace of something floral. Shampoo, perhaps. She might be sleeping in her car, but she smelled like she'd at least had a shower this morning. Actually, she smelled wonderful, reminding him of the roses his mother used to grow in her garden. Sweet and pure.

"Thank you," she whispered back, sitting down gingerly, holding her bag in her lap. Then she looked up into his face, spearing him with those dark-brown eyes and he was suddenly frozen to the spot.

He cleared his throat and straightened up.

"Good luck," he replied, his voice a little gruffer than he intended. "And don't forget to replace those tires," he added, remembering he needed to keep his official face on. It wouldn't do to let anyone else see how Aria affected him.

"Oh. No, I won't." But she said it in such a way that Jude knew she'd forgotten all about the problems with her car already.

Penny cast him an odd glance as he strode past reception, but he ignored her. He was just being nice. Making sure Aria was in the right place and in the right frame of mind for the interview, that was all. He would've done the same for any old friend who needed his help. Old acquaintances… whatever the hell she was.

Pushing open the enormous glass door, Jude couldn't help one last glance over his shoulder. Aria was still sitting alone and stiff in her chair, eyes wide, like a startled rabbit.

Just before the door closed behind him, he saw a woman exit the door to Dean's office; one of the other interviewees. She was tall, dressed in a power suit and towering high heels, blonde hair pulled back in a neat chignon. The epitome of a classy, professional woman. He saw Aria's face fall as she watched the other woman stride past, and he had to resist a terrible urge telling him to turn around and go back to her. Jude knew in his heart of hearts that a hard-edged businesswoman wasn't what Naomi was looking for. But Aria wouldn't understand that. There was nothing he could do for her now, however. It was up to her to charm Naomi into giving her the job. He crossed his fingers and loped down the stairs.

Most given mornings, Dean would've been playing the gregarious host to his guests, who were checking out. He loved to talk. He was good at using his southern charm to captivate his visitors, and they all left feeling as if they were somehow special. Which they were, in Dean's eyes. He wanted to make sure every single person who visited his ranch had a great time.

It was this quality that kept the guests returning to Stargazer over and over again.

But Dean had sounded a little frazzled on the phone this morning when he'd called to ask Jude to come out.

Jude decided to walk up to the machinery shed. He could drive his cruiser up, it'd be quicker, but he was enjoying the fresh fall air. The sun had appeared from behind a bank of fluffy clouds, lighting up the mountains in the background, making the green pastures seem almost iridescent. Five minutes later, he rounded the edge of the large, red barn structure and entered the gaping doorway. The smell of grease and dust hit him first, then he heard voices, but it took a few seconds for his eyes to adjust to the gloom. Dean and his mechanic, Cat, were at the other end of the shed, peering into the guts of an old tractor set on a square of concrete next to a long bench containing a myriad of tools.

"Surely, it's time to get a new one, Dean. This tractor is as old as the hills. You keep asking me to repair it, but I think this time it's beyond repair." Cat straightened and put her hands on her hips. Wearing a pair of gray dungarees, her spiked blonde hair stood out in the fluorescent lights. Jude knew the cost of repairs wouldn't be an issue for Dean. He was just a sentimental at heart. He loved old things and couldn't bear to get rid of them.

Cat turned and saw Jude first, smiling and waving him inside. As Dean straightened, she rolled her eyes in her boss's direction but kept her lips firmly shut. Cat had a feisty tongue to go with her give-no-shit attitude and her many tattoos. But she also had a heart of gold and would give you the shirt off her back if she thought you needed it. She and Levi, the local park ranger, were recently married in a summer wedding that'd been held at the ranch.

"I hope you've come to help me convince Dean that this old dinosaur is ready for the tip."

19

"Not on your life," Dean bellowed. "This old gal is a work of art. They don't make them like this anymore." Dean was in his late fifties, wearing his customary plaid shirt, sheepskin vest, and blue jeans. He was tall and commanding. The light sprinkle of gray at his temples, in contrast to his dark hair, might give away his age, but his face was warm and welcoming, almost childlike, so alive with humor and excitement. Jude liked Dean. There weren't many people in the area that didn't.

"Yes, with good reason," Cat mumbled.

Jude smiled to himself. Cat loved bright, shiny new machines. She rode a Triumph motorcycle, a big touring bike, all black and chrome, and Cat loved it as if it were her child; the only thing she loved more in this world was Levi.

While Dean loved nothing more than to preserve a piece of antiquity. It was one of the reasons he'd been able to bring the lodge back to its full glory, his attention to detail and the fact he didn't care how long a project took.

The two of them were like chalk and cheese, and Jude wouldn't like to put a bet on who was going to win this particular showdown. And he sure as hell wasn't going to get in the middle of it.

"Morning, Cat." He tipped his hat in her direction. "Dean, you said you had something important you wanted to discuss? Do you want to go outside and chat?"

Cat's crystal-blue eyes sharpened at Jude's tone. "What's going on, Dean?"

Anyone else might see Cat's razor-edged words as a tad insubordinate toward her boss, but Jude knew Cat's history. And he also knew that Dean thought of his staff as more an extension of his own family. Just as Jude guessed he would, Dean ignored Cat's implied accusation and cut straight to the chase.

"No, we can talk in here. I don't mind if Cat joins us, she

may even tell me I'm being overly suspicious and to stop being an old fool."

"What's going on?" Cat asked again, but Jude caught the edge of worry in her gaze.

"Two of my cattle have gone missing in the past few weeks." Dean shrugged his big shoulders. Then he held up a hand and added, "And before you ask, yes, I'm positive. We weren't sure about the first one. Sometimes a cow will find a way through a fence and get lost in the hills. But after the second one, I got Tom to do a head count. It's not unheard of to lose two cattle to mishap or an accident, and I'm probably being a worrywort," Dean said with a curl of his lip. "But after all those troubles we had with my cattle last year…"

Dean had every right to be jumpy when it came to the safety of his cattle. Nearly eighteen months ago, Dean's cattle had been poisoned. He'd lost quite a few cows that day, and was lucky not to have lost the whole herd. They'd found the culprit. A man called Cyrus had been targeting Dean in retribution for Dean having put his brother in jail. But Dean also loved his cattle like he would a family pet, so Jude knew he wouldn't lie about something like this.

"What do you think happened to them?" Jude took out his little notebook and pencil he always kept in his top pocket and began to write notes.

"We're not sure." Dean rubbed his chin. "Tom didn't find any broken fences, so whoever took them must've gone through a gate. The herd was in Selway's Pasture, but after the second one disappeared, I moved them closer to the lodge, so we could keep an eye on them. I've also brought in the mob from the back pasture, even though they seem to all be accounted for."

"What about tire tracks? Or other signs someone's been in the paddock?" Cat asked, pacing back and forth across the grease-stained concrete.

"No tire tracks," Dean said hesitantly. "But there were other signs that something might be amiss."

"Such as," Jude prompted when Dean merely pursed his lips.

"A couple of boot prints in a sandy section of the paddock near the gate. That's all. As if someone walked in and stole them. Which is ridiculous. And the reason why I'm hesitant to report it. There's not a lot to go on."

"You've done the right thing," Jude encouraged. There was one more question he needed to ask, but he hated to even raise the topic. Stargazer Ranch had been through so much already, it was almost unthinkable that Dean could be targeted yet again. "I have to ask this, Dean. Have you had any threats lately? To you or to the ranch?"

"No. No, nothing," Dean replied, but his blue eyes were worried. "I promise, I would tell you if there was anything like that."

"What does this mean?" Cat asked, staring at Jude as if he had all the answers. Worry creased the corners of her eyes, and he rushed to alleviate her fears. Cat had been an unwitting target in the first arson attack on the ranch and had nearly lost her life in a raging wildfire. If Levi hadn't rushed up there to save her, she might not have survived, and so he understood where her concern was coming from. Even though the culprit had been caught and put in jail, she was still wary about anything untoward happening on the ranch.

"I don't know yet. But I'll certainly look into it." He briefly laid a comforting hand on Cat's arm.

"I asked Tom to see if he could find any footprints leading away from the paddock. But it's been a dry fall, and the ground is hard and rocky. Tom is no tracker, but he thought he saw some marks leading up the hill toward Canyon Peak."

Canyon Peak was part of a mountain range that ran along the western edge of the Stargazer Ranch. The Bitterroot

Mountains were a series of rugged peaks, with numerous steep canyons cut into them by swift-running streams millions of years ago. They were some of the Northern Rockies' most rugged terrain. Beautiful, but also deadly, if you didn't know what you were doing. People hiked and camped in the national forest area all the time. Could it be as simple as some hikers making mischief? Someone stealing a couple of cows as a prank?

It was also the same mountain range Cat had been trapped on during the wildfire. Jude suppressed a shiver of misgiving.

He snapped his notebook shut and gave them both a bright smile. "Don't worry, I'm on it," he assured them both. "I'll let you know what I find."

"Thank you." Dean returned Jude's smile with one of his own trademark grins. "I'm sure it's nothing."

Jude hoped so, too. He gave a cheery wave and set off back down the hill toward the lodge.

CHAPTER THREE

Aria skipped lightly down the stairs of the lodge. The phrase walking on air seemed almost apt for the way she was feeling at the moment. The cold breeze was still but blowing, but she no longer felt the icy tendrils on her bare midriff. If she thought no one was watching, she'd be tempted to do a twirl, she was so happy. But guests were still milling around in the reception area. This was her first bit of good luck since she'd found out about her *little problem*. Since Beau had kicked her out of his house.

Naomi had given her the job. It was the best feeling in the world. She'd soon have money to her name and be able to put a roof over her head. And she could hardly believe she'd be working at Stargazer Ranch. Naomi was so lovely, Aria was sure she'd make a great boss, just as Jude had predicted.

Her mood was the complete opposite of how she'd been feeling half an hour ago. When Jude had taken her inside to the most opulent log cabin she'd ever seen in her life, and introduced her to Penny, the cute, bubbly receptionist, she'd just about turned around and ran straight out again, sure that she'd been making a big mistake. And then when the other interviewee had waltzed out of the office as she sat on the chair waiting, casting her an unfriendly look as she sailed on by looking so cool and stylish and in-charge, Aria knew she'd been outclassed and there was no way she was getting this job.

But just as she'd stood to get the hell out of there, the office door had opened and a woman had beckoned her in. She was petite, only just hitting five feet, but Aria had a feeling that she shouldn't underestimate her. This must be Naomi, the wife of Dean, and co-owner of Stargazer Ranch. Long auburn hair draped over her shoulders, and she wore a light-blue button-up shirt with the Stargazer logo on the breast pocket. Her smile was bright and welcoming, and Aria felt some of her misgivings drain away. She straightened her shoulders and looked Naomi in the eye. She was here now, and she needed to show she could do this job. Pushing her uncertainty down—it'd do no good to show how desperate she was—she tried to plug into that self-confident side of herself that used to inhabit her body, going over the pep talk she'd been reciting in her head one more time. She could do this. She was what this ranch needed. She might not be as classy and professional as the last woman, but her graphic design skills were top-notch, and her brain was already buzzing with half a dozen ideas on how to run a social media campaign with some contemporary branding to bring the ranch into the twenty-first century.

"Hello. My name's Naomi, do come in and take a seat." Naomi shook her hand in a firm grip, then gestured to a comfortable-looking set of armchairs beneath a big picture window, indicating she should take one. Aria glanced at the large wooden desk covered in piles of paperwork. This seemed to be the main office. It had a very male vibe; dark-wooden bookshelves lined the wall behind the desk, and a bench made of similar wood ran the length of the other wall, holding a large coffee machine and the makings of morning tea.

"Would you like a cup of coffee? Or a pastry? They're freshly made by our resident French chef, Stella. She's an amazing cook, we're so lucky to have her," Naomi gushed.

"A coffee would be nice, thank you." Aria didn't think she could eat right now; her mouth was so dry, it would stick in her throat. And the sugar from the stolen candy bar she'd eaten for breakfast was causing her stomach to swirl alarmingly.

Naomi buzzed around the coffee machine, reminding Aria of an energetic bee flitting busily between flowers. "How do you take it, Aria?"

"Cream, but no sugar. Thank you."

In less than a minute, Naomi was placing a coffee on the small table in front of Aria and sitting down with her own coffee and a pastry on a plate. "Stella is going to be the death of me. I just can't resist her delicious pastries. I'll have to spend an extra hour in the garden today, just to work off the calories. But it'll be worth it." Naomi was by no means fat, and Aria guessed that running a luxury ranch kept her trim and fit.

"Now, tell me a little about you. Where have you worked before? What drew you to this job? That kind of thing," Naomi said kindly.

The casual surroundings of the cozy nook with the two armchairs pulled together, more like two friends having a chat than a formal interview, put Aria at ease.

She took a deep breath and composed herself. She may as well start at the beginning. "Well, you may already know that I was born and raised in Stevensville." That was a good solid start. She couldn't very well lie about that part. "I left town when I was eighteen." She didn't go into details as to why she left, but she watched Naomi carefully, checking for any body language that might give away her thoughts on the Cusack family. But Naomi gave a gentle smile and nodded for her to continue. If she'd heard all the rumors and gossip about her mother—or her father—she was keeping the conjecture to herself.

"Then I...ah, traveled for a while until I ended up in Portland, where I..." *Oh crap*. Aria suddenly felt self-conscious and had to put the mug on the table before the coffee slopped over the edge. Who was she kidding? Of course, Naomi knew about her family history. Why had she ever thought she'd be able to apply for a job in her hometown? No one would want to employ her. Not when they tarred her with the same brush as her father. Not when they pitied her because her mother had chosen the easy way out. Had chosen to take her own life.

Naomi saw her hesitate and frown lines formed between her brows. She put her coffee carefully on the table, as well.

"I like that you're a local girl," Naomi said softly. "It's one of the reasons I chose to interview you. I like that you understand what it means to live in a small country town—in this particular small country town," she added.

Aria breathed in deep, letting Naomi's reassuring words wash over her, hoping they were true. Hoping she truly wasn't judging her.

"And I'm looking for someone who's down to earth and will fit in seamlessly with my team. I'm not necessarily after the flashy, trendsetting professional," Naomi continued.

Aria recalled the image of the polished woman leaving the office a few minutes earlier. Was this Naomi's way of telling her that a sharp suit and a haughty look were not going to get you a job here?

"As long as you can do the job, it's more important to me that we get along. I need a right-hand woman, someone who appreciates what I'm trying to achieve, but also someone with whom I can work closely with. Do you understand?" Naomi fixed Aria with her steady gaze.

Aria felt respect growing for this strong, determined woman as the meaning of her words sunk in. She wasn't intimidated by Aria's past, and she wasn't going to be prejudiced by rumors or innuendo; she was going to make up her own mind about Aria. It seemed her large personality more than countered her small stature. Aria had heard the talk around town that the ranch had been built as much because of Naomi's determination as it had from Dean's dreams. And now she could see every word of that was true. This woman had a core of steel.

"Thank you." Aria unclenched her fists and sat back in the chair, digging deep to find her own core of steel. Her confidence may have taken a terrible blow in the past month, but she could do this. "That's good to know."

"So. Let's start again. Your resume mentioned that you've nearly finished a graphic design course, and I can see you have a lovely reference from your last employer. You have the skills to do this job. I'd like to know why you think you can help me. Like it said in my job advertisement, I need someone to help me redesign the website, and contribute to the socials. But I also have this idea that I want to start a horse riding camp for disadvantaged children. Possibly even for blind children. Do you have any ideas about how best to market that sort of thing?"

"Oh, wow, that sounds amazing," Aria said, leaning forward, her elbows on her knees.

"Yes, I want to give back to the community. We do very well here catering for rich guests, but I feel the need for something…more."

Aria liked this woman more and more. "What a great idea." Her mind was turning over different concepts of how to let people know about this wonderful opportunity. "I'd need to know a bit more about what you're planning," Aria said. "Is this going to be a free event? Or are you going to charge? How long would it run for? How old would the kids be? Would their parents or guardians be involved? Are you going to rely on the Stargazer brand, or start your own from scratch?" Aria stopped talking and covered her mouth, embarrassed. She'd got so caught up with the idea, she'd let her mouth run away with her. "Oh, I'm sorry. I have a tendency to get carried away sometimes."

Naomi sat back and laughed. "Don't you worry. This is exactly what I need in my life. Someone to ask the hard questions. Some of those things you mentioned had never even crossed my mind before. Keep going, ask away."

Aria spent the next twenty minutes brainstorming ideas, talking almost nonstop. Her coffee sat on the table, forgotten, growing cold, and Naomi's half-eaten pastry also remained unfinished.

"I think we're going to get on just fine," Naomi said at last. "When can you start?"

"What? Oh…" Aria was so taken aback that Naomi had offered her the job on the spot that she was lost for words. "Really? Are you sure?"

"Of course, I'm sure. I like you, and I know Dean's going to like you as well. Not that I need to ask his permission, this is my decision. So, what do you say?"

"Gosh. Thank you." Aria could no longer contain herself and she leaped to her feet. "That is so great. I won't let you down, I promise." Except there was that one niggling thing that Aria had failed to mention. Guilt clawed at her belly, but she pushed it down. Now was not the time to tell Naomi about her *little problem*. There'd be time enough to sort through it later. And she needed the job *now*. Her need was greater than her loyalty to Naomi, or at least that's how she justified it to herself.

And now she was outside, reveling in her new job. She couldn't help herself; she skipped across the parking lot to her car. Just as she reached for the handle on her door, she heard a deep voice behind her.

"I take it your interview went well?"

She spun around and smiled at Jude, forgetting for a moment that she was supposed to be avoiding him. "Yes. I got the job. And Naomi is so lovely, just like you said. I can hardly believe it."

He strode toward her, and she was so taken up with the size of him as he towered over her, looking all sexy and rugged in his uniform, that she ran out of words. So tall she had to tilt her head back to look in his eyes. Nothing like Beau, who was short—only slightly taller than her, some might say he was almost chunky—and blond. She should've remembered to put her guard up, but she was so excited by the good news that she gave him another warm smile. He removed his hat to run a hand through his hair, and she marveled at his curly locks for the second time that day.

"When do you start?"

"Tomorrow." She could hardly believe it. But she was just as keen to dive into the job as Naomi was. Her life had taken a turn for the better, and she was going to grasp this opportunity with both hands.

"Did they offer you a room? They have staff quarters for single employees," he said, hazel eyes flashing in the midmorning sunshine. They were an interesting color, almost a pale green in the sunlight, with a darker ring around the outside.

Her mood deflated slightly as she dragged her gaze away from his face. That was the one fly in the ointment. Naomi had mentioned they'd normally offer full-time staff accommodation, but they were in the process of renovating the staff quarters, leaving them short a few rooms. And it also seemed they were overflowing with new staff at the moment, having taken on a new ranch hand and an extra apprentice cook. But that was okay. Aria hadn't known that accommodation on the ranch was even an option, so it was no real loss. She'd just have to spend another week or so in her car until she got her first payment. Then she could start looking for a room to rent.

"No, but that's okay. I'm…self-sufficient."

He leaned a casual hip against her car, and she could feel his presence almost as if it was a physical touch. Or was that just her mind wanting something it couldn't have? She wanted him to touch her.

"You mean your sister's place?"

She turned her head away. "Yes, that's right."

He studied her for a few seconds; she could feel his gaze boring into the back of her neck. "Well, that's great news, anyway. Congratulations." He pushed away from her car and she sucked in a breath of relief as the tension between them decreased the farther away he got. "I'll look forward to seeing you around town."

"Yes," she replied, a little too brightly. "Thank you for your help this morning. I'll make sure to get these tires fixed."

He tipped his hat in her direction and got into his cruiser. She watched him drive away, then hopped into her own car. "Come on, Gandalf, things are looking up." She started the engine and followed Jude's trail of dust down the long driveway.

She was feeling so upbeat as she drove along with the window down, listening to the gravel crunch under her wheels, enjoying the big sky so blue above, that she made a decision. Possibly a rash decision, but she was feeling invincible today, so why the hell not?

Jude had mentioned Iliana's new husband had taken over the Skyridge Ranch, and she thought she might know where that was. She had a vague idea it was farther out on this same road, right on the edge of Painted Rocks State Park. She cringed a little inside when she remembered the strange look Jude had given her when she insisted she was staying with her sister. Because if she had been, she was coming from the wrong direction to get to Stargazer. One more reason he probably didn't believe her lies.

It was time she paid her sister a visit. Time to find out once and for all if she was welcome back in this town.

Turning right onto the main highway, she drove well below the speed limit, slowing to check the names on all the mailboxes she passed. This might be a fruitless search, a silly way to try and track down her sister, but she had all day to spare, and she was enjoying the fall sunshine, the pretty fall colors of the turning leaves shimmering in the breeze.

Nearly twenty minutes later, she reached the sign posting the entrance to Painted Rocks State Park and was about to give up and turn around when she spied a large, new mailbox almost opposite the entrance, with the name Doncaster proudly displayed on top.

This was it. She'd found it. Her stomach suddenly clamped in a tight knot. What if Iliana didn't want to see her? Her car stood idling in the middle of the road as she peered down the driveway, trying to make up her mind. The roof of a large, cream-colored homestead was barely visible between the trees lining the driveway. Open paddocks stretched away on each side, a few lazy cattle grazing the last remaining fall grass. It looked idyllic. The perfect country getaway.

As she continued to dither, a car appeared in her rearview mirror. She'd either have to pull over to let it pass, or keep going.

She turned down the driveway. Peering over the top of the steering wheel, she watched as the homestead grew closer. It was as neat as a pin and picture perfect, and Aria's heart expanded just a little. Good on Iliana for finally getting her life on the right track. For finding a nice man and a nice place to bring up a family. At least one of them had managed to break free from the stink of their family problems. It seemed Iliana had finally left the past behind. She wondered if Tango had ever been out here. Had he even attended the wedding? She doubted it, he rarely left the family home. And he may not have even been invited. Iliana had left home as soon as she was able to get away from their father. Their relationship had been practically nonexistent ever since. Aria didn't think it'd ever be easily mended, certainly not for something Tango would've considered as frivolous as a wedding.

Stopping her car in the neat, circular driveway, she got out and surveyed the double-story, wooden house. A wide veranda beckoned her up the stairs toward an eggshell-blue door. Unsure, Aria bit her lip. But she was here now, this was no time to chicken out. Mounting the steps one at a time, she saw a lovely cane outdoor setting and farther along two comfy-looking armchairs set to overlook the grassy vista spreading out below. Aria hadn't heard if Iliana had had any children, but the lack of toys on the veranda or in the front yard pointed to either no children, or her sister was obsessive about cleaning up.

Shaking her hair back from her forehead, she raked her fingers through it a few times, hoping to tame her wispy locks. What would Iliana think of her little sister? She hadn't changed that much in eight years. Surely Iliana would recognize her?

There was a brass knocker in the middle of the door, so she tapped it a few times, listening to the dull thud echo through the house, and waited. And waited. Clenching and unclenching her fists by her side. There was no sound from the inside. No movement. Now that she thought about it, the place looked deserted. Nobody was home.

She expected a wave of relief, but instead she felt flat, like she'd lost the chance at gaining something good. Iliana and her husband must be out. Of course, Aria couldn't turn up on the front door without letting them know she was coming and expect them to be waiting for her with open arms.

Stomping heavily down the stairs, she stopped for a second beside her car. Then curiosity got the better of her, and she decided to take a look around the back. Perhaps they were out in a shed somewhere. If this was a working farm—which it seemed it was—then, of course, they'd be out doing jobs. Feeding cattle, or fixing fences, or whatever it was you did on a farm. She followed the gravel road around the side of the house, which led to a cleared area with a large vegetable patch running away at a tangent from the rear of the house. Two cars were parked side by side next to a large, metal shed. A big, shiny Ford F100, and a smaller compact SUV. She was pretty sure she could guess who owned which car.

So, if the cars were here, then did that mean Iliana and Craig were also here somewhere?

A tortoiseshell cat appeared from underneath the back porch and wound between Aria's legs, meowing loudly. "Hello, kitty." She leaned down to stroke the cat's silky ears. "What's up with you? Where is everyone?" But the cat merely continued to rub against her legs, meowing for attention. "Well, you're no help," Aria chuckled, standing and peering around the rest of the farm.

Past the vegetable garden, a pretty green lawn ran down for a hundred feet or so, enclosed by a wooden picket fence. It seemed Iliana had developed a green thumb, because she could see big fat red tomatoes ready to be picked, and the last few green heads of summer lettuce, along with neat rows of runner beans and what looked like radishes and carrots, all coming to the end of their growing period.

Neither she nor Iliana had taken much stock of gardening when they were younger. When their mother had been alive, she'd tended a vegetable patch, used to supplement their meagre food supply, but after she died... Well, it'd always been a choked tangle of weeds and long grass. A good place to hide when their father was in one of his ranting episodes. Aria stared at the vegetable patch, trying to imagine her sister bent over with a trowel in her hand, perhaps swiping at the perspiration on her brow. A scene of happy domesticity, something Aria had never imagined for Iliana, until now.

Right before Aria had knocked on the front door, she'd wondered if Iliana would recognize her. But now she turned that thought around; would Aria even recognize her sister? Did Iliana still have long blonde hair and that same slight stature and quick, intense gaze? The same big laugh? Aria used to tell her she sounded like a donkey when she laughed. Now she wondered how she could've been so mean. Back when they'd been children living under their father's roof, neither of them had had many friends. Most kids and parents were wary because of the rumors and half-truths floating around town about their father. About the fact that he'd belonged to some cult, and he was a man to be avoided because of his beliefs. But instead of bringing them closer together, two sisters fighting a common obstacle, they'd actually drifted farther apart, each existing—surviving as best they could—in a world of their own. At the time, Aria had never blamed her sister; she'd done what she thought she needed to do to protect herself.

Aria had never really dissected her feelings toward Iliana; she'd just boxed them up with the rest and put them away, getting through each day as best she could. But now she was struck with sudden insight. Seeing this farm, seeing everything Iliana had—her nice house, a husband, her cute vegetable garden, everything that Aria didn't have, had never had the opportunity to obtain—made her slightly resentful. Her sister had all this because she'd only ever looked after herself. Put herself first. But Iliana was the oldest sibling, it was her job to protect her younger sister, wasn't it? Deep down, Aria resented Iliana for leaving her to cope on her own. Standing there in the weak fall sunshine, Aria felt the surprising fact hit her like a blow to her solar plexus. Wow, that was an interesting revelation. How come she'd never come to that conclusion before? Was that the reason she'd refused to come to the wedding? Cut off all contact. Until now.

The cat meowed again, pulling her out of her musings, and she lifted her head. Beyond the vegetable patch sat a big, red barn, with all its doors shut up tight. She guessed this might be where the tractors and other farm equipment were kept. But it was all locked up, and so perhaps they weren't working today, after all.

Aria spent the next ten minutes checking the nearby buildings and sheds, with the cat following along, her tail held high like a flag, but they were all locked, and Aria trudged back around the side of the house.

She would've loved to have been able to tell someone about her job offer, share the good news with someone who might be interested. In addition to Jude, of course. Maybe that was one of the reasons she'd chosen to seek out Iliana today. If things had worked out, perhaps they might be sitting on the front veranda right now, having tea and chatting about all the things they'd done over the past few years. Maybe they could've mended some fences. Or at least started up a conversation to try and heal the rift. A rift that Aria hadn't truly understood until now.

But today was a dead end, and healing their relationship might well be a pipe dream. Because she wasn't sure she was ready to forgive Iliana. With her sudden revelation today, she needed more time to think about it. The tortoiseshell ran up the front steps, meowing as if she wanted Aria to follow her.

But Aria ignored her and got back into her car.

She drove away, her guts roiling, not sure if she was happy to put the meeting off for another day or sad because she was no closer to finding out if Iliana still cared.

CHAPTER FOUR

Jude pulled his cruiser up in the parking lot of the ranger station just as Levi walked down the front steps of the building. Shit. The day had got away from him. He'd been meaning to call in and see Levi all afternoon, and now he'd left it too late and the ranger would be heading home for the day. But this couldn't wait, so Jude jumped out of his car and strode across the parking lot to meet Levi as he approached his vehicle.

"Jude. Nice to see you, man." The two friends fist-bumped a greeting, but Levi's dark eyes watched him shrewdly. "I'm guessing this isn't a social call." Jude was on more than friendly terms with Cat and Levi, along with most of the Stargazer staff. They were of a similar age and often hung out together when off duty. But they also had a shared history with all the troubles at the ranch recently, and strong bonds had formed, especially with Levi, Cat, Penny, and Clayton.

"You guessed right," Jude replied, ducking his head. "You'll probably hear this from Cat tonight when she gets home, anyway."

"Oh, yeah?" Levi drawled. "It must be something to do with Stargazer, then?" He opened the door to his vehicle, threw his ranger hat and jacket inside, and turned to give

Jude his full attention.

"Yep, I'm afraid so."

Levi cocked an eyebrow, but didn't say anything, waiting for Jude to continue.

"Dean reported some cattle missing today."

"Oh, yeah?" Jude gave him a look full of meaning. He'd know without being told how two missing cattle would put Dean on edge. A normal person might be annoyed at the inconvenience, as the loss of cattle would be worth a pretty penny. But that wasn't what would be worrying Dean. He'd be concerned that something untoward was happening on his ranch. Again. Even though Stargazer was renowned as a luxury ranch with only the best experiences for guests and did incredibly well in their field, they'd also had some terribly bad luck, and it wouldn't be the first time they were targeted by a person with a grudge.

"Tom thinks he saw some footprints leading up toward Canyon Peak."

"And you want me to check it out?"

Jude liked that Levi got the gist of the conversation with minimum effort. He was a man of few words, but when he said he'd do something, you knew he'd always follow through.

"Yes, if you've got time tomorrow, that'd be great. It's probably nothing, but to put Dean's mind at ease, well, you know…"

Levi stroked his beard thoughtfully and Jude watched him consider his words. Levi was of a similar height to Jude, ebony shoulder-length hair pulled back in a ponytail, and the same ebony eyes which regarded him with a studied frown from beneath lowered brows. Even from his male perspective, Jude acknowledged Levi was a good-looking man, if you liked the outdoorsy type. Which Cat clearly did. Cat was lucky to have found him, and they made a great couple. Levi balanced out her spirited nature, with his calm demeanor. They were the perfect example of opposites attracting.

Jude thought back to Cat and Levi's wedding a few months prior. It'd been a simple, beautiful ceremony in the garden surrounding Stargazer, and Jude had been surprised by how moved he'd been by the whole thing. He blamed it on the drugs still circulating through his system from his gunshot wound—he'd only been released from hospital the day before. But he knew that deep down, he was looking for the same thing Cat and Levi had. That special spark, a special bond, a life shared with a soulmate. He hadn't found that in any woman, but he hadn't given up on love. Not yet. It was just so hard when he worked such long hours. Married to the job, some people might say.

After the wedding, Penny had taken to subtly remarking about this woman or that one, asking him what he was looking for in a partner, and generally making it obvious she was trying to matchmake him. He bore her efforts with an inward groan and an outward smile, because she meant well. But there just weren't any women in this little town he was interested in.

Until now. An image of Aria standing by her car, long hair swirling around her shoulders, smiling with delight after she got the job at Stargazer struck him with a jolt that he felt all the way down to his stomach.

"Sure, I'll borrow one of Dean's ATVs and go for a drive tomorrow," Levi said, breaking into his musings. "I'll let you know what I find."

Jude shook his head to recover his equilibrium. "Thanks." But they both knew Levi really had no choice in the matter, because as soon as Cat got home, she'd be in his ear about the missing cattle, and wouldn't let it rest until he promised to take a look. Dean and Stargazer Ranch meant a lot to her, and she wouldn't want to see either of them in danger again.

"Do you want to come and join us for a beer before dinner?" Levi offered.

Jude considered his offer for a heartbeat. "Thank you, but I've still got a few things to cross off my list before I clock off," he replied ruefully.

"No rest for the wicked," Levi said with an understanding smile.

It was par for the course. Jude often worked long hours, especially if there was a big case happening. He and the other deputy sheriff, Susan Nomad, were used to having their lives disrupted. It was part of working in a small sheriff's office in a large country town. Overworked and underpaid was their silent motto. At least the main police station in Missoula was only forty minutes away if they ever needed help.

Jude hopped back in his car. Half his life seemed to be spent driving around in this damn cruiser. Next was a visit to the local milk bar. Lizzie had filed a report of a shoplifter thieving candy bars from her store. It was a minor crime, and some people might see it as petty, but it shouldn't go unreported. In Jude's experience, these things often escalated if they were to let it slide. It was most likely one of the local kids, and a talking to by the deputy and a warning that if it happened again they'd be charged, was usually enough to stop it.

It was already dark by the time he took a spot in the angle parking outside the milk bar. The rest of the shops were shut for the night, only the milk bar and the burger joint farther down the road remained open.

"Hi, Lizzie," he called, pushing open the door, which jangled the little bell above it to let the owner know someone was coming in. The place was empty, and it looked like Lizzie was cleaning up, getting ready to close. She didn't always have set closing times, it depended on how busy she was.

"It's about time. I called the theft in this morning,"

"I know I'm sorry, we've been flat out today."

"Oh, and I guess petty little crime like shoplifting gets pushed to the bottom of the pile," Lizzie said grumpily.

Jude made no reply, just leaned up against the counter and took out his notebook. Lizzie had obviously had a long day, she wasn't normally this tetchy. She'd had a spate of things go wrong in the past few weeks. Someone had thrown a rock at her neon sign out front and smashed it. It wasn't a targeted attack, just a gang of youths, drunk and bored, working their way down Main Street in a frenzy of vandalism. Deputy Nomad had collared the leader, and he was now in jail. Then a pipe in her kitchen out back had burst, flooding the whole shop. Lizzie had taken over the milk bar five years ago and really turned it around. Redecorating in bright colors, adding a countertop and barstools, some tables and chairs on the path outside, and updating the menu to include gourmet milkshakes and hot beverages, it was now a hub for teenagers after school or the older generation to sit outside and gossip.

"Sorry," Lizzie said eventually, swiping a hand across her brow. "I need to put my feet up with a cup of tea. I didn't mean to snap."

"No problems." Jude liked Lizzie. She was mid-forties, with wild, curly red hair, and had moved to Stevensville after a messy divorce. She'd made a positive impact in the town, with her bright smile and warm welcome. "Can you give me a description of the shoplifter?"

"Not really," Lizzie admitted. "It was real busy this morning, the Men's Shed Group was all in buying coffees, and me and Clara were run off our feet. There were a few kids in buying gum and candy before school started, as well. It was Clara who saw the woman stealing, not me."

Clara helped Lizzie out in the milk bar most mornings. A retired grandmother, she'd decided she needed more stimulation in her life and taken on a part-time job in the new milk bar.

"Clara had her hands full, with a tray of coffees for the guys, so she was too late to stop the woman walking out the door."

"Yes, and a good thing, too," Jude replied with a frown. "I've already told you not to try and apprehend shoplifters on your own. You could get hurt if someone retaliates."

"Yes, yes, I know that." Lizzie waved a hand in the air. "Anyway, she told me all she remembers is the woman was wearing jeans and a crop top, with long flowing hair down her back."

Jude stopped writing and lifted his head. What? That description sounded an awful lot like…

"Clara said it was a little strange, because this was no teenager, it was definitely a woman, perhaps in her mid-twenties, which isn't our normal demographic for petty theft, if you know what I mean. And a stranger, too. Clara didn't recognize her."

"Right," Jude replied slowly, his mind spinning. Could this criminal possibly be Aria? Why would she be stealing candy bars? Then he remembered all the stuff in the back of her car. If she were sleeping rough, then perhaps it meant she also had no money. She'd seemed pretty desperate to get that job at Stargazer. "I'll post the description at the station, and we'll keep our eyes open. You let me know if you see this woman again." But would he? Would he post a description that matched Aria so closely?

"Will do," Lizzie replied tiredly. "And thanks for calling in. I know how busy you are. Give my regards to Sheriff Buchanan."

Jude tucked his notebook back in his top pocket. "You take care, Lizzie," he said, raising his voice to be heard over the jingle of the bell above the door. She gave him a distracted wave as he stepped outside.

Letting the cold evening air seep over him, he filled his lungs. Lights twinkled in the distance; Main Street was practically deserted. A couple of cars were parked near the burger joint, but that was it.

Jude sighed and pursed his lips. His leg was beginning to ache from his twelve-hour shift, telling him he still wasn't completely healed. He should go back to the station and sign off for the night. His shift was supposed to be over an hour ago. But there was one more thing he needed to do. He needed to find Aria and make sure she was okay. But was he trying to track her down because of her petty crimes? Or was he looking for her for more personal reasons?

The sheriff was constantly telling him that he needed to stop getting so involved with the people in his cases. A deputy sheriff needed to be unbiased and have solid boundaries. Hank prided himself on being able to make those distinctions, keep those margins between good and bad clear in his head, but sometimes Jude felt that the sheriff's impartiality portrayed him come across as cold and unfeeling, which wasn't Jude's way. He couldn't help it if he got suckered in to a person's story. His mother had always told him he had too much empathy, that he had a kind soul, and he'd be welcomed into heaven with open arms when it was his time. Which'd freaked him out, but also resonated somewhere deep inside. Because he knew that sometimes to understand why a person committed a crime, you needed to understand their motivations and their hopes and dreams. Sometimes crimes weren't always perpetrated out of malice or greed, but out of desperation or need.

If he hadn't taken a personal interest in Clayton and Penny's case, by taking them out to hide them in a small fishing cottage owned by a friend—going against his boss's express command—they may well have been hunted down and killed by the murderous gang before the sheriff's office even had a chance to figure out who wanted them dead and why. Afterward, Hank had begrudgingly admitted Jude had been right to put them in a safe house, but only when they were alone, and certainly not through official channels.

Jude got into his cruiser. Where would Aria park her car if she was going to sleep in it tonight? She'd want somewhere private, away from prying eyes, and safe. Jude knew there were a few places he could start looking, and he had a hunch where she might be. Should he contact Iliana? Just to check that her sister wasn't staying with her as she said? He decided that if he couldn't find Aria in the next hour or so, he would give the Doncaster place a call, even though it was getting late.

And Aria hadn't even mentioned her father, who lived over on the east side of town. Jude had heard speculation that Aria had left town because there was bad blood between them. So he discounted that idea for now. Tango was a crazy old coot. Jude had learned that from personal experience; the old man had come into the station rambling about a killer on the loose, sent to hunt him down, from some long ago feud in some long ago cult. Jude couldn't, for the life of him, see Aria wanting to stay at the family house, which Tango had let fall into utter disrepair. Nope, he was pretty sure she was out there somewhere in her car.

First of all, he checked around the back of Butterby's Building Company. There was a large area of unused land, surrounded by a line of trees on two sides, planted by a long ago rancher. The pine trees provided shelter from the worst of the weather, and homeless people sometimes gathered there at certain times of the year. Tonight, there were two vehicles parked up by the fence, and a couple of roughly constructed tent-style dwellings. But there was no sign of Aria's car, so he kept moving, not wanting to disrupt the small homeless community for no reason. It was hard to turn around and drive away; it was one of the reasons Jude rarely visited these places. He knew some of these people's stories, and most of them had a sad tale of loss or misadventure, and didn't deserve to be sleeping on the streets. But he also knew he couldn't help everyone. This homeless pandemic affected every town and every city in the US.

He thought a little harder. Where would Aria go? Then he stopped and laughed at himself. Who the hell was he to think he could possibly understand Aria's motives? Just because she'd been an acquaintance back in his youth, didn't make him an expert on how her mind worked now. And just because he was worried about her safety now, didn't mean that he was attracted to her, either. Nope. That flash of magnetism when she'd smiled at him was nothing. He needed to keep reminding himself of that.

There were a couple of rest stops down by the river, where people could go to have a picnic or swim in the shallower pools of water. It was picturesque and charming, but camping wasn't allowed overnight, and so most of the spots would be deserted by now. The closer he got to the river, the more certain he became that he was on the right track.

The first rest stop was indeed deserted. Less picturesque in the dark and even a tad spooky.

At the second one, a group of teenagers were sitting around a low campfire, smoking pot and drinking from box wine. When they saw the cruiser, they jumped up and scattered, stubbing out what remained of the joint. One tall boy hid the box behind his back as if Jude wouldn't be able to see it. Jude wound down his window and said, "Make sure that fire is out properly, and don't let me catch you down here again." He gave a grim smile as he wound his window back up. The teenagers would just move somewhere else, but he had to be seen to be doing his job.

Finally, at the third rest spot, Jude spotted a gray vehicle tucked in behind the trunk of a large Douglas fir. Not wanting to startle her, he switched off his headlights and rolled to a stop.

It was dark without the lights of his car, almost pitch-black. Was Aria frightened by the dark? It certainly took some guts for a girl to stay out here completely alone. What if someone tried to break into her car? Attack her? A shiver of goose bumps ran over his skin at the thought. Flicking on his flashlight, he walked toward the car. It was completely silent. There was no movement from within. She was probably asleep already, even though it was just past nine. How was he going to do this? Normally, he'd just go up and rap on the window, not bothered if he scared whoever was inside. So why did he think this was any different?

But still…

He approached the car carefully and peered in, but it was too dark to make out much of anything. He knocked his knuckle gently against the rear window and waited. But there was nothing. If she was asleep in there, she was a heavy sleeper. He knocked again a little louder and called out her name. Still nothing. Was anyone in there? A little perturbed now, he stood tall and knocked even louder, then shone the light into the rear seat.

The pale oval of Aria's face appeared in the window, mouth forming a grimace of fear, sleepy eyes wide in the beam of light, a small scream erupting from her open mouth.

"It's me, Aria. Deputy Wilder."

"Holy mother of God, Jude. You scared the crap out of me," she yelled through the glass. Ducking her head, she shaded her eyes from the bright light, and he quickly lowered it. There was a scuffling sound from inside the car, and then the door opened and Aria stepped out, standing onto the gravel in only her socks, wearing sweats and a T-shirt, her hair all mussed. In the illumination from his flashlight, she looked warm and heavy-lidded from sleep. And inviting. He caught a whiff of roses as she pushed her hair back from her face.

She cast him a guilty look, but said nothing, waiting for him to be the first to speak. What should he say? It was clear he'd caught her out in a lie, so what next? She wasn't even trying to deny it, because there was no point. He stared down at her, suddenly aware of her luscious mouth as she pouted at him from beneath lowered brows, and he was suddenly lost for words.

When he didn't speak, she finally said, "Where else am I going to go?" Her soft eyes turned hard. "I don't have enough money for a hotel room. That's why I needed the job so badly." She shivered and wrapped her arms around her body. "It's cold out here. Can I go back to bed?" Her tone turned slightly piteous.

But he couldn't let her sleep in her car overnight. Not out here, alone, where anyone could approach the car, and do... just about anything to her. She was too vulnerable. Too isolated.

It was the same question he'd been turning over in his head ever since he'd first decided to come looking for her. He wanted to ask why she wasn't staying with her sister as she'd insisted earlier on. But for whatever reason, she clearly didn't want to, or couldn't, go there, and the last thing he wanted to do was get involved in her family politics at nine pm on a cold, dark night.

"Look, I have a place you can stay."

"What?" Her head shot up. "I'm not staying with you. I'm fine right here. Leave me alone." She took a step backward.

He'd been debating the idea back and forth in his mind for the past hour while he'd been looking for her. But he hadn't truly known the answer until he'd seen her standing there in her socks, vulnerable and isolated.

"You wouldn't be staying in my house," he quickly amended, not wanting her to get the wrong idea. "I have a mother-in-law apartment out the back, which is vacant at the moment. You can use that for the next little while. It's completely separate accommodation, with its own kitchenette and bathroom."

Technically, he was staying in his mother's house, but she was now living full-time in the aged home because he could no longer care for her himself. Alzheimer's was a terrible disease, taking away a person's ability and character, leaving a mere husk of a body behind. His mother, Annie, wouldn't mind. In fact, she'd probably encourage him to take Aria in. She always told him he had a heart of gold, but then, so did she. She'd never told him that he couldn't bring that half-drowned feral cat he found down by the river into her house. Tabby had ended up living five more years, fat and happy in their house. And she'd even stayed up to help him with the night feeds when he brought the baby bird home that time. Even with all their attention, the poor little thing had died. But Annie had helped to dig a small grave and say a few prayers over the tiny body. She was just as much of a sucker for the destitute and needy as he was. Was Aria just another one of these lame ducks he was bringing home?

"I can't pay you. At least, not until I start getting a salary."

"I know that. I can't in good conscience leave you here. It's either that or I take you to the woman's shelter downtown." Her face blanched at the mention of the shelter.

"I don't need your pity. I'm fine by myself. And I'm not some charity case, I won't go to some refuge. I'd rather stay out here."

It was what he thought she'd say.

"Well, it's not safe, and you're not staying here." He wasn't going to let her win. She wasn't staying out here alone, end of story. He was offering her a way out, and it was just her stubborn pride that was stopping her from accepting. He was used to dealing with hardened criminals, teenage petty thieves, and everything in between, and he certainly wasn't going to let one petite woman get away with giving him *no* for an answer. He wasn't leaving until she agreed to go with him.

"What are you going to do? Handcuff me and drag me off in your cruiser, if I don't comply?"

He lifted an eyebrow in her direction. The idea had merit, she was certainly trying his patience and handcuffs might show her the gravity of the situation.

"You'd like that, wouldn't you, putting me in handcuffs? Is that what gets you going? Do you get off on power tripping and lording it over helpless females? Is that your kinky kind of crap?"

The ferocity of her attack caught him off guard. He'd never do anything to a woman that she hadn't consented to, and how dare she insinuate that he would? But her spiteful words weren't enough to make him leave her. His job was to protect the innocent and vulnerable and those who couldn't protect themselves. And she ticked all three boxes. Even if she was the most annoying person in the world, right now. He wasn't leaving her here. He stood his ground. Her outburst didn't deserve an answer and so he gave her none. She was only trying to scare him away. And he didn't scare easily. At least, he wasn't scared by big burly men looking for a physical fight. This small woman glaring up at him, however, made him feel so uncomfortable, he had to tamp down on the urge to get in his car and flee.

Aria stamped her foot on the ground and glared up into his face.

"Answer me, goddamnit."

But when he still stood there, immovable as a rock, all the

fight suddenly seemed to leave her. Shoulders hunched, she wrapped her arms tighter around her body.

"Why are you doing this? You barely know me. Why…?"

It was a good question, and one he didn't have an immediate answer for. He couldn't very well say that he felt he owed her a debt for some reason. That he'd watched her from afar back when they were teenagers at school and had wanted to reach out and offer his friendship—he had an inkling of what she'd been through already with her mother, and what she was still going through with her father—and yet he'd done nothing. Like the rest of them, he'd sat back and pretended to ignore her as she stumbled through school, painfully shy, with no one who really cared about her.

"It's my job," he replied softly

"It's not your job to offer a stranger a safe haven."

Perhaps not, but he knew was he couldn't leave her out here alone.

"Come on. I live over in Turner Street. I'll lead the way."

He waited a heartbeat. And then another, before she finally said, "Fine," in a flat voice.

He wished she'd smile again. It was such a beautiful smile. He wanted to make her smile so that her nose wrinkled in delight. He was determined to see that smile once more.

CHAPTER FIVE

Aria followed Jude's straight back along the pathway that took them down the side of the little wooden house, scuffing her feet as she went. Jude was clearly walking with a limp now, but she refrained from commenting. He needed to know that she was still not happy with this arrangement. Not happy at being told what to do. Not happy that he thought he could take over her life. A rear porch light came on as they rounded the house—it must've been motion sensitive—and illuminated a pretty cottage garden.

Completely separate from the house, in the back corner of the yard, sat a little self-contained bungalow made from the same weatherboard and painted the same cream color as the main house. She'd refused to let Jude carry her bag, he was already doing enough for her, ordering her around like she was one of his deputies, and she hoisted it over her shoulder as it slipped down again. It was big and heavy, and she felt a twitch low in her belly. Maybe she wasn't supposed to be carrying heavy things. But then he certainly didn't need to know that.

She stifled a yawn, then shivered from the cold, even after she'd thrown on a sweater. A comfy bed and clean sheets might not be such a bad thing, after all. Jude stopped at the door to the bungalow and fumbled with a key. She watched him, shoulders wide and impressive, filling out his jacket nicely. Just the mere presence of him set her on edge. But it wasn't a bad kind of *set on edge*, not like someone dragging their fingernails down a blackboard. It was more like a low thrumming deep in her stomach, spreading a warmth through her chest. Like she was acutely aware of him, but he also made her feel secure. Like no one could hurt her when he was around.

Jude stood back and held the door open, ushering her inside with a chivalrous dip of his hand. It was dark inside, and she fumbled around on the wall, feeling for a switch. Jude's hand brushed across hers and she pulled away with a squeak. Not sure if her girly sound was because of the shock of touching another human being, or from the zing of electricity his fingers left behind on her skin.

"Sorry, let me," he apologized. A light came on and a small cosy room was unearthed from the darkness. The room was decorated in soft, neutral colors, with a tan couch, a cream rug, and white-washed furniture, with added pops of color to bring it alive—blue floral cushions on the couch, a blue vase on the sideboard, a couple of big watercolor pictures on the wall.

"Oh, this is gorgeous." Aria was more than a little surprised. It definitely spoke of a woman's touch, homey and inviting, and it made her wonder if the inside of the main house was more of the same.

"It's got all the mod cons. There's a television over there." He pointed to a small wall-mounted screen. "The kitchen is small, but functional. And it's stocked with all the cutlery and crockery you should need." He moved farther into the room. "The bedroom is over here, it's got built-ins if you want to unpack your stuff. And the other door is the bathroom." He opened the door and flicked on the light to show her. "It's small, but again, it's got everything you need."

"This is great," Aria said, trying to take in everything at once. "Really great. Thank you." She tried not to sound too surprised to find this little gem in the backyard of the local deputy's house. But he seemed to catch her tone.

"This is my mother's place. She decorated this cottage. I moved back in to look after her a few years ago. She's got Alzheimer's."

Ah ha, that explained it. This was no bachelor pad. But his face grew strained as he mentioned his mother.

"Oh, I'm so sorry," she replied. What did you say to a man who had the courage and compassion to care for his own mother? Her mother never got the chance to grow old. Perhaps to some, that might be a blessing in disguise. Would Aria have nursed her own mother if she made it to old age? She liked to think she would have.

"No need to apologize, but thank you, anyway... She was moved to care home a few months ago, but I still visit her almost every day."

"That's lovely." What an attentive son. He obviously loved his mother. And for a second, she wondered what it would've been like to grow up in that sort of environment. But rehashing the past would never give her clarity, so she dropped the thought like a stinky bone.

"My mother used to rent out this cottage. It gave her extra income. But as she got sicker, people started taking advantage of her. When I found out the woman who was living here was only paying her ten dollars a week in rent, instead of a hundred, I kicked her out, and no one's lived here since. That was when it became clear she couldn't live on her own anymore, and I moved in."

Something spasmed in her heart. It was so sweet letting Aria live here, even if it was only for a short time. And it showed a certain amount of trust. It was suddenly important that she let him know his trust wasn't misplaced. She would pay him back the rent when she was able. The money might not matter to him, but it did to her. Jude Wilder was a bit of a conundrum. A pragmatic and tough deputy on one hand, with a soft spot for people in trouble on the other. Or was the soft spot just for her? The idea was both intriguing and scary.

"As long as I'm not intruding," Aria said softly, but she was only half concentrating on her answer, the rest of her focus was on his mouth. And how firm and strong his lips were. Bottom lip slightly fuller than the top, there always seemed to be a smile lurking in the corners of his mouth. As if he was ready to find almost anything amusing. A three-day stubble covered his chin, framing his lips and running up to join his sideburns melting into his curly brown hair. She almost reached out her fingertips to touch the tiny cleft in his chin. The stubble looked soft. Beau sometimes sported a sort of chin-strap beard, a thin band of hair running along the bottom of his chin, which he thought made him look hip and a bit boho, but she thought it made him look silly. Jude's three-day growth was much more rugged and fascinating. It wasn't long enough to be called a beard, but she'd love to scruff her fingers through it anyway. Were deputy sheriffs even allowed to grow a beard? She had no idea.

She looked up, just as he caught her staring. Crap. A red flush began to creep up her neck. Their eyes locked, and for a second she couldn't look away. In this light, they were more golden hazel, that dark ring around the edge was still there, but now his pupils dilated to make his eyes appear almost black. Double crap. She was the first to look away.

"No, you're not intruding. It'll be nice having someone else around. I miss her," he admitted. Then, as if realizing what he'd just said, he turned and took off out the door and up the pathway. "Don't be afraid to come and knock on the back door if you need anything. I'm a light sleeper," he called over his shoulder.

Unlike her, she thought grimly. Jude practically had to break the window to wake her up tonight. She was just so tired. The interview today at Stargazer had been stressful, even though the outcome had been positive. As had her trip around her sister's property. The whole past month had been stressful. Losing her job. Being kicked out of the house she and Beau shared. Finding out about her *little problem*. Sleeping in the car ever since. And finally deciding to come back to her hometown. She didn't feel like she'd had a proper sleep in weeks. So with the prospect of starting her new job in the morning, she'd finally fallen into a deep sleep in what felt like the first time forever. And then Jude had come and woken her up.

She really didn't know what to think about Jude Wilder. He'd always been kind and generous back when they were kids, if perhaps a little aloof. It was one of the things she'd noticed about him, one of the many reasons she'd had a crush on him. And it seemed he was still kind and generous now.

"Thank you," she called out belatedly. "This is so..." So what? Helpful. Nice. Good. Exactly what she needed.

* * *

Aria was standing next to the bed, wrapped in a towel, trying to decide what to wear to her first day at work, when there was a knock at the door. Crap. That could only be one person. She dithered for a second, but decided she had no choice other than to open the door dressed only in a towel.

"I thought you might need some breakfast." It was Jude holding a tray of food, dressed and neat as a pin in his deputy uniform. "There's no food in here, so I bought you coffee and some toast, and..." He stopped speaking mid-sentence when he saw what she was wearing. "Oh, ah, sorry. I didn't realize..." He gestured toward her attire, or lack thereof.

She couldn't very well leave him standing out in the cold,

misty morning, especially seeing as he had her breakfast on a plate. "I was just trying to decide what to wear to my first day at work. Come in."

He moved awkwardly past her and through to the kitchenette, placing the plate on the countertop. She followed him over. Then he looked up and their eyes caught and held, and suddenly, she regretted letting him in. She was achingly aware of how close he was, of how he seemed to consume all the air in the room. Achingly aware that she was only wearing a towel, completely naked underneath. Achingly aware of how the air buzzed with tension between them. His eyes went dark, the same way they had last night, as he let his gaze roam over her bare shoulders and then down to where the towel barely skimmed the top of her thighs. The heat in his eyes set off a tremor of echoing heat low in her belly. The spark between them was undeniable. Her gaze was drawn to that provocative mouth, and she licked her own lips in response. *Kiss him*, a crazy voice said in her head. *Go on, you know you want to.* The compulsion was almost overwhelming, and she found herself leaning toward him. Crap. This was the last thing she'd expected when she came back to town. And the very last thing she needed. She had so many problems to solve; she needed a fling with a man she'd once had a teenage crush on like a hole in the head.

She stepped back, clasping her towel with one hand, almost tripping over the small coffee table. Jude hadn't moved from his spot by the countertop, but she needed to put as much distance between them as possible.

But instead of staying where he was, he followed her around the coffee table, his eyes never leaving her face. She opened her mouth to tell him to step away, and instead moved in closer, his solid male body crowding up against hers as she pushed forward. She liked the feel of his lean hardness, evident even through the bulk of his uniform.

Reaching up, he tucked a damp strand of hair behind her ear, letting his fingers brush lightly over the bare skin of her neck.

"You're more beautiful than I remember," he said softly. "So much more...real."

She wanted to say ditto, that he was so much more, as well, but her mouth had suddenly gone dry. Aria's heart was pounding so hard, blood thundering in her ears, she wondered if he could hear it.

Before the next beat of her heart, he lowered his mouth to hers, searching her eyes for permission. She gave it, by standing on tiptoe and closing the distance.

His mouth was gentle, as if he didn't want to scare her, the kiss slow and sweet. She let go of the towel, no longer caring if it slipped, and slid her hands around his waist, letting herself melt into him. His mouth became more urgent, suddenly unapologetically passionate, and she liked the dichotomy of the soft and the hard, their tongues tangling as he dragged all the air out of her lungs with his intensity.

Without lifting his mouth from hers, he walked them backward until she felt the cool, solid wall at her back. Dipping his head, he kissed a slow trail of desire down her neck, and she tipped her head back to rest it against the wall, letting the thrum of arousal set her alight. Her whole body trembled with the need to touch him, and she found the edge of his jacket, stopping momentarily when she encountered his gun belt, her fingers shying away from the weapon, and moving farther around his waistband to untucked his shirt from his trousers so she could smooth her palms over his lower back. She slipped her thigh between his legs, feeling his arousal, and loving how he groaned in the back of his throat as she slowly ground against it.

"Aria." His voice was warm and husky, full of desire. Her name sounded good on his tongue, and she wanted to hear him say it again. "You drive me crazy..."

Then he lifted his head and eased away from her slightly. Uh oh, here came the but.

"And I've been wanting to kiss you ever since I saw you smile after you got the job at Stargazer. You have a beautiful smile," he added, taking her shoulders and stepping back. "And so, I'd hate to think I made you late for your first day on the job."

He was right. Of course, he was right. But now her cheeks heated at how brazenly she'd acted. Hell, she'd been about to slip the knot on her towel and let it fall to the ground. She was ashamed to admit she'd wanted this to go further. How far would it have gone if he hadn't done the gentlemanly thing and stopped it?

"Yes, yes, you're right." She needed to get ready for work. But more than that, she needed to mentally disengage herself from what'd just happened.

"And you need to get to work, as well," she added.

"That too," he agreed, but it seemed he was just as reluctant as she was to break their embrace, which made her feel a little better.

"Aria, I want—"

She cut him off, because it didn't really matter what he wanted. He'd change his tune soon enough, anyway. "Don't worry about it. I'm not sure what just happened, but it won't happen again." She had to nip this thing in the bud. After all, no man would want to be in a relationship with her when they found out about her *little problem*. Even Jude, with his generous heart, wouldn't want to get involved with a woman who was carrying a baby that didn't belong to him.

That was the reason she'd come back to Stevensville, and she needed to keep that upmost in her mind. Hoping that family might be her saviour—even though her little plan hadn't panned out properly yet. But at least she had a job now. Nothing else mattered. Including this crazy attraction to the local deputy.

She ducked under his arm and escaped to stand in the bedroom doorway.

"I need to get dressed," she reminded him, not quite meeting his gaze.

He stood for a few more seconds without speaking, and she could feel his looming presence. But there was no way she could give him the answers he wanted, so she waited until he finally got the message.

"Right. Well, have a good day at work. I'm sure you'll love it, and I'm sure you'll get on well with Naomi."

"I'm sure I will, too," she replied crisply, willing him to just go.

"I might see you this evening, then."

She doubted it; she wasn't going to initiate any more contact than was absolutely necessary.

"Remember, just knock on the door if there's anything you need. Anything at all." He put his hand on the door handle.

"Thank you." He deserved that much. He definitely had her respect and appreciation. Without him she would've spent another night in her car, and would now be getting dressed at the public toilet block outside the back of the community hall, washing her hair in the stainless steel sink. "I mean it, Jude. I owe you a debt of gratitude."

He gave a perfunctory shrug and closed the door behind him.

Aria took a deep breath, and then another, waiting for her jitters to subside. She considered the breakfast tray still sitting on the countertop. She hadn't been eating much in the morning lately, finding her stomach couldn't handle anything but coffee. But for some reason, she thought she might be able to handle the toast and honey Jude had brought. At least her morning sickness—if it could be called that—seemed to be fairly minor, and usually by lunchtime her slight nausea had disappeared. She hoped and prayed it'd stay that way, or at least not get any worse. She'd heard horror stories from other women who'd been so sick they couldn't keep anything down, or who'd been practically bedridden. She was fairly lucky, by all accounts. Not that anyone knew she was pregnant, yet. And it'd be months before she started showing, so she had time. Resting a hand on her belly, she drew in a deep breath. Everything she was doing now was for the sake of this little one. This little nine-week old peanut growing inside her.

Had she made a mistake by accepting Jude's offer to stay here? It was a roof over her head and that was top priority right now, so she needed to squash all her doubts and get on with it. But how the hell was she going to stay away from him? This attraction was so strong it was almost unmanageable. She needed to cleanse him from her mind and find the willpower to do what needed to be done.

CHAPTER SIX

Jude tried to breathe through his mouth. Even wearing a mask, the smell was terrible, and he nearly gagged. You never got used to this stink. The sickly sweet aroma of death.

He made his way through the darkened hallway toward the smell, Deputy Nomad right behind him. It wasn't hard to decipher where the body was.

The call had come in just after lunch. A delivery man leaving a box of groceries on the back step had been nearly overpowered by the smell. And then he'd noticed the swarm of flies congregating around the back door, which was hanging open. One peek inside had been all he needed before he took off at a sprint back to his van and called the sheriff's office. The delivery man was standing by the front gate now, face pale, and one hand still held to his nose as if he couldn't get rid of the smell from his nostrils.

"Oh, shit," Susan Nomad muttered as they approached the doorway at the end and peered into a kitchen.

Oh shit indeed. The room was like something from a nightmare. Blood spattered the walls, the countertop, the floor, and one of the windows. Old, congealed blood, almost black, and crawling with flies. Even in late fall, the insects were still active.

Was there a body? He quickly catalogued the layout of the kitchen. The back fly screen door still hung open on its hinges, and every time it flapped, it seemed more flies came in. The kitchen was a mess—even if you discounted the blood everywhere—dirty plates and pots and pans piled in the sink, food was left out on the counter, stacks of old newspapers in a corner, and a large central kitchen island filling most of the space in between. Jude forced himself to go farther into the room, stepping carefully and not touching anything, even though he was wearing latex gloves. Leaning forward, he squinted around the corner of the island, then recoiled before he could stop himself.

"There's a body," he confirmed to Susan. "And it's not pretty." His guts roiled, and he had to force down a wave of nausea. It didn't matter how many times he'd come across a dead body, the sight always made him sick to his stomach. The tragedy of someone's life cut short always hit hard with him, no matter who the person was, or even whether some might say that person deserved it.

Susan squinted at him, but she followed his lead and leaned to stare around the kitchen island. Her cool blue eyes taking inventory of the body and the rest of the kitchen, much like he'd already done. Susan had been on the job as long as he had. They'd both been taken in as trainees around the same time. They worked well together, and he trusted her implicitly. She was always cool in the face of danger, and they'd both seen their fair share of dead bodies, so he knew that while she might be shocked by the mess on the floor, that'd once been a man, she would remain professional and do what was needed. They both would. It was what they'd been trained for. Oh, God, how was he going to break this to Aria?

This was her father's house, and there was a partially dismembered body on the floor. They need to try and confirm his identity before they informed the next of kin. But he was in no doubt this was Tango Cusack. The old bloke was practically a hermit. He rarely, if ever, came into town, and Jude had to think hard as to the last time he'd seen him. It would've been six months ago when the man had come in to the sheriff's office raving that someone was out to get him. He'd looked almost crazy back then. Thin as a rake, long, scraggly beard and bloodshot eyes. Jude had been assigned to talk to him, but Tango made little sense, talking about a cult called InXium, and a man who was out to kill him. But he had no proof, and after an hour of listening to him ramble, the sheriff had come into the deposition room and told him to go home, because that wasn't the first time Tango had been to see the sheriff and Hank was getting tired of his staff having to listen to his delusions.

No one had followed up on the accusations, because Hank had decided there was no basis to his allegations. It was just the ravings of an insane, old man. Jude had Googled the cult InXium. It seemed they actually existed, so Tango had got that part right but there wasn't a lot of information. The biggest gathering was in Colorado somewhere, but they were a bunch of drifters, usually traveling in groups of three or four. A religious group who believed in an apocalypse, where humanity would have to account for themselves at the end of time, which was supposedly happening soon. Everyone would have to account themselves to Him when the time came. Jude assumed He was their version of God, or Jesus, but it wasn't really clear. What connection Tango might've had to this cult was unknown.

But now it seemed that perhaps Tango hadn't been wrong, after all. Maybe there was someone out to get him. Jude was a little uncertain as to how this cult might be responsible for Tango's murder, but maybe they should do a little more in-depth digging.

This murder wasn't recent. Jude guessed the body was at least four or five days old.

Shit, hadn't Aria said she'd been out to see her father when she'd first arrived back in town? Was she perhaps the last person to have seen him alive? How was she going to take this news? He knew their relationship was strained, but would she still grieve for him? Jude wanted to be the one to tell her. To be the one there for her, if she needed him.

But he was getting way ahead of himself. One step at a time.

"I'll go and call the cops in Missoula. They can organize the guys from homicide and a forensics team to get down here ASAP," he said, professional mask back in place.

"Right," Susan replied briskly. "I'll call the boss and then cordon off the area and make sure no one enters the scene."

"Good." Jude retraced his steps down the hallway, already taking his phone out of his pocket and dialing the Missoula police department. His day had suddenly become very busy.

Once he was sure the police were on their way, he went to grab some yellow tape to help Susan seal off the area. But his mind kept going back to thoughts of Aria. This was only her second day working at Stargazer, hopefully this didn't put her job in jeopardy. He didn't think Naomi or Dean would be that shallow. Surely, they'd give her a few days off for bereavement leave?

Jude had been careful not to go near the cottage since he'd barged in and found her wrapped in only a towel yesterday morning. If she wanted something, she'd have to come to him and ask, because he couldn't be trusted around her. He could still barely believe he'd kissed Aria. And he wanted to do a whole lot more than kiss her. If his mother knew, she would've rapped him over the knuckles for his ungentlemanly behavior. He'd taken advantage of the woman he'd offered refuge to. But she'd looked so...

tempting. Soft and warm, straight from the shower. The sight of her bare shoulders and elegant neck had hit him so hard. But it was the knowledge that she wore nothing underneath the towel that had him hard in a second. He wanted to run a hand up her thigh, beneath the edge of that towel. She was alluring. Then she'd licked her lips, her dark eyes boring into him and something in him had snapped. A part of him he barely knew existed surged within, driving him to touch her, to taste her. Physically, she was his perfect woman, dark and slender. If he had a type, it would be her. But this was something more than just a physical attraction. There was something a little…lost about her. Something the protective side of him wanted to safeguard, as if he could help her find that missing piece. Which was utterly ridiculous.

He'd been trying to get her out of his head ever since, without much luck. And to make matters worse, he'd never posted the description of Aria as the thief from the milk bar, which made his stomach churn in self-reproach, even now. And to top that off, now he was mixed up in her father's murder investigation. She'd require him most in his professional capacity. But he was also going to be there for her emotionally, if she needed him.

"Jude, I've run out of tape," Susan called from the front gate.

"I've got some right here." He held up the roll. Then he turned at the sound of a car engine. Sheriff Buchanan was here to oversee everything. The sheriff gave him a look as he exited his car, as if to say, *here we go again*. Jude understood that expression. This wasn't the first murder they'd attended in the past two years in this small, sleepy town. And here was yet another one with a connection to Stargazer Ranch, albeit a loose one, as Aria had only been working there for two days. But it was a connection, nonetheless.

Thinking about Stargazer jogged his memory back to

earlier today when Levi had called into the office. He'd almost forgotten his conversation with Levi because straight afterward the tip-off had come in about a suspected dead body, and Jude and Susan had dropped everything to rush over to Tango's house.

Levi had some interesting news. Yesterday afternoon, he'd borrowed an ATV from Cat at Stargazer and driven into the foothills of Canyon Peak, which ran parallel to the Stargazer Ranch boundary. And he'd found signs of at least two abandoned campsites. It was very dry up there with the fall rains yet to start, and so footprints were almost impossible to see in the dusty, rocky ground. It'd taken Levi's trained eye to spot them; whoever was camping there had done a good job of covering up any signs. Some partially flattened grass and what looked to be freshly swept earth, scattered with leaves and other debris. This would've fooled most people, but it immediately raised a red flag in Levi's mind.

"I think they might still be up there," Levi had said in his slow, considered way. "It looks like they move around every couple of days. But I ran out of time, and out of daylight, to keep searching."

"You said *they*. Do you think there's more than one person?" Jude asked.

"Yes. Two, maybe three people, from the size of the campsite. I found no sign of the stolen cattle, but that doesn't mean they didn't take them. If they were that careful to cover their tracks and campsite, they could easily have buried the remains of the cattle somewhere outside the camp and disguised that site, as well," Levi added thoughtfully. "It's a little odd, and it definitely warrants another look." Levi had scratched his beard and tipped his head to the side, watching Jude with his dark eyes.

Jude trusted Levi's judgement, which was why he'd asked him to go up there in the first place. So they'd made a plan to go back together in a few days' time, when they were both free.

Now, with Tango's murder, Jude decided there should be more urgency put on someone going into the area to give a more thorough search. Could there be a link between the mysterious campers stealing cattle and a murder in the town? It would be a tenuous link, but Jude knew better than to discount anything in an investigation.

He tossed this all around in his head as he watched Sheriff Buchanan walk toward him. He hadn't mentioned asking Levi to take a look for him to his boss yesterday, seeing it more as a favor to Dean. But now he needed to make the search official. He filled Hank in on everything they'd found today, as well as Levi's findings, as they walked toward the house.

CHAPTER SEVEN

"Mmm hmm." Aria made the sound in the back of her throat as she watched Naomi sketch out her idea on a piece of paper. It was a rough plan for a new covered horse riding arena, specifically designed to teach blind children to ride. It was like a large dressage arena, with high wooden fences and a roof to keep out the snow and rain. Aria was a little flabbergasted at the ease with which Naomi blithely threw plans around, as if money were no hurdle. Which it obviously wasn't. But it was still hard for Aria to get her head around that kind of money being so easily accessible.

"We'd have to have a covered walkway between the arena and the stables," Naomi stopped drawing and tapped the pen against her lips. "I wonder if Dean would let me build a whole new set of stables specifically for the blind riding horses, too?"

Aria silently shook her head. It was a great thing Naomi was doing, all this philanthropic development of the ranch, but she talked about building stables like they cost nothing at all, like she wasn't thinking of spending millions of dollars to achieve her goal.

Dean had been in earlier to see what they were up to, and had just grimaced when he saw how his wife and new employee were taking over his office. Drawings and papers covered in Naomi's scrawled handwriting littered the floor. Piles of reference books and articles were stacked on one end of the desk, and a set of yellow sticky notes were plastered to the window. His grimace said that he knew he wasn't getting his office back any time soon.

"Looks like you ladies are having fun," he said with a smile. Aria was fast coming to learn that Dean always had a smile at the ready. He was one of those positive, happy people who just loved his life. And why wouldn't he? With this beautiful ranch, his lovely wife, and more than enough money that he'd never want for anything.

"We are," Naomi had enthused. "Look, Dean, we could build our very own riding arena."

"We could?" Dean eyed the picture Naomi held up with mild confusion.

"Yes, I think that would be best," Naomi replied, completely serious. Naomi turned to Aria and said, "Dean is totally on board with this. He's already talking about retraining some of our ranch horses, or perhaps bringing in new horses that've been trained specially to work with blind people. They'd need to be bombproof. Gentle and extremely tolerant."

Aria held in a smile. She didn't think Dean had any choice about being on board, it seemed Naomi was running with this idea, and no one was going to stop her. But Dean gave her an indulgent smile, full of love and admiration, and Aria knew he'd give her the sun and the moon if she asked for it. What would it be like to have that sort of love? Where your man loved you unconditionally, would do anything to see you happy and smiling? It was a special kind of love that Dean and Naomi had, and Aria found herself a tad jealous.

This was only the second day on the job, but her head was already bursting with all the new information, all the projects

Naomi had lined up, and how many different ways Aria could help Naomi achieve her goals. She'd originally thought she was applying for the job of marketing and social administrator, which Naomi agreed was definitely a large part of the new position. But she also said she needed help with the practicalities of getting the blind riding school off the ground, and that would form at least half of Aria's new duties. Aria didn't mind. As long as she got to use her graphic design skills, she would be happy. And they'd already come in handy getting all of Naomi's hand-drawn ideas into readable and recognizable documents on the computer. Aria had shown Naomi a software package that could bring her drawings to life, and show her a 3D virtual reality version of the plan once it was input into the system. Naomi had been beside herself with glee when she'd seen that software, and now that Aria knew she liked what she saw, she had plenty more ideas up her sleeve.

Yesterday, Aria had spent all of the day locked in the room with Naomi, getting to know her new boss and finding out the extent of her plans. Naomi had waxed lyrical about all the different ways horseback riding could help to add meaning and structure to a vision-impaired person's life.

"Usually with a blind person, their other senses are highlighted," Naomi had told her. "Riding stimulates these other senses, through touch, the leather of the saddle, the soft horse's hide when they groom the animal, and through environmental stimuli, like the sound of a farm and the smell of dust and hay and manure. Their posture may be improved, too, as they learn to sit up straight, keep their shoulders back and look the world right in the eye, so to speak." Naomi had given a self-effacing cough at her unintended pun. But then she'd continued with her passionate sermon. "It will also give them freedom of movement, they're no longer tied to shuffling along using a stick or other implement. They're free to fly on top of a cantering horse." Naomi was so excited by this new prospect, it was hard not to feel excited, as well. In fact, Naomi was so excited, Aria could hardly get a word in edgeways.

Then finally, late this afternoon, Naomi had remembered to take Aria out and introduce her to the other Stargazer Ranch staff.

"You've already met Penny," Naomi said, breezing past the reception desk.

"Yes. Hi again." Aria waved as they fluttered past, and Penny gave her a sympathetic glance at being caught up in the whirlwind that was Naomi with a new idea brewing.

"I'll give you a quick whistle-stop tour of the place," Naomi said. "So you can get your bearings." Naomi took two jackets from inside a mud room to the side of the main entrance and handed her one with a Stargazer logo on the back. "I'll get Penny to order you your own personal jacket to fit you properly, but this spare one will have to do for now."

Practically having to run to keep up with her new boss, Aria was glad she'd decided to stick with jeans, a sweater and a pair of tennis shoes, throwing the jacket over her clothes as they trudged up the hill toward the machinery shed. The wind was decidedly icy. Fall was definitely setting in. Aria noticed a gorgeous garden hugging the side of the lodge and leading down to the parking lot, full of natives, and pockets of green oases set in amongst the trunks of enormous pine trees. There was even a stand of silver aspen, their yellow fall leaves shivering in the breeze. But she didn't have time to stop and stare, as Naomi charged up the path toward a low rise, over which she could just make out a metallic roofline.

"Cat, are you there?" Naomi called out as they rounded into a huge iron-clad shed full of farm equipment and other vehicles. A woman with bright blonde, spiky, short hair clambered out from underneath a tractor. "This is our newest staff member, Aria Cusack." Naomi pointed to Aria, who was standing with her mouth open, taking in the enormous space.

"Nice to meet you." Cat shook Aria's hand with a handshake firmer than most men, and Aria hid her shock that the ranch mechanic was a woman.

"Dean often says this place would stop functioning without Cat," Naomi said, affectionately patting the other woman on the shoulder. "She can get any piece of machinery or equipment back up and running." Aria didn't doubt it. This woman looked fit and athletic, and highly capable. Not someone to be messed with. But Naomi was clearly fond of her and so Aria decided she must not be all hard edges and sharp eyes; she'd delay her judgement until she knew the woman better.

"Are you coming down for afternoon tea?"

Cat scowled at the tractor as if it held some untold secret it wasn't letting go of. "Yes, I'll be there," she finally agreed. "I need a break from this heap of crap, anyway. Dean reckons I can fix anything, but I'm not so sure about this one."

"Good, I'll see you in twenty minutes, then." And with that, Naomi took off, leaving Aria to scurry behind her.

Next, they visited the stables where she met Clayton, Penny's boyfriend—they shared a couple's cabin and were the ranch's latest loved-up pair, according to Naomi. Poor Clayton, he tried to hide his slight awkwardness at Naomi's oversharing, but then Aria guessed you either got used to her boss's bubbly persona, where everyone was an open book, or you simply didn't work at Stargazer. She was then introduced to Tom and Emily, who'd just returned with a group of guests after having taken them horse riding through the foothills. Another loved-up couple. Aria was beginning to wonder if there was something in the water. The stables were abuzz with noise, people chatting, horses snorting as they were being unsaddled, and it was warm and friendly out of the wintry breeze. Aria had never been on a working ranch before. She might've been born in a small country town, but this was all completely alien to her. She decided she liked it; the camaraderie and the banter, the musky smell of the horses and sawdust.

Then she and Naomi went back to the lodge, just in time to join the rest of the staff for afternoon tea. Cat was already there, helping herself to a slice of delicious-looking chocolate cake and berating Dean about his old-fashioned stance on having to fix everything, instead of replace it. She was introduced to Joseph, the head chef, and Stella, the amazing French cook who'd created the pastries she'd been offered the other day, along with the new apprentice cook, Markus. Then there was Gordon, the activities coordinator, a Scottish gentleman with a smart, gray beard who reminded her of the comedian Billy Connolly. As soon as Gordon saw Naomi, he took her by the arm and dragged her aside to ask her about whether he should set up the outdoor archery kits for some of the child guests this afternoon. The ranch crew piled in through the door, Clayton, Tom, Emily and another two she hadn't met yet, but who she knew must be Steph, an older lady who'd worked at Stargazer forever, and their new recruit Jimbo, from Naomi's descriptions.

Stella took a chair next to Aria and smiled at her warmly. Aria might've had her mouth open, gawping at the group of busy, cheerful people, because Stella said, "We're like one big happy family. And this isn't even all of us. We have two ladies who come from town and help with dinner service, and an assistant cook, Violet, who'll arrive later on this afternoon as well. There's also Myrna, the full-time cleaner, who lives in town, plus a couple of other extras when we're really busy."

"Wow. It's a big crew," Aria breathed.

"Yes, it is. But everyone has their place, and we all work

well together, like the pieces of a jigsaw puzzle. You'll fit in as well, don't worry," Stella assured her.

Aria was beginning to learn that this place took a village of people to keep it running. It was a complex web of personalities and jobs, and if any one of them broke a link, it might all come tumbling down.

And Stella might just be right. She might enjoy working here. She could see herself fitting in. Perhaps this'd been the right move after all.

She had a new job and a place to stay—no longer homeless and living out of her car. They were definitely steps in the right direction. And even though she hated to be thought of as a charity case, she was glad she'd accepted Jude's offer of the cottage in his backyard. It was the best two nights' sleep she had in a long time. She was determined to pay him rent from her first paycheck, just to prove to him—and to herself —that she could indeed stand on her own two feet.

While lying awake, luxuriating in the soft bed on the night Jude had brought her back to his place, she'd even wondered if this might turn into a permanent solution. If she could perhaps start paying him rent and live in the cottage full-time. But that illusion had been shattered the following morning when he'd kissed her. Or had she kissed him? Or was it somewhere in between? Whatever the truth, she'd been avoiding Jude ever since. She wasn't in the market for a relationship at the moment. Things were way too complicated. And if he found out she was an unwed mother-to-be whose boyfriend had kicked her out when he learned about the baby, then Jude was likely to do the same. And even if he didn't evict her, he wouldn't want anything to do with her from that moment on. Of that much, she was sure. Perhaps she wasn't giving him enough credit, because he did seem like a nice guy, but her experience of men had taught her that they were often selfish beings and weren't to be trusted.

Stella interrupted her introspection by handing her a plate filled with cake and other pastries, which Aria accepted gratefully. All that weight she'd lost while living in her car was about to go back on her hips in one afternoon if she ate this lot. And if this was how they ate at the ranch every day, she wouldn't need to worry about the pregnancy showing too soon, as she'd be as big as a house before long.

Half an hour later, Naomi beckoned Aria back to the office. Aria pushed the plate away and patted her stomach. Her good intentions not to finish everything on the plate had gone out the window as soon as she tasted it. No need for dinner tonight.

Now, the two women settled back behind the desk, and Aria took the initiative to ask a few questions before Naomi got too bogged down in all her plans and ideas again.

"Is there a budget for this new venture?" Aria hardly dared to ask. But she needed to know. Naomi was talking big picture stuff, new buildings, infrastructure, livestock, and even employing new staff to help out. But Aria wondered about the smaller details, like, was there money allocated for the marketing side of things?

"A budget?" Naomi seemed surprised. "Well, no, not really —"

There was a knock on the door, and both she and Naomi looked up from their papers to see Penny standing nervously in the doorway.

"Deputy Wilder and a detective are here to see you," she said hurriedly before Naomi could ask.

Aria's heart skipped a beat at the mention of Jude's name. He was here. In the flesh. Crap. She needed to stop that reaction. This was no longer a schoolgirl crush. She needed to remind herself to keep her distance and stay cool. It never occurred to her that a deputy and a detective arriving together could mean anything sinister.

Naomi straightened and replied, "Well, send them in. Can you clear a pathway for the two gentlemen?" she added to Aria, pointing at the papers strewn all over the floor.

Just as Aria got down on her hands and knees, Penny said with an awkward grimace, "Um... It's actually Aria they've come to see."

CHAPTER EIGHT

Jude sat in the passenger seat next to Detective Brady as they drove out to Stargazer Ranch. Jude kept his face blank, but inside he was seething. Brady was the homicide detective dispatched from Missoula to investigate Tango's murder, and already Jude didn't like him. Tall, clean-shaven, dressed in designer jeans and dark overcoat, the man was cocky and sure of himself. He'd marched into the Cusack house demanding to know if anything had been touched or moved, demanding to know if the next of kin have been told yet, then grilling the sheriff to make sure protocol had been followed to the letter, and generally treating the sheriff and the deputies with the disdain he thought they deserved. He'd even winked at Susan when he'd asked her to go and retrieve a piece of equipment from his car for him, as if she were some topless waitress at a local strip joint and he'd asked her to go and get him a beer. The other two officers that accompanied him treated Brady with professional regard, but Jude could see their equal distaste hovering beneath the surface. At least Jude knew he wasn't alone in his dislike.

Brady had recently been transferred to the Missoula office, and this was the first time they'd had the pleasure of working with him. Jude hoped it'd also be the last, as did Susan, if her glower at the man was anything to go by. Susan hated any form of male chauvinism and this guy was handing it out in spades. And if the man kept up his obvious lack of regard for the way the sheriff's office conducted their business, it may well be his last job in Stevensville. Hank didn't take kindly to being told what to do, or treated like a snot-nosed kid fresh out of deputy training. Hank's mustache was getting a workout as he tugged viciously on the ends every time Brady made a comment.

After a thorough examination of the body, the house, and the surrounding garden, Brady had called in his findings to his superior. The guy was doing everything correctly by the book, and Jude couldn't fault Brady's procedure, it was just his attitude that stank. By that stage, the sheriff had left in a huff, ostensibly to go and handle a fender bender up by the local gas station, telling Jude and Susan to keep him updated.

The detective had asked for the names of the next of kin because he wanted to talk to them immediately. Susan had told him that Tango had two daughters currently in town and Brady wanted both home and work addresses. Jude thought about Aria, who'd be nearly finished her second day at a new job and had argued they could at least wait another hour and a half until she came home. He knew without having to be told that she'd be mortified if her new boss, as well as everyone at Stargazer, were to see two police officers arriving to talk to her.

Jude had argued until he was blue in the face, but Brady wouldn't be swayed. He wanted to talk to Aria Cusack as soon as possible, and then Iliana. But Aria was first on his list, especially after he found out that she'd only returned to town a few days ago. Around the same time as her father was murdered, in fact. In Brady's words, *he wanted to confront her*, which Jude didn't like the sound of, as if Brady thought she had something to do with Tango's death.

Susan, along with one of the corporals from Missoula, had been dispatched to break the news to Iliana and her husband and take down any details that might be pertinent to Tango's death, find out if their father had any enemies in town, that kind of thing. Susan had cast Jude a sideways glance as she made her way to the police cruiser, and he knew she was thinking, *if you listened to Tango, just about everyone in the county was an enemy.*

"I just want to get this completely clear," Jude said, turning to study Brady in the driver's seat. "We're just informing the next of kin about the death of their father, aren't we?"

"Yep, that's why you're here," the man said, flicking him a raised eyebrow. "You're going to break the sad news to her. I'm just tagging along because I'm interested in her reaction to the news."

Jude bristled at his tone. And not for the first time today, he wished Missoula homicide had sent someone else to work this case. Anyone else. "You're not about to drag her in for questioning, are you?"

"Not unless she gives me cause to." This guy was infuriating. Jude had the sense that Brady suspected Aria had something to do with her father's murder. As if. It was ridiculous. Yes, he could see why Aria might be on the suspect list, family were nearly always at the top when it came to the death of a loved one. But this murder had been so shockingly violent, Jude knew Aria wasn't capable of something like that.

Although, in Brady's eyes, the violent way in which Tango died spoke to him of a deep passion. Hate. Often the more violent of killings were rooted in deep-seated emotions, perpetrated by people close to a family member who'd been hurt in some way, or who were holding a grudge. All of which applied to Aria.

Jude squared his shoulders and led the detective up the

stairs to the reception area in the lodge. It was never easy telling someone that their loved one had died, even if that loved one wasn't particularly…loved. It was still a shock. But because it was Aria, it'd be much harder for him to utter the words and then stand by and watch as the meaning hit. To a bystander, it might look like as if he and Aria were mere acquaintances. Old friends renewing an attachment from their school days. They'd effectively only known each other for a few days. But to Jude, their connection went much deeper than that. From the first time he'd seen her sitting in her car, staring up at him with those big, brown eyes, it was like there was a force from somewhere deep inside pulling him toward her. A recognition of who she'd once been and the woman she'd now become. An attraction. But also more than that. More than just owing her a debt from when he'd been a dickhead teenager. He didn't want to see her get hurt, which was inevitable with the news that he brought today. Jude braced himself.

"Hi, Penny. This is Detective Brady. Is Aria around?" Jude dispensed with his normal friendly greeting. It was enough to show Penny that he was here on business.

Penny's eyes widened as she studied the detective standing slightly behind him, a smug smile hovering on his lips. "Oh, ah. Yes. She and Naomi are in Dean's office." Penny indicated the door behind reception.

"Good. Can you let her know we'd like to speak to her privately, please?" At least they could break the news in the seclusion of Dean's office, a small concession, but better than nothing.

They followed Penny to the door, and he glimpsed Aria kneeling on the floor, picking up piles of paper. His guts tightened at the sight of her.

When she looked up, her face was pale, almost as if she knew he was about to deliver some terrible news. Slowly, she stood and shuffled back a few steps, her eyes never leaving his face.

"Thanks, Penny," Brady said, pushing past Jude and striding into the room. "You can go now," he added brusquely as Penny continued to hover in the doorway. Jude clenched his fists by his sides. This guy seemed to have his default constantly set at *rude*. Jude was yet to hear a considerate word to come out of Brady's mouth.

He shot Penny an apologetic glance as she went back to the reception desk, and she waggled her eyebrows as if to say, *don't worry about it*.

"I'm Detective Brady." The man stood in the middle of the room, sizing the two women up, but not offering his hand in greeting.

"And I'm Naomi Williams, joint owner of Stargazer Ranch." Naomi stood a little taller, almost like David squaring off against Goliath; she was so petite next to the tall detective.

"We're here to see Aria Cusack, so if you don't mind, we'd like the room for a moment."

Aria flinched and nearly dropped the pile of papers she was hugging to her chest. "What...? Why...?" Her eyes darted from the detective to Jude and back again.

"What's going on here, Jude?" Naomi turned to him, ignoring the tall man behind her.

"We have some...news we need to share with Aria," Jude said, taking a step forward, effectively placing himself between Brady and the women.

"And some questions we'd like to ask," Brady added from behind him.

"What news? What questions?" Jude could see slight tremors running through Aria's body and had to stop himself from reaching over and touching her arm, telling her everything was going to be okay.

"If Mrs. Williams would leave the room, then we can tell you," Brady said haughtily.

Naomi completely ignored the man towering over her. "Would you like me to stay with you, honey?" she asked, taking one of Aria's hands in hers.

Aria looked at her new boss in confusion. It'd be better for her if Naomi stayed. It'd force Brady to be more circumspect in his questioning, but Jude couldn't explain that to her. Instead, he inclined his head ever so slightly, hoping she'd take a hint.

"Yes, please," she finally said.

"You can't—" Brady began, but Jude cut him off.

"She's entitled to have someone here as a moral support." He turned around to glare at Brady, hating the fact he had to look up to meet the man's eye. Brady pursed his lips but said no more.

"Come and sit over here," Naomi suggested, leading Aria by the hand toward the two comfy chairs by the window. Jude followed and hunkered down next to Aria's chair.

"Tell me what's going on. You're scaring me." She turned wide eyes to him, lips trembling slightly, and again, he had to stop himself from reaching out.

"I'm sorry to have to inform you that your father was found dead this morning at his property on Manning Road."

"What?" Aria's eyes clouded, as if she hadn't quite understood what he'd said. "My father? Dead? That's impossible. He's so…" She shook her head. "I saw him just a few days ago, he was fine."

"Well, I can assure you he's not fine anymore, Miss Cusack. He's definitely dead. It probably happened around four days ago." Brady trained his beady eyes on Aria, searching for her response.

Jude wanted to stand up and punch the detective right in the face. What was with this guy? He seemed to have no compassion whatsoever.

"Oh, I'm so sorry, honey." Naomi reached over and covered Aria's hands with her own. She glanced at her boss, but it was as if she didn't really see her.

"How did he die?" All the color had drained from Aria's face.

Jude hesitated for a second, but she deserved to know. And if he didn't tell her, then Brady would probably take great glee in dispensing the information. "We think he was murdered."

"Oh, no." Aria removed her hands from Naomi's and covered her mouth, hunching her shoulders as if folding in on herself. "That's terrible." She stared up at him with a pained expression, eyes remaining dry, but the lines around her mouth were pinched and deeply etched. He hadn't really expected tears from Aria over her father. But the anguish was clear in her face. Even though she might not have liked her father very much, she plainly never wanted him dead.

"Yes, it's terrible, and that's why we need to ask you some questions. Maybe you can help us capture the murderer." Brady was still standing, looking down at the trio huddled around the coffee table, but then he pulled the chair around from behind the desk and sat, looking intently into Aria's face. Couldn't the man see how distressed she was? He was a homicide detective, surely he should be good at gauging when a person was genuinely upset. But it seemed not, because Brady went on to say, "Tell me about the last time you saw your father. Alive," he added, then leaned in closer, as if Aria might actually be about to admit to being the killer.

Jude was so disgusted with the other man's blatant disregard for any sort of compassion that he stood and glared down at Brady. "This woman has just received distressing news. I think your questions can wait until later."

"I agree," Naomi chipped in. "You need to give her time to

process this. Jude, I think you should take her home, back to your place. She can answer your questions tomorrow morning. Don't you agree?"

Jude was about to say he thought that was a good idea when Brady interrupted.

"Wait, are you telling me she lives with you, Deputy Wilder?" Brady's eyes narrowed dangerously as he fixed Jude with an accusing stare. "Why didn't you reveal this information beforehand?"

"Because it's not pertinent to the case." *And you didn't ask,* but Jude kept that thought to himself. "She's renting a little cottage in my backyard. She needed a place to stay, and I had the room to spare, that's all."

"Really." Innuendo dripped from the detective's words as he sent an assessing gaze flicking over Aria, who was still hunched in the chair. "This sheds a different light on things. Perhaps you shouldn't be part of this investigation anymore, Deputy Wilder."

"I beg your pardon," Jude said, his voice suddenly low and husky. He stood up to his full height, and Brady backed the chair away so he could also stand. "I don't like what you're implying. There's nothing going on between me and Aria Cusack. I want you to note that on record. I'm merely helping out an old friend from school. You don't get a say in whether I work this case, anyway, it's up to the sheriff."

"We'll see about that." The two men stood staring at each other like two alpha dogs, sizing each other up for a fight.

"Excuse me." Naomi inserted herself between them. "I'm not sure what's going on here, but my main concern is Aria's mental well-being." Even standing on tiptoe, Naomi only came halfway up Brady's chest. "So you can just get out of my office." She stared at Brady and then pointed to the door. "And do your questioning elsewhere."

Jude wondered if Naomi hadn't gone a step too far,

ordering a detective around like he couldn't just arrest her on the spot for obstructing an investigation. And thinking about arrests, Jude hoped that Brady didn't get it into his head to take Aria into custody, either. He was within his rights, according to the book. But most police officers knew that ethically and morally it was unhealthy and unwise to bully someone who'd just been informed of their father's death, even if they were a potential suspect.

The man's gray eyes glinted like they were made of steel, and Jude almost held his breath.

"I'll expect you at the sheriff's office at nine am sharp tomorrow morning." Brady stepped around Naomi and Jude and walked out of the office without even one backward glance, shutting the door loudly behind him.

"What a nasty piece of work," Naomi said, even as the door closed. "I'm so sorry, honey." She got down on her haunches next to Aria and placed an arm around her thin shoulders. "This must be a terrible shock."

"I'll drive you home," Jude said softly, holding out his hand.

Half an hour later, Aria was propped up in bed in her little cottage. He'd made her a mug of hot tea, but it sat untouched on the bedside table. After they got home, Aria had complained of feeling cold, and when he took her hands in his to try and warm them, they were like blocks of ice, so he'd decided bed was the best place for her. She was probably suffering shock, and she really wasn't wearing the right clothes for this weather. Her thin sweater and battered denim jacket did nothing to keep out the bitter wind. Maybe she'd forgotten how cold fall got here in the Bitterroot Mountains. He'd taken off her shoes, like she was a child and he was the parent while she sat on the end of the bed. It was like she was in a sort of trance, which again could be the shock.

They'd hardly spoken on the drive back into town. At one

stage, Aria had asked if he was really, really sure that Tango had indeed been murdered.

"Yes. I saw the body myself," he'd replied. "There's no doubt in my mind."

She didn't ask for details, for which he was grateful, just took his word for it, but then she asked, "Do you have any leads on who did this?"

"No," he replied simply, and silence had fallen over them again. There were a million questions burning brightly in his mind, but he knew better than to ask them. Unlike that prick, Brady. He wondered if she was thinking the same as him? If she was remembering her father's crazy claims that someone was after him. He tried to think back to when Tango's paranoia had first become evident. It was hard to recall what Tango had been like back when Jude had been a teenager. There were rumors, even back then, about Tango's weird notions, but Jude didn't think he was openly spouting his theories to the sheriff at that stage, and everyone tended to ignore him. So when had his delusions become worse? When had they become so bad he'd began asking the sheriff for help?

Jude had interviewed Tango six months ago, when he'd come in with fresh accusations that someone was out to kill him. That was when Jude had first heard about the cult InXium. But before that, the sheriff had handled things. Tango had probably been spouting his delusions for many years. But that was well after Aria had left town. So how much did she know?

She was huddled into the passenger seat, looking frail and alone as he ground the gears of her Subaru, unused to driving a stick shift. Her bright, bubbly smile was nowhere to be seen. People had turned to watch as he led her down the stairs from the Stargazer lodge to her car, and he'd wanted to tell them all to mind their own business, to shield her with his body from their scrutiny and their judgement.

Looking at her now, he hated that he'd have to leave her alone. "I'll need to go back to work tonight," he said into the silence. It would be all hands on deck at the sheriff's office over the next few days. As much as he wanted to stay with Aria, there would be no way Hank would let him take a day off right now. He'd probably need to pull an all-nighter, as it was.

"Fine. I'll be fine," she said, the blank stare not leaving her face. He didn't want to abandon her, but he didn't see many options. He'd stay another half an hour, and then he'd go back to work.

"I'll just call in and update my status." Aria didn't seem to hear him from her spot huddled into her bed, so he took out his phone and dialed Susan, wandering out of the bedroom to the far end of the cottage where Aria wouldn't overhear. Susan should be back from breaking the news to Iliana, and he wanted to find out how it'd gone. Where he stood in the corner of the cottage, there was a high window to let in light, but would keep out the prying gazes of the neighbors. He was just tall enough to see over the windowsill to the view of the house next door's back garden; and he considered the neat pretty space thoughtfully, deciding it was time he got back into his mother's garden, he'd been letting it go lately.

Susan answered on the fifth ring. "Jude, I was just about to call you. Hank wants you in the office straight away," Susan said, and he could hear the strain in her voice.

"I'll be in soon," he promised. "I just want to make sure Aria is really okay before I leave her."

"Hmm, she didn't take the news well, then?"

"Not really. And I needed to get her away from that... detective."

"Say no more," Susan sighed. "He's at the station right now, poking his nose into places he's not wanted, and just being a general meathead." Jude could tell by the slight high pitch in Susan's voice that if he tried any more of his condescending shit on her again, she might well have to put him in his place. And Susan had tricks; she knew how to hurt a man where it mattered most. "But, Jude, I've got some news, and it's not good. I was expecting to see you here at the office when I debriefed the sheriff about my trip to see Iliana, and then Brady got all up in my face and I haven't had a chance to talk to you."

Jude stilled and held the phone a little closer to his mouth. "Why? What happened?"

"Iliana and her husband seem to be missing."

"What? Where have they gone?"

"We don't know, the place was deserted when we got there, apart from a hungry cat who wouldn't leave me alone." Susan had a soft spot for cats; she had three of her own, and was considering fostering a fourth. "Everything was locked up tight, two cars parked neatly around the back, all the sheds and the barn closed up," she continued. "But the back door was unlocked, and when I looked inside, I noticed signs of a struggle, so we entered the premises. It seemed like the couple had been eating breakfast, then something had gone awry. Plates and glasses were scattered on the floor, and there were a few drops of blood near the sink."

"Shit." It was taking Jude a while to get his head around this new scenario. "Do you mean you think they've been abducted?" he finally asked. It was the only scenario that fit.

"I don't know what it means. But Brady is just about frothing at the mouth with the news. He's gone out there himself to take a look." Fuck. Jude wouldn't mind taking a look himself. Sometimes it helped to put the puzzle pieces together when you saw a scene with your own eyes. "Hank is just about having a conniption, he was looking forward to Stevensville going back to being a sleepy little country town again, but it seems like we might have a whole shit load more trouble brewing."

Jude didn't have time to feel sorry for the sheriff. Yes, this town seemed to have more than its fair share of crime over the last few years, but this was their job. This was also the last thing Aria needed to hear. Should he tell her? Even as he listened to Susan give him more details about the missing couple, he was internally debating whether to let her know or not.

Susan told him everything she and the police officer from Missoula, Sergeant Camden McMurdo, had found in the Doncaster house. It was giving him chills just listening to her. The house was neat as a pin, except for the kitchen, which'd been trashed. Iliana was clearly house-proud. Susan was about to go back out and start door knocking the neighbors to see if they'd seen or heard anything unusual. It was difficult to put a timeline on the abduction—he couldn't see how this could be anything other than an abduction—the leftover food was definitely a day or so old, at least. And the biggest question of all. Was this new crime somehow related to Tango's death?

"Right, thanks, Susan," Jude finally said. "I'll be in as soon as I can." He ended the call and huffed out a breath. He turned around to see Aria staring at him.

"What's going on? Were you talking about my sister?" Damn, she'd overheard him. Now what?

"Tell me." She advanced on him, her movements jerky, and he reached to take her arm, afraid she was about to fall.

"I'm sorry, Aria." He led her to the couch and forced her to sit. He sat beside her and took her hands in his. They were cold and clammy. "Iliana and Craig are missing."

A groan escaped her from somewhere deep inside. "I heard you ask if they'd been abducted. Is it true? Has someone taken them?"

She deserved the truth. "The evidence points that way, yes."

Aria moaned again. "I went out to see her two days ago, straight after the interview at Stargazer." She lowered her gaze, fixing it on their hands entwined on her knee. "I wanted to try and fix things between us, but the place was empty, so I left. I never even got to see her again. And now she's missing." A small part of Jude's brain that wasn't focused on Aria and her highly distressed state catalogued the fact that she'd just provided him with a slightly better timeline for the abduction. A sob broke from her throat, and she laid her head on his chest. Aria hadn't cried at the news of her father's death, although she had been in shock, but here she was crying for her sister who she hadn't seen in eight years, and Jude suddenly got a better idea of where Aria's allegiances lay.

He pulled her closer as she spoke muffled words into his jacket. "My sister and I were never close, but I was hoping to fix that. I was hoping that by coming back to town, and me getting a job, we might be able to reconnect. And she might help me with the—" Her words cut off suddenly, but Jude had no time to wonder what she'd been about to say, as her sobs got louder, almost hysterical.

He held her tight as she cried, trying to work out this complicated woman. She had a tangled history with this town and a tragic past, losing her mother when she was so young and then stuck being raised by a man who had his own demons to fight. It must've been lonely and confusing, and it was interesting to hear that she and her sister weren't close. These types of family tribulations often brought siblings together. But then he remembered Iliana had moved out of home the second she'd finished high school, while Aria remained living with Tango for another three years, until she was also old enough to finish school and leave. He wondered how hard that'd been, living with a half-crazy father and no support from a sister who'd by all accounts abandoned her.

But Aria was about to have a lot more problems than just a shitty childhood. It didn't look good, Aria admitting to visiting Iliana's place, perhaps on the very morning she and her husband were abducted. Adding to that fact, she'd also been at her father's house on the day of his murder. Could it be just a simple coincidence she was connected to two crimes scenes? Brady was going to be all over this. Jude could imagine the barely restrained relish with which Brady would receive this news.

Aria's sobs lessened slightly, and she pulled back, wiping the sleeve of her denim jacket under her nose.

"Wait here," he said, and was back a few seconds later was a box of tissues he'd noticed beside her bed.

"Thank you," she snuffled, wiping her eyes and blowing her nose. He remained sitting close, watching her intently. He was sitting so close, he caught the smell of roses from her hair, and he had to remind himself not to lean in so he could draw that smell deep into his lungs.

"I know how this looks," she said carefully. "I know me being at Iliana's place makes me suspect number one." She was one smart cookie. But she didn't have anything to do with this; he knew it deep down in his guts.

"You're right," he admitted. "This news is certainly going to make the police want to take a closer look at you." He didn't add that Brady, in particular, would most likely be one of those police pointing the finger in her direction. "But I know you didn't have anything to do with this. And I believe in the justice system. I believe that if we let it take its course, you'll be proven innocent. And I want to say right now, how sorry I am for the loss of your father. You might not hear this from many of my colleagues, but I want to acknowledge your grief and let you know you can count on me if you need any support." Jude knew this to be true, once a person became a suspect in a crime, an officer of the law found it hard to show compassion toward them, lest they be seen as taking a bias or not being able to disconnect their personal from their professional feelings. Jude knew he was in jeopardy of doing exactly this. Letting his growing personal feelings for Aria overshadow the job he still had to do.

"Thank you, Jude." Aria sat up straight, blowing her nose one final time. Her eyes were red-rimmed, her face blotchy from crying, and her hair was a tangled mess around her shoulders. In this moment, she looked so alone and defenseless. And beautiful. The most beautiful thing he'd ever seen.

"But you need to know something else," she said. "I've been sitting in my bed trying to work out who would do this to my father." Her gaze drifted to stare out the window at the darkening garden, and Jude was shocked to notice the encroaching dusk. He hadn't realized the time. Aria took a deep breath and said, "I admit, I was shocked by the news of his death, but you may have already worked out, I wasn't overwhelmed by grief. Our relationship was tricky, at best. Hate is probably too strong a word, but I definitely didn't love him. Unlike my sister. I love her, and I wish things had been different between us." She looked back at him and he saw the truth in her eyes.

"Anyway, what I'm trying to say is that Tango was always scared of something, or someone. You probably know most people think he's delusional, and I probably agree with them. He's always had plenty of different conspiracy theories to keep him occupied. But the one about someone wanting him dead has never changed. He was always spouting that same story, even when I was a small child. I know he and my mother used to argue about it all the time." A shadow of pain crossed her face at the mention of her mother. "So, now I'm wondering if I should've listened more carefully. Tango never truly believed that my mother killed herself."

This was interesting. At least Aria had confirmed that Tango had been saying these things for a long time now. He hadn't been a deputy at the time Dimitra had died. But he had read the case file, however, and he knew that Hank had never bothered to look into Dimitra's death. It'd been an open and shut case of suicide. There was a note in Dimitra's hand, and Tango had been cleared of any wrongdoing, as he'd had an alibi that put him out of town on the day she died. The girls had both been at school. Iliana was the one to find her mother hanging in the barn at the back of the property that afternoon. Jude vaguely remembered Dimitra, because he'd seen her around town as a child. She'd had long, dark hair, much like Aria's and a captivating smile, also like Aria. It seemed Aria had much of her mother's Greek blood in her veins and took after Dimitra, even if she didn't realize it.

But if Dimitra truly hadn't killed herself—which Jude found hard to believe, the coroner had ruled it a suicide and who was he to doubt that?—then who had? Was she actually murdered? And if so, could that murder be tied to Tango's? The implications were astonishing, and Jude's mind began to whirl. He made a mental note to take another look at Dimitra's file.

But something else was topmost in his mind right now. Aria had brought up the conspiracy theory thing, so maybe now was the time to ask.

"Yes, I've heard about his...severe paranoia," Jude admitted. "Tango even came into the sheriff's office early this year to make a report that he thought his life was in danger."

Aria lifted one eyebrow, as if to say, what else was new.

"I took his statement, because Sheriff Buchanan was...busy. And he mentioned a cult called InXium. Have you ever heard him talk about this group before?"

Aria sat up straighter, pursing her lips. "Maybe," she said eventually. "He was rarely ever specific when he was on one of his tirades. But... I think I remember him and my mother arguing one night, when they thought us girls were asleep, and I heard my mother say that word a couple of times. But my mother especially was very careful not to enable my father in any way when he was in one of his paranoid moods. She'd change the subject or take us out of the room. She clearly didn't want us to be infected by whatever was haunting him. Sorry I can't be more specific." She shrugged. "Do you think it's relevant?"

"I don't know." It was his turn to shrug. "At the time, I Googled the group, but then we got busy and I put your father and his crazy cult delusions out of my mind. Perhaps we need to take a closer look. Do you think your parents were involved in this group? Perhaps before you were born?"

"Anything is possible," she replied. "I was too young to remember when we first moved here, and I have no recollection of where we lived before. It's funny, isn't it, how little we often know of our parents' past lives? Iliana might recall more, she was three when we came to Stevensville."

Jude doubted that a three-year-old would remember much. Was Iliana a victim of this same misadventure that'd plagued her father? And perhaps the mother, too? Had something from his past come back to haunt Tango and his family?

Aria was talking again, and Jude tilted his head to listen. "But I was trying to make a point earlier." She prodded his knee to get his attention. "After my mother died, my father warned me and Iliana a few times to be careful, that we might be next. But of course, we never took him seriously. Should I be taking him seriously now? Now that Iliana is missing. Am I a target too?"

Jude stared at her. He'd never even considered this aspect before. Should Aria be in protective custody right now?

CHAPTER NINE

Aria felt faint. She hadn't eaten anything all day and her stomach was like a deflated balloon flapping around inside her. This morning, she hadn't been able to stomach anything more than a cup of coffee. Either her morning sickness was getting worse or, more likely, it'd been the impending trip to the sheriff's office to give her statement to Detective Brady that was making her feel ill.

Now it was past one in the afternoon, and she was regretting her decision not to eat even a single slice of the toast Jude had brought to her. So far, neither Brady nor his offsider, another police officer from Missoula, had thought to offer her anything more than a glass of water. She wondered where Jude had got to. She knew he was busy, but it would've been nice to catch even one glimpse of his friendly face.

Brady said something, but she didn't catch it.

"I'm sorry," she said. "What did you say?"

"I asked if you could be more specific about the exact time on Tuesday morning that you called in to see your father," Brady said slowly, as if speaking to a moron.

"You've asked me that question three times already," she snapped, finally having had enough of his constant badgering.

"Yes, and you've been unable to give us a clear answer every time," Brady snapped back. "First, you thought it was nine o'clock in the morning. Then you changed your mind and said it was closer to ten. Which is it, Miss Cusack?"

Aria glowered at him. "I don't know," she grated out between clenched teeth. "I already told you, the clock on my car dashboard is broken." More to the point, she hadn't looked at the exact time, because she had nowhere else to be that morning. No appointments to be at, no job to be ready for, just the day stretching out ahead of her with only the prospect of sleeping in her car that night on an empty stomach. She hadn't even bothered to open her phone to check the time. She barely looked at her phone anymore. Why would she when no one was messaging her, or texting her, or phoning her? And she was certainly staying away from social media. She wasn't about to broadcast her downfall to anyone, and she didn't want to see any of her so-called friends back in Portland going about their happy, carefree lives.

"When is this going to end? I've told you everything I know." Aria slapped a hand on the table. She'd had enough of this bullshit.

Just as Brady turned cold eyes toward her, the door opened and the face of the female deputy—Aria couldn't remember her name—appeared in the crack. "Time for a break, gentlemen?" The deputy raised her eyebrows, but even Aria knew it wasn't really a question.

"I still have a few more—"

The deputy held up a hand, stopping Brady mid-sentence. "I've had lunch delivered for everyone, it's in the break room. The milk bar down the road does these amazing sandwiches. I'm sure everyone will benefit from a break. You can always recommence in half an hour," she said brightly.

"Thank you," Aria said gratefully.

"I could do with some food," the second police officer said, plainly ignoring the frown Brady shot him and smiling brightly at the deputy.

"Right," Brady said ungraciously. "Interview suspended at one-oh-seven pm," he said into his little recording machine.

The deputy beckoned Aria over, and she stood, her legs threatening to buckle beneath her as she walked across the room.

The other woman grabbed Aria by the arm, almost as if she knew Aria needed the support, and steered her down the corridor. "I'm Deputy Susan Nomad. Jude left me with orders to look out for you. I could see you were just about ready to faint from hunger in there."

"Thank you" was all Aria had the strength to say in reply.

"Come and sit in my office. I stole us a couple of sandwiches. Then you won't have to sit there and look at those two..." Susan trailed off with a little cough.

Aria let herself be led down the corridor and around to the right, then up another long corridor and into a large, windowless office.

"I share this office with Jude and our trainee, Lance," Susan said by way of explanation, waving her hand at the three desks shoved haphazardly into the open-plan office. Susan pulled out an office chair on wheels from beneath one of the desks and let Aria down gently into it, and then scooted her across till she was in front of the desk nearest the door.

"Would you prefer turkey, pesto and salad, or roast beef, lettuce and homemade relish?" Susan asked.

"Turkey please."

The deputy handed her a wrapped sandwich and a can of soda. "Tuck in," she suggested.

And Aria did, taking great bites of the delicious sandwich, almost moaning in pleasure, it tasted so good. Susan did the same with her sandwich, taking a seat on the opposite side of the desk, only the sound of chewing breaking the silence.

After she'd devoured half the sandwich, and the growling tiger in her stomach had been reduced to a cat-sized hiss, Aria looked up. So this was where Jude worked.

The words, *do you happen to know where Deputy Wilder is*, were on the tip of her tongue when the man in question rounded into the office. Aria's heart rate shot up a few beats when she recognized his handsome face. He looked so good, striding through the door in his uniform, clear gaze fixed on her. She hadn't realized how much she'd missed him, missed his unwavering support, missed the way his eyes always found her wherever she was in the room, and she wanted to reach up and touch him. He returned her gaze, and for a split-second, it felt like they were the only two people in the room.

"Sorry," he apologized. "I was meant to be back an hour ago. Thanks for intervening, Susan. And thanks for lunch," he added, reaching for the wrapped sandwich on his desk.

"I got you your favorite: meatballs on rye," she replied through a mouthful.

"Thanks, you're a star." Jude pulled up another chair and began to unwrap his sandwich. Then he stopped and fixed Aria with his clear, hazel gaze, reaching over and touching her arm.

"I'm not going to ask how it went, because I know Brady is a—"

Susan coughed, drowning out his derisive remark.

"What? You know he's a…" Jude replied.

Susan merely raised her eyebrow, as if to remind him to keep his thoughts to himself. Brady was a dick, but he was also a police detective doing his job, and Aria understood that a certain amount of propriety needed to be maintained; otherwise he wouldn't be able to do that job if his work colleagues undermined him to a suspect in a case. Even if that job was taking him down the wrong pathway, and he was letting his bias against her—unfounded as it may be—direct his investigation. Jude had told her last night that he believed justice would prevail in the end, and she could only hope and pray he was right. She was innocent, and surely Brady would discover that, eventually.

"Anyway, I'm sorry you had to go through that. And I'm sorry I wasn't here to help." His simple touch meant so much to her, reminding her how he'd held her in his arms as she cried for her sister last night. Sudden tears pricked at her eyelids, but she blinked them back. She was not going to cry. What was wrong with her? She didn't normally cry at the drop of a hat. Could it be hormones? Could she blame the baby for her sudden uncertainty, for the fact that every emotion she had right now seemed to be magnified a hundredfold? She was normally a much stronger person than this. Even when Beau had kicked her out, she'd remained dry-eyed and logical.

Being pregnant was something alien and new to her. She'd never read any books on the topic because she hadn't planned on getting pregnant, and she didn't know anyone else who was pregnant. Of course, she'd heard the stories of pregnant women complaining they were being ruled by their hormones, but she had no idea if it was true. Forcing the lump back down her throat, she turned to look at Jude. She didn't know where he'd been all morning, but if he'd been out near the Doncaster house, he might have heard something.

"Any news on…" She couldn't bring herself to say Iliana's name and ducked her head, immediately regretting the question when she saw the shutters come down in his face.

"Sorry." He shook his head. "You know I'd tell you, if we heard anything. Anything at all."

"I know. Thank you. It's just so hard, all this not knowing." She put her sandwich down on the desk, suddenly no longer hungry. One good thing about the interview this morning was that it'd kept her mind off her sister's predicament. But now the same questions that'd been circling her head all last night came back with a vengeance. Who had taken Iliana? Why had they taken her? Was she still alive? Was it more than one person, or someone working alone? Jude had agreed with Aria's summation that it was probably more than one person to be able to take both Iliana and Craig at the same time. By all accounts, Craig was a strong, fit and athletic man who wouldn't have gone down easily.

And last of all, was it the same person, or people, who'd murdered her father? And if the two were connected, should she be worried about her own safety? She'd raised this question more than once to Brady and his offsider in the interview, but he'd merely pursed his lips and said that, of course, they were looking into every alternative. She could tell by the slant of his eyelids that he wasn't taking her seriously, however. The last thing she wanted to do was go back into that room with that man who was trying to pin her as suspect number one.

"Can I go home now?" she asked in a small voice. Surely the detective had other people to question, other leads to track down. "I've answered all his questions, haven't I?"

"It sounded like he wanted to continue after lunch," Susan said quietly, attracting a glare from Jude.

"I'll take you home in a minute," Jude replied, shifting his gaze to Aria.

Susan made a noise and Jude looked up sharply. "And if Brady has any problem with that, he can talk to me."

Susan raised her hands in the air, but Aria caught her worried frown. Was Jude making an enemy of Brady because of her? And more to the point, should she let him? Maybe she could go back in there for another hour, that wouldn't be so hard, would it? And then a sudden wave of nausea made her clutch at her belly and double over.

"Are you okay?" Jude was off his chair and kneeling beside her in a flash.

She started to say she was fine, but another wave of nausea rolled through her and she knew she wasn't. Shaking her head, she said, "I'd really like to go home." She hated this weakness, how her voice wobbled, and how she sounded like a gutless woman afraid to face up to her responsibilities. Even if it was the baby hormones making her feel this way.

Gentle hands helped her to her feet, and Jude gripped her elbow to lead her out of the office. "I'll take her," he said to Susan. "I'll be back in half an hour." His tone said that he'd brook no argument, and Susan nodded, giving him a tight smile.

Jude took her out the back door. Aria could only assume it was so they could avoid seeing Brady on the way out. As soon as she took a few deep breaths of the cleansing mountain air, she felt revived. Perhaps all she needed was to get out of that sheriff's office. He led her to his private car, a little four-door sedan, which was parked in the rear lot.

"Are you going to get into trouble?" she asked, buckling her seat belt.

"Nope. You're not under arrest, you're giving these statements of your own free will. He has no right to hold you, or make you stay any longer than you want. Okay?"

"Okay," she replied. But she still wondered if he was stretching the boundaries of the law. He probably was, in Brady's eyes at least.

They sat in silence for a few moments, but there were things Aria needed to ask, and she had no idea when she'd next see Jude.

"That young police officer told me that I can't organize a

funeral for my dad until the coroner releases his body. But I'm not sure what that means," she said, turning to stare at his profile as he drove through the back streets of town. She studied the outline of his full lips, the curve of his ear, the way his hair curled just slightly on top, his strong neck beneath the collar of his jacket, and square jawline. So familiar, but how could that be? She'd only known him a few days.

Jude gave her a sympathetic look. "They still need to finalize the cause of death. An autopsy has already taken place, but we don't know the results yet. We're waiting on toxicology reports, that sort of thing. Depending on the findings, the coroner may not release the body for another week or more, until they're absolutely certain."

"Oh." Crap, that didn't sound promising. "I thought you said it was obvious he was murdered, I thought..." She assumed that meant he'd been shot, or—God forbid—stabbed, or had some other sort of physical wound that was proof of how he'd died. Jude had refused to tell her of his injuries, saying they were distressing and all she needed to know for now was that he'd most likely died quickly.

"I was going to ask Iliana to come and help me with Tango's stuff. I guess we need to clear the house out at some stage. But I mean, I wouldn't even know where to start. And now that she's missing..." Aria couldn't finish the thought. She had no idea where to begin with the property, with wrapping up Tango's life. What were you even supposed to do when someone died? Did he even have a final will and testament? She had no idea. But she guessed the first thing to do was to search the house, to see what legal papers he may have left behind, if any. But now, everything felt like it was hanging in limbo. She couldn't even plan a funeral. Not that she wanted to. And with Iliana missing, it was too much to think about.

"Do you have any other relatives who could come and help? Any friends that might come and stay with you?" Jude asked helpfully.

Aria shook head. "No other family that I know of. I've probably got aunts and cousins and stuff in Greece. But I've never met them. Mom never took us to visit her family. I'm not sure why." Dimitra had always dismissed any talk if Aria ever brought up her mother's side of the family. Aria would've liked to know if she had Greek grandparents somewhere, but it seemed her mother had been disowned by them for some reason. Some sort of family scandal had caused a rift. Maybe she'd decided to marry Tango against their wishes? But she guessed she might never find out.

"Tango has family down in Colorado somewhere. He has an older brother, I believe. I guess that'd make him my uncle. Mom said he and my dad were close for a while. We even lived in the same town. But then something happened, I don't know what. That must've been before we moved up here. Before…whatever happened to make Tango so scared."

Jude shot her a sympathetic glance. "No grandparents on your father's side? No other cousins?" Jude queried.

"Nope," she replied. "I think my grandparents died before I was born." She gave a shrug and stared out the window. That was all she knew. Aria had never thought it strange growing up that they hadn't been surrounded by family. Yes, she noticed other families congregating together at Christmas and other holidays. She'd just taken it for granted that was how other families worked, but hers was a little different. It was all she knew; she'd grown up with just the four of them, never seeming to need anyone else. She probably did have cousins down in Colorado she knew nothing about. But that wasn't going to help now.

"Tango's house is still a crime scene at the moment, but I can't see why Brady shouldn't release it soon. When the time comes, and you want to take a look inside your family home, just let me know, and I'll come with you."

"Thank you." Those two simple words seemed inadequate for what he'd just offered. She could hardly believe how much he was prepared to do for her. It felt…kind of right, there was a connection between them that couldn't be denied. And she would've done the same for him had their situations been reversed. So, perhaps she needed to stop second-guessing herself and just let him help her.

Sooner than she expected, Jude pulled into his driveway. Without comment, Jude came around the car and opened the door for her, then waited until she got out, before shutting it again. It was such a show of old-fashioned manners, something that was rare to find in a man nowadays, and something Jude did without even thinking, probably drummed into him by his mother. Some women were determined to be treated as equals, and frowned upon anything they saw as being condescending. But Aria liked it. It felt respectful somehow. Caring. One more thing that she liked about him.

They walked down the driveway and around the side of the house to the cottage. He waited as she unlocked the door and then made her stand outside, while he went in first to check everything was as it should be.

She could hear him rattling the window in her bedroom, checking everything was secure and locked up tight while she remained standing just inside the doorway.

Returning from his perusal of her bedroom, he said, "Sorry, I can't stay with you at the moment. I'll make sure I'm home by seven tonight." He didn't say it, but she knew he was worried about leaving her alone, especially after dark. She wondered how he was going to make that happen, when he'd only been telling her last night that they'd all be pulling extra shifts over the next few days. "You have my number, if you need anything." He stopped on his way through the front door and bent at the knees so he could look her directly in the eye. "I mean it, Aria. If you feel at all unsafe, I want you to call me. I don't care if you feel stupid or if it turns out to be nothing."

She froze. He was so close, dominating the small space, and she was suddenly hyper-aware of him, of his male physicality. Hyper-aware of how his lips had felt on hers when they'd kissed the other day. And her stupid brain wouldn't stop wondering if he was about to do it again.

"Okay," she whispered, unable to turn her gaze away from his golden eyes.

"And make sure you lock your door after I leave." He regained his full height, a worried frown marring his perfect features, and she sucked in a wobbly breath. No kissing, then.

"I will." She stood a little awkwardly in the doorway, watching him walk up the driveway. "I'll make dinner, if you like," she blurted before she could pull her words back. It was the least she could do to repay him for his kindness, but she was suddenly wondering if it was a good idea to spend more time confined with him in the cottage.

Jude turned. "That'd be nice, thank you. As long as you're up to it?"

"Definitely." She needed to do this, even if it was just to prove that she wasn't some weak, pathetic girl who crumbled under the weight of a few hours of being interviewed by an overbearing detective. She was stronger than that. Besides, it'd give her something to do to take her mind off her predicament. "See you at seven, then." She waved and closed the door, making sure she locked it.

What could she possibly make for dinner? On her way home from her first day working at Stargazer, she'd stocked up on the basics from the local grocery, using her small stash of money that she'd been keeping for an absolute emergency, figuring that she had a job now, and money wouldn't be a problem soon. She'd bought pasta, flour, milk, sugar, salt, cheese, a few tins of beans, and some cookies. Not a lot to choose from if she were to make even a half-decent meal. But then she remembered seeing a few remaining tomatoes still clinging to a vine in the back garden. The garden was full of weeds, as if Jude hadn't tended to it for a while. Perhaps that'd been his mother's thing. But surely, Jude wouldn't mind if she picked some of those. If she was lucky, she might even find some basil in the little herb garden she'd noticed by the back door. She knew a pasta recipe that incorporated all those things. Yes, that would do nicely.

CHAPTER TEN

Jude knocked on the door of the cottage. He'd just arrived home and was yet to change out of his uniform, but he was desperate to check on Aria first. His mind had been only half on his job all afternoon as he worried about her, and he'd worked himself up into a lather of anxiety. The more he'd thought about Tango and Iliana, together with what he now knew about Dimitra, the more agitated he'd become. Something was going on. This was connected somehow, he just didn't know how.

"Coming," a voice called from inside, and his hands unclenched from where they'd been rammed up against the door. If she hadn't answered in another two seconds, he might well have busted the door down. He took a deep breath and straightened his jacket, running a hand through his hair. Perhaps he should've taken the time to change. But then it was too late, as the door opened and light spilled out onto the doorstep.

"Hi," Aria said brightly. "You're right on time," she added as he remained rooted to the spot, staring at the vision in front of him.

Backlit from the cottage, her slim, willowy figure made him catch his breath. She'd answered the door in bare feet, wearing a pale green midriff top with long sleeves, and jeans, her long hair a halo around her shoulders. She looked like an angel come to life. The bare strip of skin around her waist called to him, and he could hardly tear his gaze away. He wanted to place his hands on her hips and pull her close, rub his thumbs over the exposed skin of her stomach.

"Are you coming in?" She gave a slight shiver as a cold wind gusted in past him.

"Sorry, yes," he apologized, stepping into the bright warmth of the cozy cottage. She closed the door behind him and then rushed back and busied herself in the small kitchen. Quickly removing his jacket and gun belt, he placed them over the back of one of the wing chairs and strolled over to lean against the kitchen island.

"Something smells amazing," he said.

"It's just spaghetti pomodoro. Nothing special." She shrugged lightly. "And some homemade biscuits."

"Well, it smells special, even if you say it's not." He caught her eye and smiled, trying to remember the last time a woman had cooked for him, apart from his mother. His last serious relationship had ended over two years ago. And Samantha had been the first to admit she wasn't good in the kitchen. The best she could manage was eggs on toast, breakfast cereal and heating frozen meals. Which hadn't bothered him at the time; their relationship had many other problems, and her lack of cooking was at the bottom of the list. But still...to have a partner who cooked would be something.

The kitchen looked like a bomb had hit it. There were unwashed dishes piled in the sink, plates and utensils scattered all over the countertop, an open packet of spaghetti had spilled near the stove, and there were dustings of white flour everywhere. She might be a good cook, but she sure was a messy one.

"Can I give you a hand?"

"Gosh no, you've been hard at work all day. You just sit down and put your feet up. If I had a beer, I'd give you one." Then Aria clapped her hand over her mouth. "Oh. My. God. I'm so sorry. I realized how much I sounded like a clichéd wife just then. That wasn't my intention, at all." Her cheeks colored a lovely shade of pink, and he couldn't help it, he erupted into laughter. It felt good to laugh after his stressful day. It was the first time he'd really let go all day. She was funny, and he liked it.

When she saw that he hadn't taken offense at her faux pas, she picked up a knife, turned to the bench with her back toward him, and began chopping tomatoes on a small wooden board.

He stared at the back of her head for a few seconds. "Much as I appreciate being told to put my feet up, I couldn't just sit here and watch you cook." That wasn't his style, never had been. "So, put me to work." As he spoke, he sidled around the corner of the kitchen island.

Aria hesitated for a second, still not quite meeting his eye, and he studied her profile, noticing that her cheeks were still pink. Was she still embarrassed?

As if coming to a decision, she lifted her head, her back still to him. "Okay, you asked for it. I found a few salad items in your garden, if you could chop them up for me, that'd be great." Then she quickly added, "Oh, I hope you don't mind that I raided your garden?" She whirled around at the same time he came up behind her. Instinctively, he flinched backward as she nearly sliced him with the knife that she still held in her hand.

"Oh. My. God," she said for the second time, dropping the knife with a clatter to the floor. "I'm sorry. I don't know what's the matter with me. I'm not normally this much of a motormouth. Or this much of a klutz."

As he bent down to retrieve the knife, he finally figured it out. Aria was flustered. She was cute when she was flustered. And it made his chest expand that *he* was the reason she was flustered.

Holding the knife in one hand, he took one of hers with the other, and said, "I don't mind that you raided the garden. My mother would love that you're using up the veggies she planted. And while my knife skills aren't quite chef quality, I can at least make a salad for you."

"Oh, good." She released her breath in a gush, then looked down at their hands still entwined. And back up at him. He suddenly forgot all about the food, forgot they were even standing in a kitchen, as their gazes locked. Then her cheeks went that gorgeous shade of pink once more, even as she tugged her hand free. "I, ah… I better stir the sauce. I don't want it to catch on the bottom."

"What? Oh, sure." Reluctantly, he let go of her hand and turned to the chopping board to attack the tomato that Aria had left half-chopped. Great, now he was the one getting flustered. She was making him feel like a teenager again.

He stood with his back to her but could feel her presence as she flittered around the kitchen, opening the oven to check on the biscuits and rattling some plates as she set the small table in the corner. There was a pile of climbing beans on the bench, which he proceeded to top and tail when he finished with the tomato. He added them to the bowl that Aria had already filled with late-season endive lettuce that must've self-seeded from the early crop his mother had sown this summer. This whole thing felt suddenly so domestic. Him and Aria preparing dinner together, like they were some old, married couple.

He turned and leaned his butt against the countertop, watching her openly. She was bent over the table, making sure the knives and forks were lined up against the plates.

"What?" she asked, straightening up.

"Nothing." He raised an eyebrow.

She went back to fussing with the table, rearranging a posy of pink daisies—which must also be from the garden—in the middle of the table.

"What?" she asked again, the corner of her mouth twitching as she glared at him.

"Shall we eat?" he said, deflecting her question. Because if he stopped to think about his answer, he might have to admit that he liked watching her. Liked what he saw. That he liked her.

"God, yes. I'm so hungry," she admitted. "And I'm sorry, but I meant it when I said I didn't have any beer to give you. All I have is water."

"That's fine." He didn't need alcohol, he felt like he could get high on Aria's presence alone tonight.

Together, they put the food on the table. Aria pulled the steaming tray of biscuits out of the oven and put it on another wooden board on the table with a knife. Then she poured the sauce over a large bowl of pasta and let Jude carry it to the table, where he pulled out a chair, waiting till she was seated before he took his own.

"Thank you." She looked like she was about to say something more, but closed her mouth with a snap instead, piling a heap of spaghetti on both of their plates, while he helped himself to the salad. There was companionable silence for a few moments, as they sucked spaghetti into their mouths in unison.

"This is so good," he mumbled around a mouth full of pasta.

"I had an Italian friend in Portland, Luciana. She taught me. This is her favorite dish. It's so simple, but so tasty."

"Well, here's to your Italian friend." He raised his glass of water, and they clinked them together in a salute to Luciana.

The biscuits were good, too. Hot and nutty, slathered with butter. The pasta pomodoro tasted fresh and heavenly, the slightly peppery flavor of the basil adding to the simplicity of the dish. The good food and the good company almost made him forget the day he'd had at work. Almost. But then Aria placed her glass on the table and her face sobered, and he knew what she was going to ask before she even opened her mouth. He was surprised she'd lasted this long; the questions must've been eating away at her.

"I guess you would've already told me if you'd heard anything on Iliana's whereabouts?" she said, and he hated the slightly hopeful tone of her voice. God, he wished he had some good news for her.

"I'm sorry, Aria. Nothing else has come up. We still have people out there doing their job. Brady might be a dick, but he's conducting a by-the-book search for your sister. If she's out there to be found, he will find her." Even as he watched Aria for her reaction, Jude winced quietly inside, because that wasn't all together true. He knew that when the sheriff had passed on Levi's information about a group of strangers camping up in the hills, Brady had discounted any further investigation, saying he didn't have the manpower to be following every hunch and half-baked lead the locals threw his way. Which might be technically true, but Jude knew that hunches were often right, and anyone who discounted information because it was a hunch and not a solid lead was a certain type of fool.

"I feel like I should be out there searching for her," she said softly. "But I wouldn't have a clue where to start. Maybe I could go and knock on doors, ask around to see if anybody's seen her, that sort of thing?" She raised an expectant gaze to his. He didn't want to dash her hopes, but there was really nothing she could do. "You're right. I'd be more a hindrance than a help," she replied when she saw his blank stare.

"That's not it, Aria." He leaned across the table and captured her hand in his. "We have trained professionals out doing that exact same thing right now. You need to be somewhere close by, so when we do find her, we can contact you." He didn't add that he had a personal vested interest in ensuring she stayed somewhere safe, so he knew where she was, making it easier to protect her.

"Yeah, leave it to the professionals," she agreed. "I just feel so helpless." She retrieved her hand from his and rubbed the back of her neck.

"I know, but I wouldn't lie to you. I will tell you as soon as we find something."

"Thank you." Lifting another forkful of pasta to her mouth, she studied him for a moment.

"And no new developments in my father's case?" She paused to save a coil of pasta that threatened to fall off her fork. "No idea who the killer is yet?"

"No," He shook his head. "We have a range of options and leads we're following up at the moment, but nothing new to report." It was a glib line that he'd use on any normal member of the public, and he knew she saw right through his ruse. But he didn't want to worry Aria, or scare her, if he didn't have to. There was one piece of good news, although he wasn't sure if Aria would view it as such.

"I did hear that Brady has released your father's house—actually, it's your house now—as it's no longer considered a crime scene."

"That's good, I guess," she replied but screwed up her nose in distaste. He surmised she needed to get used to the idea that the house truly belonged to her now. Her and her sister…when they found Iliana.

"Like I said earlier, I'll come with you to your father's house when you're ready to go." It was probably stretching professional courtesy, and Brady wouldn't like it one bit, but

Jude was determined that Aria shouldn't go into that house on her own. And if he happened to be her one true friend, then he was more than happy to bear that burden.

"Thank you," she replied, staring at her dinner as if it no longer held any appeal.

He put his fork down and reached across the table to touch his fingers to her wrist. Ignoring the sparks that flowed up his arm at the contact, he said, "I can't imagine how hard this must be for you. Especially with no family around to help you through it."

"You're already doing too much for me," she said in a small voice. "It's not your fault I don't have any family or friends here. I'll get by." She offered him a wobbly smile. "I just have to remember that, as the saying goes, this too, shall pass."

He leaned back. "It's good wisdom to live by," he agreed.

"Naomi called me this afternoon to see how I was doing. She offered to help me in any way I needed. She said that I'm part of the Stargazer family now. It was nice of her." Aria gave one of her special smiles as she thought about Naomi, the one that wrinkled her nose so sweetly.

"They are nice," Jude admitted, letting go of Aria's wrist before he did something stupid, like entwine his fingers with hers. "You couldn't work for a better family."

"I told Naomi I'd like to come back to work tomorrow. It'll help take my mind off things, and there's nothing much else I can do sitting here."

"That's a great idea, as long as you feel up to it," Jude encouraged. It'd solve one of his problems. If he knew she was safely ensconced at Stargazer, then he could breathe a little easier and get back to working without being distracted.

"I do." Aria retrieved her fork and began eating again, as if the decision to go back to work tomorrow had eased the weight on her mind. She sucked in another strand of spaghetti and his attention was momentarily drawn to the purse of her lips.

"So, tell me, Deputy Wilder, what's it like being in law enforcement in a small backcountry Montana town?" Aria was trying to change the course of the conversation, and he admired her for not wanting to dwell on her own problems.

Taking her cue, Jude started reciting an anecdote about old Bill Mitchell, who he'd picked up last week, wandering down the street buck naked. It made Aria laugh when he described in great detail the man's pale, hairy buttocks wobbling along in front of his cruiser. "The poor old guy was freezing his pecker off," he told her, and his heart lifted when she giggled, the mood in the room changing to a more lighthearted one.

They talked, and they ate, and before he knew it, the meal was finished, and Aria was collecting the plates and stacking them in the sink.

"At least let me wash the dishes tonight," he pleaded with a grin. "It's only equitable after all this wonderful cooking you did."

"Fair enough," she replied. "I'm all for equal rights. Despite what I stupidly said earlier tonight."

He waved her away from the kitchen, and she took to the couch, curling her long legs up beneath her and watching him with her dark eyes.

Soon, he had his hands plunged into soapy water, but it didn't take long to finish, and the mess wasn't as bad as he first predicted. They talked about his mother's garden while he washed and stacked. She said it was a shame the garden had been let go, and he agreed. She went on to say that if he didn't mind, she'd love to have a go at fixing it up. She wasn't promising miracles, but he replied that anything she did would be much appreciated. It was one of the reasons he'd been hesitating about bringing his mother home for a visit. If she saw the garden, she'd be devastated. But he was just too busy at work, and he'd never really had a green thumb or been overly worried about the state of a few weeds. So he welcomed Aria's help. Who knew, perhaps between the two of them they could get the garden back to shipshape condition, and he could bring his mother home to share Christmas dinner. That reminded him he hadn't been to see his mother today. Would she even remember when she last saw him? But that wasn't the point, he reminded himself. He'd make sure to pop in and see her tomorrow, perhaps on his lunch break.

Folding the dishcloth, he sat on the opposite end of the couch, his hands still red from the hot water, and they talked about other things, like the people she was getting to know at Stargazer. She asked about Levi, and his brother, Wyatt, both of whom she was yet to meet, but had heard so much about. Their talk drifted to the Indian Reservation, where Levi and Wyatt were born, and the state of the social and communal side of living on the *res*, as the locals called it. How the community was at odds right now with a growing crime rate, but no real solution on how to fix it. Most reservations had their own form of law keepers, and the police or sheriffs were rarely called in, unless there was a murder, and even then it was often impossible to get witnesses to come forward.

She wanted to know about Penny and Clayton and their recent trouble with the local crime boss and how their love had grown stronger because of it. She'd seen how friendly he'd been toward Penny that first day and knew they were good friends, and had already decided that she liked Penny, telling Jude how helpful, open and friendly Penny in particular had been over her first few days on the job.

Cat, on the other hand, well, the jury was still out on Cat, Aria told him. Jude assured her that Cat had a heart of gold beneath that layer of bikie-chick belligerence, she just needed to take her time and get to know her.

Aria was sharp-witted and clever, and Jude was drawn to her mind, as much as he was drawn to her body. He watched her face become animated when she talked about her time in Portland. Watched her hands glide through the air as she punctuated meaning to her words. About how much she loved going to university, feeling like she was part of something bigger than just herself. About the student lifestyle, how everyone was passionate about something on campus. How she was excited about learning every new technique to further her graphic design skills. How branding had become such a big thing nowadays, you couldn't run a marketing campaign without proper branding anymore. He could barely tear his eyes away from the flash of her white teeth or stop himself from drowning in her chocolate gaze. The way she wrinkled her nose when she smiled was just the cutest thing ever, and it made something inside his chest inflate whenever she did it.

He'd known plenty of attractive women, both before and after his last serious relationship. In the past two years, he'd had a couple of one-night stands and one lady who'd lasted a few weeks. But none of those women made his guts cramp up tight the moment he laid eyes on them. None of them made his inner protector growl like an angry bear when he thought she was in danger.

It was hard when the community watched his every move. Being a deputy, his life was always out on display, it was part of the job, but not one he necessarily liked. And that included his love life. The members of the over-eighty knitting brigade liked to stop him in the street and tell him about their pretty niece, or their widowed daughter, who were looking for a man just like him. Stable and dependable and nice. It felt as if he was their property, to matchmake to whomever they pleased. He always politely declined. Because he knew there was more to him than just being a stable and dependable man. That was merely a front he projected to the world; something that was expected from the man in his position. But beneath the façade, he wanted more. He wanted spice and heat and perhaps even a little risk. And he also knew when the right woman came along, nothing would be able to stop him.

Aria's hair kept falling across her shoulder, covering her face, and her arm kept brushing across his as she talked, so his entire body thrummed with awareness of her.

"Jude?" Aria was staring at him and he was suddenly aware that she'd been talking for quite a while now, but he hadn't heard a word she'd said. And right now, he didn't care, just continued to stare at her, drinking in her curves, the soft line of her jaw, her pink lips, so plump and luscious.

She stopped talking and gazed at him, as if her words had dried up and blown away in the heat of his stare. He didn't know what to say, so he did what his body had been urging him to do all night, and he closed the gap between them and kissed her.

Her lips were soft and pliant, welcoming him in. Then she gave a small groan in the back of her throat and the sound unleashed a surge of lust for this gorgeous woman.

This wasn't like the first kiss they'd shared. That'd been rushed and clandestine, with a faint sense of being wrong. There'd been an edge to it, as if he'd been taking advantage of her. She'd been wrapped in a towel, after all, and not too many hot-blooded men would've been able to resist. This kiss, however, felt different. More fully developed, not just based on pure lust. It felt right, as if destiny, karma, whatever you wanted to call it, had been leading him here, to Aria.

He pulled her closer, their thighs touching, and he reached around behind her, finding the bumps of her spine and running his fingers over the dips and valleys of her back. Her skin bared by the crop top jumped and twitched beneath his touch, and her teeth grazed his bottom lip. His hand dropped lower and before he knew it, he'd scooped her up and pulled her closer until she was almost sitting sideways in his lap.

Her tongue slid along the seam of his mouth, and he swept his hands higher up underneath her top and he followed the line of her bra, tracing the underside of the lace covering her breasts with his palms. She sucked in a breath and made a low humming noise deep in her chest. He liked her reaction and cupped her breast with each hand. They were plump and heavy and he suddenly wanted to strip her clothes off, so he could see her revealed in all her glory.

Her thigh pressed against the thickness of his erection and the agonizing sweetness was almost too much to bear. If they didn't stop now... He might not be responsible for his actions. His fingers worked their way down and into the waistband of her jeans, and she turned to straddle him, settling herself over his crotch, causing his breath to catch as blood surged like a mini-volcano in his groin.

Aria suddenly drew in a deep breath and shifted back a little so she could look into his eyes. There was a question hovering in the depths of her dark-brown irises. Did he know the answer?

"Should we be doing this?" she asked, voice husky.

He blinked and thought about it.

"I'm attracted to you," he admitted. "More than just attracted to you." He desperately wanted to say this was the best thing he'd ever felt. Wanted to urge her to keep going. But his conscience, that annoying little bloody voice in his head, was telling him to get a grip. She was a suspect in a homicide. She was also under his protection.

As if on cue, his phone, which was on the kitchen countertop, started to ring. A sharp, insistent sound that shattered the mood around them. He grabbed Aria by the hips, desperate to stop her getting off his lap, but it was too late, her eyes had become shuttered, her mouth a tight line of apology.

She gave him a lopsided grin, full of regret. "Saved by the bell, I guess."

"I don't need to answer it," he said, desperately grasping at straws.

She hovered halfway off his lap as the phone stopped ringing. They locked gazes, and for a second, he thought she might relent. Then the phone started its tenacious, shrill noise again.

"Shit," he mumbled, levering himself off the couch. This better be bloody important. As he crossed the short distance to the countertop, he eased his jeans away from his groin. Lucky this wasn't a video call, he thought with grim amusement.

He checked caller ID. It was Lance.

"Yep," he said, short and to the point.

"Sorry to disturb you." Their trainee was on shift till midnight, helping Brady sort through witness statements. Brady had asked—no, demanded—that Jude work late too, but he had looked Brady square in the eye and told him no. Jude knew Hank would back him up, as he hated it when out-of-town detectives thought they could bully his staff. Lance, however, was young and inexperienced, and easily swayed. But he was also enthusiastic and mature for his age and would make a good deputy.

"We just got a call from the medical examiner doing the autopsy on Tango Cusack, and I thought you might want to know the results." Brady had requested a rush on toxicology, and so Tango's bloodwork had been sent to the lab yesterday. But a twenty-four-hour turnaround was good by anybody's standards. Brady either had a connection he could lean on in the lab, or he'd been his normal bloody annoying self and they'd rushed it through just to get him off their back. It was late in the night to be getting this sort of information sent through, and so Jude decided Brady had been particularly annoying, until the results had finally been faxed through.

"Yes, please. Go ahead."

"The cause of death wasn't through the knife wounds. Those were mostly inflicted postmortem. Directly following death, but not the cause of death."

"Okay," Jude said slowly. This was interesting. But perhaps a few things were making sense now. Tango's body had been badly mutilated and there'd been blood spattered everywhere. To an untrained eye, it looked as if he must've bled out and died. But when forensics had come to inspect, they'd spent time going over the blood spatters in the kitchen, and Jude had overheard one of them say it looked too random, as if someone had thrown blood against the wall. If the blood had spurted from a severed artery in the neck, or arm while a person was still alive, then there would be a certain pattern to it. But that pattern was missing, according to forensics. So if the mutilation had happened very close after death, then the blood would still have seeped out, but not flowed or spurted.

"Cause of death was by poison," Lance stated simply.

"Oh, shit." Jude closed his eyes. This complicated things.

This would put Aria squarely in Brady's sights.

He turned to find Aria watching him with those intense, dark eyes, waiting to find out what this turn of events might mean.

CHAPTER ELEVEN

The highway out to Stargazer wasn't busy at this time of the morning. She could count on one hand how many cars she'd passed, and Aria drove almost on autopilot, her mind buzzing with Jude's revelation last night.

Her father had been poisoned. It was completely nonsensical to her. Why poison someone and then inflict physical wounds all over their body just as they were dying? It was barbaric, and the more Aria thought about it, the more confused she got.

Jude's face had gone ashen as he'd listened to his trainee on the other end of the line, and he'd turned to stare at her, compassion and something else written in the lines on his face. Then he'd sat next to her on the couch and told her the terrible news, stroking the back of her hand and watching her carefully. But this news didn't clarify anything for Aria, instead it made the whole thing more puzzling.

The other day, Aria had asked Jude if he thought her father's death was connected to Iliana's disappearance, and perhaps even to her mother's death so many years before. But she couldn't see how they could be connected. Her mother had died by being hung from the rafters in the barn— whether she did that to herself, or it was done to her, was still to be proven. Her father had been poisoned and his body mutilated as if by someone in a terrible rage. And Iliana had merely…disappeared. There was no pattern to these deaths, Jude had himself admitted. None of it made sense.

That wasn't the only thing her mind was buzzing with. She also couldn't get images of that scorching kiss to leave her alone. They flickered behind her eyelids every time she closed her eyes. As if she didn't have enough to worry about with this new development in her father's case, now she also had to deal with her body's untamed reaction to Jude's second kiss. If his phone hadn't rung, what might've happened?

Surely she wouldn't have been brazen enough to sleep with him? She couldn't start a relationship with him. Not with anyone. Not with the mess her life was in. And not with the baby growing inside her. She couldn't do that to him; lead him on or form an attachment, before he knew the full truth about her. Even one night of hot sex wouldn't be fair to him. Although, the idea had a certain kind of merit. One night, where she took everything he had to offer and gave everything she had to give, before she had to tell him the truth. Would it be worth it? Maybe. But there were other things to take into account. She also had no idea if it was a breach of protocol for a deputy to be dating a suspect, or a witness, or whatever the hell she was.

Her mind drifted back to those moments they'd spent on the couch together, where he'd almost overwhelmed her senses. There was a pure masculine aura around Jude. No other man had ever caused such a visceral reaction in her. An insistent tug deep down in her belly, telling her to get closer. Press him tight to her body. Tighter still. So close she wouldn't be able to tell where her body ended and his began.

Then he'd looked at her, hazel eyes going dark, and her pulse had thudded in her neck as time seemed to slow. She knew he was going to kiss her. And oh God, she'd wanted him to.

She'd stared into his eyes, which were as deep as the ocean; and then she knew how people drowned.

If she got involved with Jude Wilder, she was surely going to drown.

Aria's gaze was suddenly drawn to something farther down the highway. A figure was standing in the middle of the road, waving their arms in the universal signal for someone requiring aid. As she drew closer, she could see a white van pulled over onto the verge and the figure morphed into a tall man. She slowed, studying the scene in front. Crap. Should she stop?

Jude would be along any moment, he said he'd follow her as she pulled out of the driveway of his house. Said he had business at Stargazer this morning and he may as well escort her out there. Aria knew his behavior went deeper than that. He was worried about her and wanted to make sure she got there okay. She'd seen him caught at a set of traffic lights that'd turned orange as soon as she went through the intersection. She wasn't worried, and had continued driving, knowing he'd catch up with her soon.

The man was still waving madly as she approached, not attempting to get out of her way. So she either stopped to help him or ran right over him. She guided her car onto the verge behind the van.

"Thank you. Oh, thank you." The man ran over as she stepped out of her car. "The last person wouldn't stop," he puffed. "My van broke down and I've got my pregnant wife in the back. I think all I need is a jumpstart. I have jumper cables, come and take a look." The man looked to be in his mid-fifties, smartly dressed with a black sports coat over black trousers, his longish hair was well groomed, with gray speckles peppering his designer stubble. His eyes were light-blue and kindly. He looked like the guy next door, so she nodded that she would follow him. But as he turned back toward the van, something in the line of his jaw, the slight upturn of his nose, was somewhat familiar. But the flash of familiarity was gone as soon as it'd appeared. She must've been imagining things.

She walked along the edge of the road to where the man had his head inside the engine bay and was pointing to the battery. "I'm sure it's just a flat battery," he said. "The car just sort of died, and I had to pull over."

"Hmm." Aria wouldn't have a clue what was wrong with the car, but if it was as simple as a jump start, she could help. "As long as it's quick. I'm on my way to work. And I don't want to be late."

"Sure, sure," the man agreed. "Come and help me with the jumper cables." He beckoned her toward the sliding door in the side of the van that opened into a cargo bay behind the front seats.

Where was his wife? He'd mentioned a pregnant wife, hadn't he? There was no one sitting in the passenger seat. She shrugged and followed him, walking between the edge of the road and the side of the van. The man had his hand on the door handle when he looked up and muttered something under his breath.

"We'll just wait till this car passes," he said brightly.

But the car slowed and then came to a stop, idling in the middle of the road. The four-wheel-drive had the ranger logo on the door. The man behind the wheel rolled down his window. This must be Levi, Aria thought suddenly. He matched the description Jude had given her; long, dark hair pulled back in a ponytail, a short beard the same color as his hair, watchful eyes sizing up both her and the man.

"Need a hand?"

"Oh, no." The man waved Levi's question away. "This lovely lady is going to help me jump my car, that's all."

Levi's gaze zeroed in on her, almost as if he recognized her.

"I can do that," Levi replied, already directing his vehicle onto the verge in front of the van.

"There's no need, it's all under control," the man replied, and Aria wondered if that wasn't a hint of desperation in his tone. Why would he refuse the offer of a ranger? He'd surely know more about the car than she did.

Levi stepped out of his truck and went to look beneath the hood, poking something Aria couldn't see. The man in black grimaced as he looked between her and Levi. Then he stomped to the front of the car and began to talk in an excited, high-pitched tone.

Aria hovered, wondering if she was free to go or if she should go and introduce herself to Levi when another car appeared over the slight rise. It had the unmistakable shape of a sheriff's cruiser. Finally, this must be Jude. She let out a gust of relieved air. With these two capable men around, she wouldn't be needed.

Jude drifted the cruiser to a halt behind her Subaru. It was becoming quite crowded on the verge. He got out and stalked along the edge of the road.

"What's going on?" he asked crisply. "Why have you stopped?"

"This man waved me down. He said he needed help. But then Levi turned up, so I guess I'm not needed."

"No, you're not," Jude answered, his gaze fixed on the van in front. "You get going. I won't be far behind you," he promised.

She got back in her car with a sigh of relief, and pulled out onto the highway after checking her rearview mirror, glad there were two strong, capable men to look after the hapless man and his pregnant wife.

Ten minutes later, Jude caught up with her just as she turned into the Stargazer driveway. They bumped along the gravel road in convoy and he pulled into a spot next to her in the parking lot. He was standing beside her car as she got out.

"Will that man be okay?" she asked, pulling on her borrowed Stargazer jacket over her sweater.

"Yes, Levi will look after him." His words were clipped, even as he gently took her elbow to lead her past a large pothole in the gravel. "But, Aria, I need you to be more careful than that. You can't just stop for any old stranger. We talked about this."

"Yes, but...he was harmless."

"Maybe. But who knows next time...?"

"Okay," she mumbled. Jude was only looking out for her. And really, she'd been the one to ring the alarm bells in the first place, wondering if her life was in danger now that Iliana was missing. "Sorry, I wasn't thinking. It won't happen again," she promised.

"Aria." He turned her to face him, using his grip on her elbow. "I don't want to scare you. But until we have more information on your father's killer, I want you to keep a low profile. There's a lot going on, and..." He stopped and pursed his lips. "Some things I can't tell you, I'm sorry. It's not just strangers you need to be wary of. You need to stay away from Brady as well."

"What? Why?" Not that she minded his advice; she couldn't stand the detective, and would quite happily stay far away from him if possible.

He drummed a tattoo with his fingers on his thigh as he considered her words, his other hand still gently holding her elbow.

"I'm worried that he might want to...question you again. And I don't want him near you if I'm not around."

"Okay." Jude might be taking this protective thing a little too far, but Aria would go with it, for now.

Before she could ask any more, Levi's truck pulled into the parking lot. He leaned out the window and said, "I sorted that guy out. It turned out there was nothing wrong with his van, after all. It started first time." Levi shrugged but the light frown hovering on his forehead showed he was more worried than he was making out.

"Thanks, that's great." Jude let go of Aria's arm and backed away a few steps. "This is Aria, by the way. I'm not sure if you guys have been formally introduced."

Levi tipped his chin up by way of greeting. "I thought that might be you. It's nice to finally meet you. Cat has mentioned the new marketing guru who's helping Naomi bring her dreams to life."

"Nice to finally meet you, too," Aria called through the open window, although she doubted it was just Cat who'd mentioned her name to him recently. Her name was probably on most of the town folks' tongues after her recent reappearance and the sudden death of her father. She wondered if Jude had talked to Levi about her. He was good-looking, with his olive skin and dark eyes, big, capable hands resting on the wheel, and she could understand what Cat saw in him.

There was a short, awkward silence.

"You wanna jump in? We can drive up to the machinery shed together." Levi's words cut across her next question; she'd been about to ask if Levi had seen the man's pregnant wife. The whole thing was a little odd, and it was bothering her. Why had the van started first time? Was there actually nothing wrong with it?

"Yeah, thanks," Jude said, turning to give her a quick look that warned her to stay out of trouble.

"Where are you going?" she queried.

"Levi and I are just checking out something Dean reported a few days ago. He's had some cattle go missing," Jude added, replacing his hat as he spoke, so Aria could no longer see his eyes. Then he jumped in the truck and she was waving them away in a cloud of dust.

It wasn't until Aria had reached the top of the steps and was just about to open the front door when it finally occurred to her to wonder why it would take a ranger and a deputy to work on a simple case of missing cattle. And why the recent murder wasn't taking precedence. Why would Brady send Jude off on a wild goose chase? Was there something else going on here? Maybe Penny would know?

Aria walked in through the door, her mind still on the reasons Jude was on the ranch, and so she was shocked when Penny practically knocked her over as she rushed to hug her.

"I'm so sorry, Aria." Penny pulled back and Aria could see the sincere sympathy in her eyes. "I can't imagine how you're feeling right now."

So much had happened in the past few days, it was hard to keep track of who knew what; the timeline was fuzzy in her head. Naomi had called a couple of times yesterday to make sure she was okay. Her boss had been so genuinely concerned, Aria had to convince her not to come round; that she was fine and Jude was taking good care of her. And of course, Penny hadn't seen Aria since she'd left in a daze with Jude the other day, the news of her father's death still ringing in her ears. Not since Iliana had been declared missing.

People must have an inkling that Aria and her father weren't close. A person didn't spend eight years away, with no contact, if they were close. But none of these doubts showed in Penny's face. And Aria was swept away by the other woman's genuine consideration. Why was it that you always felt remorse when a person passed away? Felt like you could've done more, said more, to try and heal the rift. Because now her dad was dead, the possibility of finding out what was truly going on in his head was gone forever. Aria would never get the answers she needed. Had her father loved her in his own peculiar way? Where did all his crazy theories stem from? What'd happened to him before she was born to turn him into the man she knew as her father? Losing a parent changed something indelibly inside you.

"Thank you," Aria replied simply as Penny turned and looped her arm through Aria's as they walked together toward the office.

Aria looked up to see Naomi watching them from the doorway. She bundled Aria into her arms as soon as she got close.

"Oh, baby girl, I'm so sorry for your loss. Losing a parent is a hard thing to go through, for anybody." Naomi drew back and looked her in the eye, brushing away the hair that'd fallen over her face with a motherly touch. The sincerity and warmth Naomi showed had a lump forming in Aria's throat. The way she treated her, so much like she was special and fragile; worthy of love. It made Aria pine for her own mother. Naomi tucked her under her arm and led her into the office, motioning to Penny to come in and help her make coffee.

"You take a seat and we'll get you a coffee and something to eat." Naomi lowered her into one of the comfy armchairs and patted her hand, taking the seat opposite. "If you need anything, anything at all, you just have to ask. With the funeral arrangements, with help in settling your father's affairs. I know it can all be overwhelming, but we know the right people to talk to in town. And you also take as much time as you need off work," Naomi added.

It struck a chord deep inside Aria. These people hardly knew her, yet they were being so nice to her. They were good people, decent people, and she was glad to be surrounded by these caring humans. It suddenly showed her that what she thought she'd had with Beau had been a paltry example of a genuine relationship. She'd thought she loved Beau, and that he had loved her. But the fact he could send her away without a second thought showed her exactly how shallow he was. Perhaps she could blame her deficient upbringing, where her mother had died too early to really show Aria what true love was supposed to look like. And her father was so preoccupied with his own problems, he just didn't have it in him to be capable of love.

She'd thought she was the one who was broken, but maybe it wasn't her fault, after all. The idea hit her like a hammer blow to the chest.

"Thank you," she said, surprised to hear the wobble in her own voice. "I seem to be saying that a lot at the moment, but I mean it. You've been so supportive." Most bosses wouldn't have been this accommodating after only two days of work.

Penny placed a mug of steaming coffee in front of Aria, the lines around her eyes still crinkling up with concern. Kneeling down, so she could look Aria in the eye, she said gently, "That's what friends are for."

So, this was what it was like to have true friends.

"I'd better get back to reception." She stood and Naomi nodded at her. "I know Jude has been doing a good job of looking after you. But like Naomi said, anything you need, just give us a yell."

"I will," Aria replied, brushing away a tear that had somehow formed without her knowledge.

Neither of the two women had mentioned Iliana, as if they were worried Aria might shatter if they said her name. She was a tad embarrassed by all this attention already, and tears were close to the surface. She knew talking about Iliana would tip her over the edge, so she said, "When the time comes, I would appreciate your help." She lifted her chin slightly and straightened her shoulders, hoping that Naomi got the hint. *Please don't ask me about Iliana. Not yet.* "But at the moment, everything is all in limbo." Jude had said her father's body might not be released for burial for weeks yet. And the problem of Tango's house and all his belongings could wait. There was no rush to do anything. A part of her that she didn't like to acknowledge also hoped and prayed they found Iliana soon, then she wouldn't have to do this alone. "So until it comes to the stage where I need that help, I'd love to keep busy, to keep my mind off everything, if you know what I mean."

"I know exactly what you mean," Naomi replied sagely, thankfully getting the hint loud and clear. "Idle hands are the devil's work. I'm the same as you. If I have a problem, or a worry, I like to knuckle down to work, because sitting around worrying about a thing never got me anywhere."

"Yes," Aria agreed. Today was Friday, which only gave her today to bury herself in the work. But she'd wonder about how to keep herself occupied over the weekend later.

So after they finished their coffee, Naomi opened her laptop and Aria got out her iPad, and they began to talk about Naomi's project. Aria soon lost herself in the world of how to brand a riding camp for the blind. It needed to have that special quality that could only be found at Stargazer Ranch.

They spent the morning cocooned in Dean's office, and Aria asked if she could have lunch at the desk. She wasn't up to facing the rest of the staff, and Naomi seemed to get that, so she left Aria to her sandwiches, saying she needed to talk to Dean, and wanted to catch up with Clayton about something, as well. Aria stared out the window at the low clouds gathering over the mountains as she ate. Which reminded her, she still hadn't had time to get herself a proper warm jacket yet, and winter was clearly just around the corner. Naomi had told her earlier that the first winter storm was on its way. They were predicting a bad one and Naomi had been worried that Aria's car might not be up to handling the freezing weather to come. Aria remembered her broken taillight and bald tires, which were still yet to be fixed, and felt a twinge of guilt. Jude hadn't said anything about them since, but she knew what he must be thinking about her driving an unsafe car.

Naomi returned to find Aria looking at different fonts on her iPad, trying to decide which would suit the new brand they were creating for the riding camp. Stargazer already had a logo, using a particular color palette, and so Aria had asked if she could use that logo and redesign it to incorporate the new theme. The two women spent the next hour shuffling images around, adding new colors, trying to find the best fit for Naomi's new brand.

It was nearly two pm when Aria became aware of something going on outside in the reception area. It sounded like a group of people had gathered and were all talking at once. There were voices on the verandah outside and on the steps leading up to the lodge.

She stood, and both she and Naomi went over to peer out the window down into the parking lot below. She could see her Subaru and Jude's cruiser with the sheriff logo on the side. But now other cars swept into the lot as they stared. Two police cruisers, followed by a phalanx of black sedans, and lastly a white van that had *crime scene unit* splashed across the side.

"What's going on?" She turned to Naomi, who looked equally flummoxed.

All of a sudden, there was a knock at the door, and then, without waiting for an answer, Jude stumbled in, closely followed by Detective Brady.

Aria's heart plummeted to her stomach, and Naomi reached a hand over to grasp hers, as the two women stared.

"Aria." Jude came to stand right in front of her while Brady hovered in the doorway, glowering from beneath his eyebrows. "I'm so sorry, but I've got some more bad news." Aria felt her knees want to give way, but she locked them in place and continued to stand, not saying a word, just waiting. Jude's eyes were fixed on hers, and he swallowed hard, once, twice. Then he cleared his throat.

This wasn't going to be good.

"We found your sister and her husband."

For a split second, Aria was elated. They'd found them. That was great. She couldn't wait to finally take Iliana in her arms and tell her a thousand times how sorry she was that she'd never made it to the wedding. But then she remembered Jude had said it was bad news.

"They're dead, aren't they?" she said flatly. "My sister is dead."

"I'm afraid so," he replied softly.

"I need to sit down." She suddenly felt faint.

Jude grasped her around the waist, and she sagged against him. He led her to the armchair and lowered her into it.

So that must've been what he was doing today. Had he known he might find her sister? Why hadn't he told her? Warned her so she could be ready.

"Where did you find them?" she asked, her voice still in that strange, flat tone.

"Up in the foothills of Canyon Peak. Buried in a shallow grave. I'm so sorry, Aria."

He went to take her hand, but she pulled it away, suddenly feeling terribly alone. Iliana was dead. Her whole family was dead. She looked up to see Brady staring at her, his face unreadable.

CHAPTER TWELVE

Jude knocked softly on the door to the cottage. It was bitterly cold outside. If this was any indication of the winter to come, it was going to be a frigid one indeed. A few seconds later, Penny opened it and peered out at him, looking half asleep, and he felt a twinge of guilt. It was past eleven, and he'd promised he'd be home by nine.

"How is she?" he asked, pushing past her.

"Asleep," she whispered, catching his arm to stop him from going in farther. "She only fell asleep fifteen minutes ago. Poor thing, she's exhausted, but she wanted to wait for you."

"Sorry I'm late," he apologized, keeping his voice low. "Things got a little…crazy." That was an understatement, but Penny didn't need to know the details. "Thanks for staying with her," he whispered back, gaze roving around the room until it came to rest on the lump barely visible under the blanket on the couch.

"Any time," Penny replied. "How was it?"

Jude grimaced. Recovering two bodies from a shallow grave in the hills was a grisly, sad job, and it didn't make it any better that he knew how it'd rip Aria apart to see her sister's face, mottled and blue, streaked with dirt. It also

136

didn't help that Craig had been a friend of sorts, and that he'd been to their wedding, watched the young couple dance together with their whole lives in front of them.

Levi had found them. He'd called Jude over, but Levi had been the one to undercover the patch of dirt and discover a hand, and then an arm, a torso, and finally a face.

The first thought running through Jude's mind when he saw that face was he had to be the one to tell Aria. She trusted him. They were friends. They were close. She couldn't hear it from anyone else.

Jude had called in the discovery on his sat phone, then he and Levi had marked out the scene with police tape, and he'd jumped back on his ATV to hightail it back to the lodge to meet Brady and Hank and the rest of the crew. And to find Aria.

After he'd broken the news, Penny had offered to take Aria home and sit with her until Jude could get off work. Because there was no way he could leave the crime scene. Levi had stayed the whole afternoon and into the night, as well. They had to drive the forensics guys back out to the site in Levi's ranger truck; their specialized van wasn't equipped for mountain tracks. Levi was as shocked as Jude at their find. The last thing Jude had expected to find was Iliana's and Craig's bodies. All he was hoping for was perhaps a clue, a fragment, a hint that the people camping in the hills weren't just simple hikers exploring the wilderness. And that they were somehow connected to what was going on in Stevensville. They'd found a connection, all right, but significantly more than what they'd been hoping for. A small part of him had been holding out hope—for Aria's sake—her sister would be found alive. As an officer of the law, he knew it was unlikely, but this grisly discovery… It blew the case wide open.

"Forget I asked that," Penny said, shaking her head. "I

don't need to know, and you don't need to relive it. At least not for my sake."

They both looked over as a ruffled head of hair appeared above the backrest of the couch. Aria swiveled to look at them and offered Jude a drowsy smile.

"Sorry, I didn't mean to fall asleep."

"No, I'm the one who's late." He turned and gave Penny a swift hug. "Will you be okay to get back to the ranch?"

"Of course. Don't you worry about me."

Jude had no doubt that Clayton would be waiting up for her in their little couple's cottage, no matter how early his start might be tomorrow morning. Yet another reason for Jude to feel guilty about his late arrival, but it was part of his job, part of who he was, and his friends understood that, and they were more than happy to help.

"Thanks, Penny," Aria called out as Penny gathered her handbag and jacket from the hook beside the door. She sat up a little straighter, pushing her hair out of her eyes.

"Any time." Penny turned and caught Jude's eye. "Let me know if you need a hand tomorrow. Clayton and I both have the day off."

Jude nodded. Most of the Stargazer staff only had one day a week off, and as the weekends were often busier than during the middle of the week, they were lucky to get a Saturday off. Naomi would make sure to schedule time off together for the two lovebirds, and Jude was touched that she would offer her alone time with Clayton to help Aria out. But then, he wouldn't expect anything less. It was part of the community spirit that was Stargazer; everyone looked out for everyone else.

There was no way he was leaving Aria alone tonight; he'd already planned to sleep on the couch. There were too many unknowns still out there. Too many unanswered questions. The topmost in Jude's mind being who had taken Iliana and why.

Brady didn't agree that Aria might be a target, and he wasn't so sure there was a link between the father and sister's murder, either, unless that link was Aria, which was preposterous. Jude could hardly believe that Brady was still looking at Aria as a main suspect. The guy had a screw loose if he thought she could single-handedly have had anything to do with murdering two people, then dragging them up the mountain and burying them.

The door closed softly behind Penny, and the atmosphere in the room seemed to change.

Jude removed his jacket and gun belt and laid them carefully over the back of the armchair. This was the moment he'd been both dreading and waiting for. To be back by Aria's side. She sat up and scooted to the end of the couch, tucking her hair behind her ear, watching him intensely.

"Sit," she commanded when he hovered, undecided on the other side of the coffee table. He drew a deep breath, steeling himself for what was to come. He sat down, close, but not touching her.

"Tell me," she demanded, her lips in a thin, firm line. "I need to know. Tell me right from the start."

"Okay." But before he began, he reached over and took one of Aria's hands in his, needing the physical contact. Her fingers closed tightly around his, but she never let her gaze drop from his face. "I think I already told you, Dean reported two cattle missing a few days ago," he began.

Aria gave a shrug that indicated she did, in fact, know that part.

"A few days ago, I asked Levi to go take a look up in the hinterland, to see if he could find traces of the missing cows," Jude relayed quickly. She had asked him to start at the beginning, but this was for his benefit as much as for hers, to get things straight in his head.

"Mmm hmm," she prompted.

"He reported back that he'd found signs of perhaps two or three people camping up there, but they were doing their utmost to keep their whereabouts hidden, which raised a few red flags for me."

Aria tilted her head on the side, looking confused, but didn't say anything. Jude couldn't explain to her what'd led him to decide there might be a connection between the people hiding out in the hills and the goings on in town.

"I wanted to go back and re-examine the sites, see if we could discover anything more about their movements. Perhaps even see if they were still up there. So, this morning Levi and I borrowed a couple of ATVs from Dean and went back up the hill."

"Mmm hmm," Aria said again, leaning slightly forward so that her long hair dropped over her shoulder.

"Levi showed me the two campsites he'd found the other day. Both of them were old, perhaps weeks old. I half thought the campers might come back and reuse the same site, but that didn't turn out to be the case. On a hunch, we followed a hiking trail higher up the mountain, and found where it connected with a fire trail. You know, the County Fire Services uses it to monitor the area, conduct burn offs, that kind of thing?"

Aria nodded.

"Levi had driven that trail a few times, but it's very rough, you need a good truck to navigate it, and there's a padlocked gate at the entry point. Anyway, we saw fresh tire tracks. Levi said those tracks hadn't been there a few days ago. So we followed them. And to cut a long story short, we found a third campsite. This was the same as the first two, heavily concealed, and all traces of anyone being there had been carefully erased. But the act of erasing, in itself, leaves other signs that a good ranger, who's been brought up hunting and living off the land on a Native American reservation, can perceive."

"So, Levi found it, even though they tried to hide it?" Aria asked softly.

"Yes. He's damn good at what he does, it was one of the reasons I sent him up there in the first place."

"And you found the..." Aria swallowed tightly. "The grave?"

"Yes. It was around fifty feet outside the camp. We figured they must've brought Iliana and Craig up in a car. Up until that point, they were probably walking in and out. It's about an hour and a half trek back to the main road."

"How long had they been dead? Do you know how they died?" Her words were so soft he barely heard them.

"I don't know." He squeezed Aria's hand. "I'm sorry, I'm not qualified to guess. And I really shouldn't even be telling you this much."

"How did you know? I mean, what made you suspect the missing cows were somehow connected to my father's murder?"

"Call it intuition, that gut feeling you get sometimes when a clue doesn't always seem to fit."

"Did Brady send you up there?"

"God, no," Jude scoffed.

Brady had been livid when he first found out that Jude gone against orders, and the sheriff hadn't been too happy either. But Jude had come up with the goods and they'd both had to concede in the end that he'd been right. Jude still expected some form of penalty from Hank. His boss didn't take kindly to his deputies taking things into their own hands. He'd probably be put on night duty for a full month once this all died down. But he'd handle that when it happened.

Aria's face, which had been pale before, went ashen.

"I still can't believe she's dead." He took her other hand and shifted slightly on the couch so he was facing her.

"I'm so sorry. I'm sorry that I had to give you this news."

"No. No. Thank you," she said, her voice regaining some strength. "Thank you for finding them. For at least giving them some peace. Giving us a chance to catch their killers."

"You've had a rough couple of days," he said gently.

"That's putting it mildly." She lifted her head and looked at him. "But at least I've got you. I can't begin to say how grateful I am, Jude."

Tonight she was wearing sweatpants and a baggy T-shirt, but he still thought she looked magnificent, long hair draped loosely over her shoulders, the outline of her willowy body clear beneath the worn fabric of the tee. She wasn't wearing a bra, and his cock twitched at the thought.

The air between them seemed to thicken, and Aria stilled as she caught his eye.

"It's all so much. I don't want to think about any of it tonight. I just want…"

The heat between them was undeniable. It'd been constant from almost the first second they'd met. A tension buzzing between them that was impossible to ignore.

Without breaking their stare, Aria slid her hand up his chest and began to unbutton his shirt. "I want to be with you tonight. I don't want to think about anything else, except the way you make me feel."

His breath caught in his throat at her words. Should he let her continue? She was clearly doing this because she wanted a distraction. A distraction from her mounting sorrows. Was it fair of him to let her use him as that distraction? One button, then another, and another, her eyes still fixed on his, daring him to tell her to stop. Until she had the shirt undone and had untucked it from his trousers. Her small hands found the indentations of his abs, tracing each one before sliding up over his pecs and pushing the shirt off his shoulders. This wasn't a good idea. He could list at least a dozen reasons why he shouldn't be doing this with Aria, aside from the fact she was using him to divert her sorrow. But was that such a bad thing? And ever since she'd come into his life, he couldn't stop thinking about her. Couldn't stop the way his body clenched every time she was near, how one touch from her set him on fire. But this was insane.

"Are you sure?" he rasped, hoping that she might come to her senses at the sound of his voice.

"Yes." She leaned forward to breathe against his neck. "Yes, I'm sure." Then her head fell back, baring the sensitive skin of her neck and collarbone. And there was no stopping him. He gently pressed his lips to her heated skin, and she moaned softly as he worked his way up her neck. God, she tasted so sweet, like honeydew or freshly mown hay. Just the same as last time, but better somehow. She drew him to her like she was the sun and he was a sun worshiper on a hot summer's day.

One hand slid from her hip to explore under the T-shirt, discovering the shape of her slim waist, running around the top of her waistband and reveling in the way her skin twitched beneath his touch. He curled his fingers into the hem of her tee and slowly dragged it over her head and then feasted on the sight of her.

Her breasts were perfect, pert, and slightly plump above her toned stomach.

"Magnificent," he whispered.

There was a smattering of pale freckles over her shoulders, a reminder of the times she'd spent in the sun as a child, and he leaned in and kissed each one. So magnificent.

He had to kiss her on the mouth now, and his lips skimmed up her neck to reach for her. He took her in a kiss so deep and raw, like he was a desperate, wild animal, but she met his desperation equally as her teeth grazed his lip, and they kissed for what felt like forever.

Her hands fumbled at his belt; and then she was pushing his trousers down past his thighs.

"Wait," he groaned into her ear. Then he stood and toed each shoe off, kicking them away in a rush. She sat up and watched as he tugged his trousers and boxer shorts the rest of the way off, until he stood before her, naked.

Her gaze burned into him like fire, scorching his skin as she looked him up and down, and he knew she liked what she saw.

"You do me," she said, lifting her hips seductively and waiting for him to free her from her sweatpants. Which he did in one swift tug.

She wasn't wearing any underwear.

"Oh. My. God." He could barely breathe.

She smiled at him, slow and sexy. And he could no longer think of anything but her. Of anything but making love to her. Of caressing her body. He knelt next to the couch and ran his hands up her thighs and over her stomach like he was giving devotion. She slithered farther down the couch, so she was practically lying on it, tugging him up so that he was lying along the length of her. He was so hard; he wasn't sure if he'd last, and her breathing was so fast it was coming in short pants.

Were they going to do it right here on the couch? Should he pick her up and carry her to the bed? He could do it; he bet she weighed nothing at all. But then she tilted her dark eyes at him and pulled him closer, arching her back so that her hips met his, and he guessed they were staying put.

Uh oh. "Condom," he muttered, freezing in place. He'd completely forgotten about protection. Never thought that he —

"In the drawer beside my bed," she panted.

In less than half a minute he was back, not stopping to wonder why she had a box of condoms, instead applauding her forethought, because without it, they wouldn't get any further tonight. He was a stickler for safety, and it seemed so was she. He knelt and sheathed himself, then smiled at her as she reached up to grab him by the neck.

"I've never watched a man put on a condom before. That was the hottest thing I've ever seen," she purred.

"Really?" He had no time to ponder her statement, as she slowly opened her legs for him, hooking one knee around his waist, and he lost all logical thought. She wanted him, and he *needed* her. She was the most beautiful woman he'd ever seen.

He pushed inside her, and her eyes slid closed as she welcomed him in. Then she opened them again as he began to rock against her. They moved together, a little faster, a little deeper, and he watched her, listening to her moans of delight, which were driving him too quickly toward the edge.

He gritted his jaw, not wanting to go without her. Her eyes were so dark, they were like pools of molasses, and her gasps became louder as she lifted her hips to his every thrust.

She came so suddenly, he almost missed it as she cried out his name, and he let himself tumble over the cliff with her, sparks of sensation like pricks of electricity going off all over his body.

He levered himself to the floor and sorted out his condom with the box of tissues he'd also snaffled from her bedside table. Then he draped himself beside her on the couch, letting her snuggle into him. She kissed him, her eyes closed, and he luxuriated in her touch, in the feel of her small hand resting possessively on his abs. Their breathing slowed to normal, and they lay together, entwined. Now that he had time to think about anything else besides Aria, he felt the cold nip of air against his bare skin.

"It'd be much warmer in bed," she suggested, as if reading

his mind.

"Your wish is my command," he said, lifting her in his arms and carrying her to the bedroom as she giggled and clung to his neck. She was light as a feather, her skin hot against his.

They made love again in bed, this time slowly, languidly, awakening each other with their hands and tongues and bodies. This time he had more control, and now he was beginning to understand her signs, he waited until she was close before letting his own climax build. He didn't want to question this night, merely accept it for what it was. If this was to be their only time together, then he needed to treasure it. Push aside all thoughts of dead sisters and a group of killers prowling the hillsides. But he really, really hoped there would be more… Because he knew once wouldn't be enough with this woman.

Later still, she pulled the sheet away from his body. "I want you to stay perfectly still," she commanded. "I want to taste you." She explored his whole body with her fingertips and her tongue. He shivered with anticipation, not sure if he'd be able to lie motionless when her touch seared him like a brand wherever she went.

She started at his feet, and quickly finding the scar on his calf, she asked, "When did this happen?"

"Earlier this year. Around five months ago. I was involved in a shoot-out trying to protect Penny and Clayton."

"Wow." Her mouth formed a circle of surprise, then she leaned in and kissed the scar. "So brave."

"Not brave, just doing my job."

"Brave," she proclaimed, biting his thigh with her teeth. "Not too many people would put themselves in danger to save someone else, whether it was their job or not."

He shrugged.

She continued to explore his body with her tongue.

"What's this scar?" she asked, stopping her excruciating investigation when she got to a ragged mark halfway up his left thigh.

"Fell off my bicycle when I was twelve," he replied, then grunted as she sucked the scar gently, her tongue doing lazy circles around the spot, moving slowly higher and higher. Much to his disappointment, she skipped over his crotch, and continued her inspection to where the trail of hair arrowed down from his belly button. She was setting him on fire with her wicked tongue and it was all he could do not to roll her over and plunge deep inside her.

"And this one?" she asked as she found the next scar, just above his left pectoral.

"Sliced with a knife while I was trying to arrest a man who was drunk and disorderly," he ground out between clenched teeth, his blood pounding so hard in his veins he could barely talk.

"Your body has quite a story to tell," she said quietly. Lifting her head, she stared at him and he could see her eyes glisten in the dim light.

"There's so much I don't know about you," she said, and he heard the hint of wistfulness in her tone. "So much we don't know about each other. So much you don't know about me," she clarified; then she lowered her head to his chest so he could no longer make out her expression.

It was true, he realized. They'd really only met four days ago. But it felt like a lifetime. He had no idea how she really felt about what they'd just done. Had it been as intense for her as it had for him? Had the intensity shocked her, or had he just imagined that look of awe on her face earlier as they both climaxed together?

"I'd like to find out more about you, if you'll let me," he said, catching a handful of her glorious hair and dragging her mouth up to his so he could kiss her and look into her eyes.

"Maybe when this is all over…" Her face took on a sort of faraway, slightly sad look. Then she seemed to come back to herself. "But we still have tonight, let's not waste it." Her mouth met his, hot and demanding, and he forgot all about what might happen tomorrow, wholeheartedly agreeing with taking what was on offer in the here and now.

The third time they made love, she took control, taking the condom from his hand and rolling it on him herself, slowly, with agonizingly nimble fingers. Then she pushed him back onto the bed and straddled him, her hair falling over her shoulders and breasts as they moved to an ever-increasing rhythm.

They stared into each other's eyes while they made love, and it felt like he was staring right into her soul. Which scared him a little. Because he didn't know if he was ready to bare his soul to this woman. Or if she was, either.

Finally, they fell into an exhausted sleep, tangled in each other's arms. Jude had to be at work early in the morning, but for those few, short, sweet hours they had left, he cradled her body protectively and let the soothing rise and fall of her chest lull him to sleep.

Barely two hours later, he was jarred awake by a god-awful banging on the door. It was still dark when he jerked upright, cursing himself that he'd been stupid enough to leave his weapon in the living room, out of reach.

"Open up, it's the police. We know you're in there."

That was Brady's voice. Jude recognized it, even in his half-asleep state.

"Whaaa…?" Aria sat up in a daze, the blankets falling away to reveal her pale breasts, partially covered by her sleep-tangled hair.

"Stay here," he commanded, already swinging his legs out of the bed.

The banging got louder, and Brady said, "If you don't open

this door, we'll be forced to break it down."

What the fuck was going on? Jude pulled on his trousers as he stumbled past the couch. He had no time to grab his shirt as he yanked open the door, letting a blast of freezing morning air in. Brady stood on the doorstep, flanked by four other officers, all with that serious, blank cop stare on their faces that didn't bode well.

"What the fuck, Brady?" Jude said.

"We have a warrant to search this premises," Brady ground out, his gaze flicking around the interior of the cottage before finally coming to rest on Jude.

"Let me see it." Jude held out his hand and Brady placed the paperwork in his palm. He felt at a disadvantage standing there in only his trousers, chest bare, but he squared his shoulders and looked the detective directly in the eye.

"It's all there in black and white, Wilder." Brady beckoned his men inside, pushing past Jude into the small living area.

"What are you looking for?" But even as Jude asked, he knew he wouldn't get an answer. Some other cops might've given him the professional courtesy of giving him at least the bare details, but not Brady.

Jude wanted to smash that small, smug smile off the detective's clean-shaven face. He was so angry, it felt like his guts were full of boiling lava. What were they looking for? Something must've happened overnight, some new evidence come to light that made Brady suspect Aria was indeed involved.

Jude walked over and snagged his shirt from the floor beside the couch, but didn't have time to put it on before Aria emerged in her doorway, wrapped in a sheet.

"What's going on?" she asked.

The smile on Brady's face only got more smug as his eyes came to rest on Aria.

Jude was in front of her in a shot, shielding her from view

with his body.

"Come and get dressed," he said, leading her by the arm into the bedroom and shutting the door.

"I don't understand," she whispered. "What are they looking for? Why are they doing this?" She pulled on a pair of jeans and an old sweater as she spoke; her other clothes were still where they'd dropped them beside the couch.

"I wish I knew." He stopped doing up his belt and went over and gathered her up in his arms. "I'm sorry this is happening to you. But I will get to the bottom of it, I promise."

She melted into him for a moment, receiving his proffered comfort, before she straightened and pushed her hair out of her face.

"Whatever they're looking for, they're not going to find it. I had nothing to do with either my father's murder, or my sister's and her husband's abduction and death."

"I know you didn't," he replied. And he believed her with all of his heart.

There was a bang on the bedroom door. "Hurry up in there. If you don't open the door, I'm sending in an officer, whether you're dressed or not."

Jude took one more look at Aria to make sure she was decent before he stalked over and opened the door, glaring at Brady who stood on the other side, impassive.

He finished putting on his shirt and buckling his belt; then he perched on the edge of the bed, Aria beside him, and together they read the search warrant. Suddenly, he surged to his feet.

"This says you have the right to search my house, as well." Jude stormed out of the bedroom, waving the paperwork in Brady's face.

"That's right." Brady's eyes went ice cold. "And you'd better not get in my way." The other four police officers were turning the small, cozy cottage upside down. Searching every drawer in the kitchen, opening every cupboard, ripping the cushions off the couch, tipping the chairs upside down, even crawling beneath the table.

What the hell was going on? Was he a suspect now? Or if Aria was the main suspect, did they think she'd left some sort of clue or evidence in his house? But she'd never even been into his house.

Jude retrieved his phone from his jacket pocket and took it back to the bedroom, where one of the cops was now going through the dresser drawers. He could take Aria outside, or into his house, so she didn't have to witness this ruination, but he wanted to be here to make sure everything went by the book, and if they did find something—God forbid—that he was here to see it.

Aria looked at him wide-eyed, a hint of hysteria in the curve of her lips. He wrapped an arm around her waist and tucked her under his shoulder.

"It'll be okay. Everything will be okay," he crooned. God, he hoped everything would be okay.

With one hand, he dialed a number on his phone. The sheriff answered after the second ring. "Jude, I'm sorry, I just found out myself. I'm on my way over." Well, that answered one question. Brady had gone behind the county sheriff's back to obtain this warrant. He was a sneaky sonofabitch. It wasn't against protocol. The sheriff's office and the local Missoula police were separate entities, working together most of the time, but they didn't have to report back, if they didn't want to.

"Do you know what they're looking for?" Jude snapped.

"No. But I heard that Brady fast-tracked the autopsy of the sister, pulled some strings to get the lab to stay open all night. Something in the medical examiner's report must be the catalyst for this search, I'm sure of it."

"Right. Thanks," Jude replied.

"I'll be there in ten minutes."

Jude ended the phone call, tapping the phone against his chin as his mind raced ahead. What could Brady have been looking for? It must've been something specific for him to get the results so quickly. Then it came to him.

"Shit. I think your sister might've been poisoned, too."

"Really. Why?" Aria stirred from beneath his armpit, looking up at him with dark eyes.

But Jude didn't answer her straightaway. That might be what they were looking for, evidence of poison. Brady must have something stronger than that. Surely, he couldn't be raiding Aria's house on such a flimsy hunch.

Aria came to the same conclusion as Jude. "And they think I did this? Why?"

"I have no idea." Jude shook his head as Aria stepped away from him.

"Could I go to jail?" Her beautiful face paled, her bottom lip beginning to tremble. "I can't go to jail. What about the baby?" She placed two hands protectively over her abdomen.

Jude blinked twice, slowly. What had she just said?

CHAPTER THIRTEEN

Aria sucked in a breath. Crap, she hadn't meant to say that. It'd been an instinctive reaction. Because she couldn't go to jail. She'd heard what happened to women like her in jail. It was a place of violence, and gangs, and deprivation. She wasn't street tough; she'd never survive. The baby would never survive. The baby was her top priority now.

And besides, she was innocent.

"You're what?" Jude stared at her incredulously.

She stepped away from him and hung her head. "I'm sorry, I was going to tell you." Was she, though? She hadn't made up her mind whether she was going to reveal her secret to Jude. Not just yet anyway. She was going to try and hide it from everybody for as long as possible, so that she could set aside some money from her new job, enough to get her somewhere safe and comfortable where she could have the baby if everything fell apart again. A small fragment of her had been holding out hope that Naomi may even let her return to work after the birth. If she did a good enough job. If she could show Naomi that she was irreplaceable and convince her she could still be valuable to the project, even after she had the baby. A sliver of hope that she might be accepted as part of the staff family at Stargazer. But she was

153

also a realist. And that kind of thing didn't happen in real life. You were fired and sent on your way at the slightest hint of misbehavior.

Jude moved to put space between them. "But we…" He turned toward the bed. "But you…" His handsome face was creased with a frown, and he stared at her as if she'd grown two heads. As the realization hit him, they'd shared a bed, been intimate all night, and all along she'd been keeping this terrible secret from him.

He had every right to be confused and perhaps even angry and disappointed. She probably should've told him before they slept together, but it'd all happened so quickly, and part of her hadn't wanted to scare him off. Wanted that one night with him, if that was all she was allowed. She was pretty certain he would've refused her if he'd known beforehand.

"When were you going to tell me?" he finally asked.

"Eventually. But it wasn't significant, at the time." Which was true from her point of view, even if not from his.

Now wasn't the time to have this argument with Jude. She was sorry he had to find out this way, but he was going to find out sooner or later, anyway. And now she understood that putting it off wouldn't have mattered in the long run. He would still have looked at her with that utter betrayal in his face.

"It wasn't significant?" His face was a mask of astonishment. "After what we just did? After what I felt for you? Last night was—"

"Aria Cusack, I'm arresting you on suspicion of murder in the first degree of Tango Cusack." Brady strode into the room, handcuffs dangling from one finger. "You do not have to say anything, but anything you do say may be given as evidence in a court of law."

"What?" she squeaked. Her mind was still replaying Jude's words. What'd he been about to say? What did he feel for her? It took her a second or two to comprehend the detective's words. He was arresting her? Her worst fears were coming true.

Jude was faster, reacting with lightning speed, stepping between her and Brady.

"Don't you dare," he growled, getting right up into Brady's face. Even though the other man was taller, Jude had a tension around him that exuded menace. She could see the rigidity in his broad shoulders, his fists balled at his side as he glared up at the other man, not backing down one bit.

"Don't get in my way, or I'll arrest you, too, for obstruction," Brady growled, glaring at Jude with undisguised contempt.

"Well, you might just have to do that. Because you're not taking her."

Jude was putting himself in harm's way for her benefit. She couldn't let him do this. Much as she didn't want to go with Brady, it'd help no one, especially Jude, if he ended up in jail.

There was no room for her to step between the two men, so she laid a hand on his arm. "Jude, don't," she said. "It's okay, I'll go with him."

It took a few seconds, but Jude finally tore his heated gaze from Brady's face to look at her.

"No, you won't, this is ridiculous."

Please don't, she implored him with her eyes. *And please don't tell them I'm pregnant*. She willed him not to let her secret out. *Please stop talking*. Willed him not to say anything more, so he didn't give Brady an excuse to arrest him. Or give Brady one more excuse to treat her with disdain. She hoped like hell he kept his mouth shut on both points.

"No, I'm sure Brady's just doing his job. Just like you should be," she reminded him. He needed to do his job. And if that job included watching her get arrested, then he'd have to stand back and let it happen. It wasn't his fault this was happening to her, and she didn't want to see him put his job in jeopardy just to protect her.

"On what grounds are you arresting her?" Jude growled, but Aria was relieved when he took a step back.

"We found evidence pertaining to the crime," Brady replied blandly.

"What evidence?" Jude ground out.

"You'll find out soon enough. She's going to need a lawyer." Brady advanced on Aria, motioning her to put her hands behind her back.

"There's no need to put her in handcuffs. She's not a flight risk, and she's not a danger to anyone." Jude stepped in front of Aria again.

"I second that," said Sheriff Buchanan, walking into the bedroom and filling it with his presence. "If you handcuff her, I will put in a formal complaint of police brutality." The sheriff and Brady eyeballed each other for a few seconds until Brady finally scowled, but dropped his arm.

Aria hadn't really taken to the sheriff on the few times she'd met him. But this morning she could've kissed him.

"This way, Miss Cusack," Brady said stiffly, pointing toward the door.

"I'm going to organize you a lawyer," Jude said loudly from behind Brady. "Don't say anything to anyone until that lawyer gets there. Do you understand?"

"Yes." She craned her neck to look around the bulky form of the detective, catching a last glimpse of Jude's anxious face.

"I'll be there as soon as I can."

Everything happened at what felt like warp speed after that. She only had time to grab her jacket from the hook by the door before she was bundled out into the freezing cold and led toward a police cruiser parked at the top of Jude's driveway. Dawn should be breaking around now, but dark, oppressive clouds covered the sky, and there was no sign of the sunrise. Naomi had mentioned that the first storm of the season was forecast for today. It was earlier than usual and predictions warned it might be a bad one. But Aria had no time to worry about late fall cold snaps as Brady got into the back seat with her and one of the other Missoula police officers drove them silently through the streets. But they didn't go to the sheriff's office, as she was expecting.

"Where are we going?" she asked numbly.

"You're going to be questioned at the Missoula Police Station," Brady replied, not even turning his head to look at her, and his words hit her like a blow to the chest. He was taking her away from everything she knew. There would be no friendly faces in Missoula. No Susan to save her from the endless interviews, no Sheriff Buchanan to pull on his mustache and keep Brady in line merely with his presence. No Jude to come to her rescue. Just her, in a cold, sterile, antagonistic room with no one who believed in her.

The rest of the forty-five-minute trip was completed in silence beneath the low, sullen clouds.

Once they arrived, she was escorted to a room deep inside the police station with only a metal table and chairs, gray walls with no window, and the red light of a camera mounted high on the wall blinking at her like an eye. Exactly the type of room she'd expected. Here, she was left alone, with no explanation as to how long she'd be here, or what would happen next. They removed her jacket, took away her phone, and checked her pockets. She huddled in the cold chair, arms wrapped around herself, and waited. And waited. What was going on out there?

She began to pace, not able to sit still any longer. Was Brady doing this on purpose? Hoping she'd get so agitated that she'd break and tell him everything in the first five minutes? And was Jude organizing a lawyer like he'd promised? Her mind was a maelstrom of worries and visions.

But time and time again, the same image kept settling in her mind. The look on Jude's face when he'd found out she was pregnant.

It wasn't quite the same look Beau had given her when she'd told him. Back then, she'd been naïve enough to think that Beau might've been pleased with her surprise news. Or at the very least, if not pleased, perhaps stoically accepting. Accepting that he was going to be a father, telling her that he would support her and the baby. Perhaps they'd even get married. Aria hadn't wanted to get pregnant, it'd been the last thing on her mind, in fact. Nor had she thought much about marriage. Even though she'd been dating Beau for over a year, and they'd been living together for nearly that long, she wasn't really sure where the relationship was headed. She loved Beau, and she thought he loved her, but they were both caught up with their busy lives. But she'd missed a period, and she was always as regular as clockwork, so she'd taken a test and was flabbergasted to find it positive. It was straight after she'd been laid off from her job, and it felt like the world hated her right then. It'd taken her a few days to work up the courage to tell Beau.

The look on Beau's face had been hard for Aria to comprehend. So many emotions had flickered across it. He'd just returned home from work and she'd been waiting for him, seated at the kitchen table. She offered him a beer, but when he asked her why she was only drinking water, she'd blurted it all out, then sat nervously waiting for his reply. She'd expected him to have to work through the same emotions she'd had when she first found out: shock, despair, anger, elation, and finally acceptance. And she expected he might need a few days to process.

But Beau's first and only reaction had been one of anger. How dare she let this happen? He wanted nothing to do with this baby, or her. This was her problem, not his. He probably wasn't even the father anyway, he'd shouted at her. She needed to get out of his house before he did something he might regret.

She'd been so hurt and surprised; it was like he'd set off a bomb underneath her world. She'd packed her things and jumped into her car and sped away without a single thought as to where she was going or what she would do next. Which was how she'd ended up back in her hometown a month later. Driving aimlessly all over the country wasn't getting her anywhere, and she'd run out of options.

Jude's face, however, hadn't been full of anger. There'd been betrayal, hurt, surprise, disquiet, but also resolve. What did that mean?

She hoped he didn't think she'd slept with him just to entrap him. Because that'd never been her intention. All she'd wanted was some of the human comfort he was offering. A chance to feel loved and needed, if only for one night. To be close to someone without having them judge her.

Truth be known, she liked Jude Wilder, liked him a lot. And she thought he might like her, too. But she'd never expected anything from him. Not a long-term commitment. Not even a short-term commitment. Something completely unexpected had happened between them, something that was special and right, and it'd been unplanned. But now she'd had a taste of Jude, she was going to find him hard to let go.

But let go she must, because she was having a baby, and she was pretty sure he wouldn't want to be part of that. If only they'd met in a different time, a different place, perhaps they might've been good together. As things were now, however, it was messy and complicated, and she wouldn't blame Jude for a second if he wanted nothing more to do with her. Could they still remain friends? She hoped so. She'd be proud to call him one of her friends, along with Penny and perhaps Naomi, and even the rest of the Stargazer staff. A sad longing filled her chest, because she wanted to be so much more than friends with Jude. But at the moment, she'd be happy with anything he offered.

The door banged open, breaking her conflicting emotions.

"Miss Cusack, you are to come with me." It was one of the young police officers who'd been with Brady this morning at her cottage. A redhead, with freckles and a scar on his chin. A glance at his badge confirmed he was Sergeant McMurdo.

"Where are we going?" she asked, slightly surprised. She'd been expecting a lawyer, or at the very least, Brady.

"I'm under instructions to move you." She didn't like the way he looked at her, kind of sideways, like he was only half watching her.

"Move me where?"

But he didn't answer, instead he forcibly turned her around and snapped handcuffs on her wrists behind her back.

"Brady didn't see the need to handcuff me before," she argued, twisting in his grip.

"Well, things have changed," he replied, dragging her toward the door. He opened it and then took a quick look into the hallway before pushing her out and practically frogmarching her down the dark passage. No one else was around. At the end of the hall, he turned right, pushing her so quickly, she almost had to jog to keep up. At the end of the next passage, he turned right again.

"Where are we going?" she asked. This was getting weirder by the second. Was he just changing rooms? Was he taking her to a jail cell?

"Shut up," he snapped.

At the end of this hallway was an exit sign, and he made a beeline for that. Before she knew it, they were outside, and she stumbled down a step into a dank alleyway.

Where were they?

"What are you—" McMurdo clapped a hand over her mouth, and her stomach flipped over. What the fuck? This didn't feel right. She began to struggle, but he bent her arm up behind her back until she would have cried out in pain if not for his hand muffling her scream. She had no choice but to go where he directed, walking quickly down the alleyway toward a square of light. They must be at the rear of the police station. She'd only seen the front entrance when Brady had brought her in. A part of her registered how cold it was outside, and she didn't even have her jacket on to keep her warm. Icy rain was falling, hitting her in the face with small, stinging drops.

A figure appeared in the square of light, beckoning them toward him. As they approached, the figure morphed into a man. It took her a few seconds, but she realized she recognized this man. It was the same guy who'd flagged her down by the side of the road the other day.

"You took your time," the man stage-whispered, as they emerged from the alley into a loading bay area.

McMurdo merely grunted in reply, keeping his hand firmly over her mouth as he led her toward the same white van that'd supposedly been broken down with the man's pregnant wife inside it. The guy, who she'd pegged as your friendly neighbor-next-door slid the van door open, revealing an empty, dark space, and she began to struggle for real this time. Then it hit her. Was this why the man had pulled her over the other day? Was he trying to abduct her back then? She was *not* getting in that van.

But then she had no choice, as the sergeant bodily lifted her legs out from under her and slammed her down onto the cold metal floor of the van. The wind was knocked out of her, and instead of screaming as his hand left her mouth, she struggled to breathe. Before she could regain her breath, a figure manifested out of the gloom in the rear space of the cargo area and plastered a length of duct tape over her mouth.

Real fear bloomed in her chest, and she thrashed, rolling herself over, kicking out at whatever and whoever she could. Even while a small section of her brain said this couldn't be happening. Even as that same small section of her brain told her to stop struggling in case she hurt the baby. But fear was a wild animal in her chest, overriding all logical thought.

"Hold her still," she heard a voice say. Then rough hands grabbed her ankles and soon both her feet were also wrapped in duct tape and she could barely move. She lay on her back, struggling to draw enough air in through her nose, eyes goggling at the two men staring at her from outside the van while the other figure hovered over her feet, tying off the last of the tape.

"I've done what was required," McMurdo said from between gritted teeth. "My debt is more than repaid. Please, just send Stacy home." He glared at the man, but Aria heard the way his tone turned pleading, before he turned his back, and without another glance, strode back the way they'd come into the alleyway.

The neighbor-next-door slid the door closed with a bang, leaving her trapped in the dark with the strange figure still crouched over her.

She whimpered in fear, tears leaking from her eyes.

CHAPTER FOURTEEN

"What do you mean, she's not available?" Jude slammed his fist on the front reception counter. "I have her lawyer here, and I'm a county deputy. We have a right to see her. Now," he added, leaning over the counter and glaring at the young female cop manning the desk.

"Sorry, Deputy Wilder, but those are my orders. No one is allowed in to see her at the moment."

"Who gave you those orders?" Jude practically roared, and the man standing beside him put a restraining hand on his elbow. The bespectacled man in his mid-forties was the same height as Jude and turned a flat stare in his direction, but his warning was clear; it'd do him no good to lose his temper. Stuart Ladley was the best criminal defender in the county, and it'd taken a few hours for Jude to track him down so that he could bring him to the Missoula Police Station. Dean and Naomi had offered to pay his retainer fee, which was substantial, and even though Jude knew Aria would be mortified when she found out how much it cost, he wasn't about to haggle prices with her when her freedom could be on the line. Dean and Naomi had more than enough money, and they would do the same for any of their staff.

And now that he'd finally arrived in Missoula with Ladley

in tow, they were telling him he couldn't see Aria.

"Get me Detective Brady," he demanded.

"He's on a call to the—" Jude cut her off.

"If you don't get him out here right now, I'm going to climb over this desk and go and find him myself. Are you prepared to physically stop me?" The young police officer paled slightly, and he felt a twinge of regret that he'd had to threaten her but not enough to make him rescind his words.

"Deputy, you need to calm down," Ladley said, and Jude knew he was right. But his blood had been boiling ever since Brady had arrested Aria, and he knew he wouldn't calm down until he got to see her. Got to see she was all right with his own eyes. Until he got her out of this place where she clearly didn't belong.

Aria was pregnant. The notion kept rolling around in the back of his consciousness, even as he went about doing everything necessary to get her out of this stupid mess.

The ramifications of her simple slip of the tongue—because that's what'd it'd been, she hadn't intended for him to know —were huge. Had she been keeping the secret on purpose? Trying to ensnare him? Picked him as a soft target? Planned to get him to fall in love with her so that he couldn't bear to kick her out of his home when he found out the truth? He didn't know her well enough to be entirely sure, but he didn't think that was her style. He sincerely hoped that wasn't her style, otherwise he'd been played for a fool. His mind kept replaying all their interactions, to see if he could find a hint of falseness, a hint that she might've been leading him along.

He didn't even know how far along she was. Probably no more than three months at the most, because she certainly wasn't showing. Her stomach had been as flat as a board. If he'd known beforehand, would he still have slept with her? He didn't know the answer to that question. He didn't know the answer to the other million questions crowding his brain, either.

One thing he did know was that she'd become special to him, and he needed to see her safe. All his other doubts could wait for another day.

"I'll get him for you," the young cop said, eyeing him warily. "But you have to take a seat and wait over there." She pointed to the row of white plastic chairs lined up along the wall.

"Thank you, Corporal Miller," Ladley said, reading the woman's name badge; then he took Jude by the arm and led him over to the chairs. But Jude was too agitated to sit and began to pace, hands shoved in his pockets, glancing up now and then at the front desk. He was aware he looked slightly unhinged, but right now he didn't care. He'd apologize to Corporal Miller after he'd talked to Aria. But at the moment, he was ready to break every rule in the book if it meant he could see her.

Five excruciating minutes later, Brady appeared through a door to the side of the reception desk.

"It's about time," Jude snarled. "What's this bullshit about no one is allowed in to see Aria?"

"I'm letting her cool her heels."

"What the...? What does that even mean?" Jude got right up in Brady's face, but Brady used his height to tower over Jude. "Is this some fucked up kind of way to get into her head? You asshole," Jude growled. "She's not one of your hardened criminals. She's a young woman who's scared out of her wits, and—" He'd almost blurted out that she was pregnant and needed to be treated appropriately, but the look Aria had given him right before Brady arrested her stopped him. She didn't want anyone to know, and he had to respect her wishes, even if he really wanted to throw that little tidbit in Brady's smug face.

"It's common procedure," Brady ground out, eyes

glittering dangerously. "And I won't have some snot-nosed, upstart deputy tell me how to run my cases."

Jude sucked in a breath. This had just become personal, and he didn't care that Brady was technically his superior, he was going to have to punch the guy in the—

Ladley inserted a hand between them and said calmly, "That may all be well, Detective. But if you're refusing my client the right to an attorney, you know I will be all over you like a rash that you'll never get rid of. I will have you up on so many harassment, unreasonable force and misconduct charges, you won't have time to scratch your ass, let alone investigate any more criminal cases." He gave Brady a dead-eyed stare, and Jude could suddenly see why this man was the best in the county.

Brady looked between Jude and Ladley, then back again. Out of the corner of his eye, Jude caught the corporal goggling from behind the desk. She clearly hadn't seen anyone stand up to Brady like this before.

"Fine. It's time we questioned her, anyway." Brady took a step back, straightening his sports coat and brushing a nonexistent piece of lint from his arm. "Follow me," he said curtly.

The young corporal buzzed them through the same door Brady had come out of, and Jude and Ladley followed him down a long hallway. He stopped in front of a door near the end and punched a code into a keypad, pulling the door open.

"After you," he said ungraciously.

Jude was too eager to see Aria to care, and barged past him into…an empty room. What the hell kind of trick was Brady trying to pull?

"Where is she?" he demanded as Brady trailed in through the doorway behind the lawyer. Brady stopped and for a split-second looked dumbfounded. Recovering quickly, he brought his cell phone to his ear.

"Someone must've moved her," he said. "I'll find out. Just cool your heels for a second."

Jude paced around the room, shooting a worried look toward Ladley, who gave a shrug. They both listened to Brady's one-sided conversation, and Jude became more worried by the minute.

"Where is she?" Jude ground out when Brady ended his phone call.

"Wait here. I'm going to look for her."

"You're what?"

"Please tell me you haven't lost the defendant, Detective Brady," Ladley demanded, becoming almost as agitated as Jude.

"No. Just...misplaced." Brady marched out of the room and Jude followed him. There was no way he was letting that man out of his sight.

* * *

Two hours later, Jude sat in Brady's office with his head in his hands, not really listening to what else the detective had to say. All he could think was that Aria had gone missing. There was no way she could've just walked out of a fully manned, well-guarded police station. So something else had happened to her. But what? He opened and closed his fists, wanting to smash something to get rid of all this rage and misery. But he knew he needed to hang on, keep himself together, for Aria's sake.

Jude was sick to his stomach with all the ifs, buts, and maybes plaguing him. He really wished he'd had time to delve a little deeper into that cult he and Aria had discussed the other day. But then they'd found Iliana's and her husband's bodies and things had developed so quickly, he simply hadn't had time. And now, Aria had gone missing, just like her sister had three days ago. This was fast becoming a pattern. But he wished he knew who was pulling the strings of this particular puzzle. He had a growing suspicion that it had something to do with Tango's mysterious past. Something to do with this InXium group, whoever, or whatever, they were.

The first thing Brady had done when they'd discovered Aria was nowhere to be found was order a review of all the security footage from all the cameras in the police station. Only to find that somehow, the cameras had mysteriously been turned off for around five minutes at the same time Aria was thought to have gone missing. This might well be an inside job, but Jude had no clue who to look at first; there were over forty people involved in manning this station, it'd be like looking for a needle in a haystack. Now Jude just glared at everyone around him, suspecting everyone and anyone.

Earlier, Jude had demanded to know what had caused Brady to request a search warrant for Aria's house this morning. At first Brady wouldn't tell him, but as it became increasingly clear that Aria may well have been abducted, he relented.

"I asked for a rush job on the toxicology report for the sister and the husband," Brady said begrudgingly. Hank had already revealed that in his early morning call, and Jude had a sneaking suspicion he knew what was in that report, but he needed Brady to confirm it.

"And," Jude prompted when Brady offered no more information.

"It came back showing they both had the same poison in their system as the father. Arsenic. The ME won't confirm it as cause of death yet, but we all know the truth."

Jude let out a sigh of frustration. "And so you decided because poison was used, that Aria was number one suspect." Poison was often the murder weapon of choice for women killers. It was less messy, required less physical force, and usually gave a satisfactory result.

"No, that wasn't it." Brady bristled at the accusation, but Jude knew he'd been thinking it. "We got an anonymous tip-off late last night from a member of the public, saying that he'd seen on the news about the three murders in Montana, and he recognized Aria Cusack. He said he didn't want to be identified, but she'd recently bought Arsenic from him, and he thought that might be pertinent to the case. It sounded like he was some kind of dodgy, backyard pharmaceutical dealer, which was why he probably wanted to remain anonymous," Brady admitted. "But it was enough to make me want to search her house and belongings."

"You what?" Jude could hardly believe his ears. Brady had been blinded by his own bias, hoping that this case could be solved by a simple family dispute. But he didn't know Aria like Jude did. This whole scenario was impossible.

"We found an empty arsenic bottle in the boot of her car," Brady said defensively, as if that had indeed been the answer to all their problems.

"And you think that justifies it?" Jude could hardly believe his ears. "Don't you see? It was a setup," Jude said scathingly. "Didn't you stop to think about how damn convenient that anonymous tip-off was? Pointing the finger directly at Aria. You played directly into the murderer's hands, giving them exactly what they wanted. They wanted you to arrest Aria. They obviously had a plan to take her from the station." Jude was so incensed, he could barely look at the man.

He continued to harangue Brady until Ladley had to pull him away before Brady ordered him to be to put under guard and led away to a jail cell to cool his heels, and now Jude was left to wonder at the complete ineptitude of the detective. How he'd only seen what he wanted to see; an easy solution to this case, so he could move onto the next one. Once Iliana's and Craig's bodies had been discovered, this had become a high-profile case, with lots of eager eyes watching from higher up. Brady was hoping for a promotion, and so he'd been happy to sacrifice Aria, if that's what it took.

Now, Jude found himself listening, but not really hearing, as Brady continued to outline the protocol for the missing suspect search to ramp up once the storm had passed.

To compound matters a hundred fold, the big storm the weather bureau had predicted was now pummeling the state. The first big winter storm to hit the region and, of course, it had to be today. All staff had been recalled to the station unless they were responding to an active call; it was too dangerous for them to be outside in this weather. It'd been raining when Jude had first arrived in Missoula. Cold, stinging sleet that was turning the roads icy and dangerous. The temperature had been falling rapidly, as well, and the conditions looked like they might make for a perfect storm. An ice storm. Where the temperature dropped so low that the rain and snow were frozen solid, covering every exposed surface with a sheet of ice. Some locals called it a silver storm because after the storm had passed and it was safe to go outside, it looked as if everything was coated in the lustrous, precious metal.

Ladley sat on a chair in the corner of the office, staring stoically out of the window. He'd followed the way the police station had come alive, like someone had stirred a hornet's nest once they found Aria missing, with a sort of morbid fascination. But in the end, he couldn't be of any more help than the rest of the confused and slightly angry team. They were just as perplexed as to how a suspect could vanish out of a locked room from a well-guarded building. Even Brady's constant shouting couldn't miraculously make Aria reappear. It was a complete mystery.

"I'm going to see if the local motel has a spare room,"

Ladley said. "Anything is better than sitting here and drinking this awful coffee all afternoon." Ladley glanced over at Jude. "I think you'd be wise to come with me. There's not a lot you can do here right now. This storm is going to stop everything in its tracks. Neither of us will be able to get home today."

Jude merely shook his head. He couldn't leave, not without knowing where Aria was.

His phone vibrated in his pocket, and he almost didn't answer. But it could be someone with information about Aria, and so he reached into his top pocket and withdrew it, noting Levi's name on the caller ID.

"Hi. I've just had some interesting news I thought you might like to hear." Levi launched into his speech before Jude even had a chance to get out a greeting. But he didn't have time for this, whatever it was.

"Look, Levi, something's going down here. They've arrested Aria on suspicion of murder. But she's gone missing from the Missoula Police Station."

"Shit." There was silence down the line as Levi digested the news. "I didn't know. I'm sorry. Anything I can do to help?"

"As soon as this storm abates, Brady's promised he'll have this whole squad out looking for her." Jude ran a hand through his hair. "He's already put out a BOLO and alerted all the other stations in the state." God, what if whoever took her had already crossed state lines? The thought was too much to bear. "I'm not really sure what else we can do right now. Where on earth would we even start looking?"

There was another studied silence on the end of the phone before Levi said, "Maybe this information I have might help more than I thought it would."

Jude doubted it, but he said, "Go on."

"I got word that a white van was abandoned in a rest stop

halfway between here and Missoula around two hours ago. A couple who'd stopped there in their Winnebago to weather the storm called it in. When they saw it was empty, they were scared that whoever owned the van might be out hiking in the storm and got caught, so they rang the station. The main ranger station in Missoula runs CCTV cameras on all large rest stops, so I asked them to check the footage. Most people don't even realize the stops are being monitored, but you wouldn't believe some of the illegal shit that goes down in those places, and so the cameras are often hidden. Anyway…" Levi hesitated slightly, as if searching for the right words. "The van registration matches the one on the side of the road the other day. You remember, the guy who flagged Aria down with a supposed flat battery, and then the car started without a hitch after you guys left? I recorded his rego plates, mainly because something felt a little off."

Jude went completely still. Awareness spiked up his spine. Call it his sixth sense, his cop intuition, but this felt like something. Something big.

"The thing is, Jude, I decided to replay the footage in the rest stop right back to twenty-four hours ago, and there was a four-wheel-drive parked up there for that whole time. It was backed right into the forest, almost as if someone was trying to hide it from view from the main highway. I kept watching all the way through today's footage, and the white van appeared, parked right in front of it, so part of the truck was obscured, but I could see at least two men and it looked like they moved something into the four-wheel-drive, then drove away, leaving the van behind. The other couple in the RV arrived around fifteen minutes later, and that must be when they called it in."

Jude didn't speak. He couldn't speak. Was the *something* those men had transferred from the van to the truck actually Aria? He was also wondering if the man by the side of the road was connected with the three murders. Had he and Levi been that close to the murderer and let him slip through their fingers? Had that man been about to abduct Aria on the side of the road that day, and he and Levi had come along in the nick of time?

Levi filled the silence on the other end of the phone. "But even if this is the connection you're looking for, I'm not sure how far they'll get. This weather is really closing in. The roads will be treacherous. The Department of Transport is warning everyone to stay at home and shelter in place. As is your sheriff's office. Roads are closed all over the county. They're predicting a huge ice storm."

Jude still didn't speak; the ice storm wasn't even on his radar right now. Instead, he was coming up with a preposterous plan. Suddenly, all the puzzle pieces seemed to drop into place.

"Not sure what that all means, but I thought you might like to know, because..." Levi trailed off, probably not sure if Jude was still listening.

"Levi, I know this sounds outrageous, but do you think that four-wheel-drive could be the one we were looking for? The one that left the tire tracks up on Canyon Peak?"

There was utter silence on the other end of the phone, but Jude could almost hear the cogs turning in Levi's mind. "It's hard to say," he began slowly. "Are you thinking that the people who've been camping up on the mountain are possibly the same people who killed Iliana and Craig? And they might also be related to the people who just abducted Aria? I don't know, it's a bit of a stretch," he mused.

"But not an impossible one," Jude said, his gut tightening in anticipation. He suddenly knew what he needed to do. "Levi, I think they might've gone back up the fire trail. That rest stop you mentioned, how far is it from the turnoff onto the trail?"

"Not far," Levi admitted slowly. "But would they really be stupid enough to return to the scene of the crime? Won't the site still be under guard? They can't have finished all their investigations up there already?" Levi pondered out loud.

"I'll check with Brady, but I'm guessing with this weather closing in, all his staff have been recalled. If there was a guard at that gate or at the gravesite, they won't be there now." Jude felt a triumphant surge of heat in his chest. He was right, he just knew it. "They know that area well. They'll feel safe up there. They'll need a place to shelter from the storm that's off the highway and out of sight of prying eyes. I'm going up there," Jude said, knowing it was probably the most stupid thing he'd ever done in his life. Maybe he was grasping at straws. But if he was right…

"I don't think that's wise," Levi prevaricated.

Jude said nothing; he was too busy sorting through what he should take with him. Warm clothing, blankets—if he could get them—whatever he could garner from the police storage.

"If you can wait a few hours, I'll go with you," Levi finally said. "But I've just had a call come in about a tree down on one of the roads along the river. It's trapped a carload of fishermen trying to get out after the storm hit. Although, God knows why they left it so late," Levi said brusquely. But both of them knew there was no accounting for stupidity. It wouldn't be the first time either of them had to rescue someone because they hadn't listened to the weather report or had simply thought the inclement weather couldn't possibly affect *them*.

"Thanks, mate," Jude replied. "But I'm going now."

"I thought you might say that," Levi sighed. "Stay safe." There were a million unsaid comments behind those simple words.

"Will do. You too," he replied, because Levi would also be

putting himself in danger by getting in his vehicle and driving out in this terrible storm just to save a group of fishermen too dense to heed the warnings properly.

Just as Jude ended the call with Levi, Stuart Ladley stood up and announced that he'd procured a room at the Travelodge Inn and was off to weather the storm down there.

"Wait," Jude called, lunging toward the lawyer. "I need to ask a favor. And it's a big one."

The man eyed him cooly. "Anything to help my good deputy," he replied after a few seconds.

"I need to borrow your vehicle."

"Hmm." Ladley stroked his chin as he considered Jude. Then he pushed his glasses up his nose and said, "Okay. As long as you tell me why you need it. And as long as you drop me down to the inn on the way. And as long as you can promise my car will be returned to me in one unharmed piece."

Jude wasn't sure he could promise the last one, so he kept his mouth shut. In his spare time, Ladley was a die-hard hunter and fisherman. Not that you could tell if you met him during the work week. When he was wearing his neat tan suit and tie, with smart woolen overcoat, his face clean-shaven, and glasses perched on his nose, he looked the epitome of the wealthy lawyer. Jude knew about his alter-ego because Dean had showed him a picture once of Stuart Ladley dressed in hunting attire, his foot resting on the head of a large deer he'd just shot. And Jude had also seen Ladley arrive in his big, kitted out Chevy truck that'd go just about anywhere. Including up a fire trail on Canyon Peak.

"Thank you." Jude could almost hug the man.

When he told Brady his plan, the other man just sneered at him. "You can't seriously be considering going out in this weather? I highly urge you not to," Brady said cooly. "I think you're barking up the wrong tree. There's no way in hell that whoever took Aria would take her back to the scene of his first crime. If indeed the two crimes are even linked."

"Screw you." Jude knew it was childish and uncalled for, but he no longer cared what Brady thought. And besides, it felt good. He was going. End of story. And Brady couldn't stop him.

"Well, you're going alone," Brady said, with a challenging lift of his eyebrows. "I'm not asking any of my valued team to risk their lives on some wild goose chase."

"That's just fine by me." Jude hadn't expected anything more, and he and Ladley left the office as Brady shut the door in a waft of self-righteousness.

CHAPTER FIFTEEN

Aria was cold. So cold. She was folded into the fetal position in the back of some four-wheel-drive truck, trying to keep herself warm. To keep the baby warm. Oh, God, the baby. She hoped with all her heart that the baby was still okay. Those men had manhandled her. Pushed her into a van and slammed her on the ground. Then they'd driven for around twenty minutes before stopping and lifting her into the rear bay of this truck, leaving her bound and completely powerless. She'd never before felt this helpless. This alone. Or this cold. She wished she had her jacket, but that was back in the Missoula Police Station. God, how she wished she were back in that little interrogation room. She'd take her chances with Brady any day over this nightmare scenario.

After they'd changed vehicles, they'd driven for another twenty minutes up some steep, rocky road, and she'd had to brace herself against the rest of the equipment jammed in around her to try and stop from rolling around. Then they'd stopped the vehicle and got out without a word to her. The rear bay seemed to be filled with camping equipment, some of which had been moved to create a small space for her. She wished there was a blanket in the mix somewhere, but even if there was, she wouldn't be able to get to it with her feet and hands still bound.

Who were these men? What did they want with her?

She was beginning to shiver harder. The temperature in the vehicle had been okay until they stopped and turned off the engine. And the heat. But now the temperature was dropping quickly. She had no idea even what time it was. How long had she been sitting in that room before the crooked cop had taken her out the back? It couldn't be past lunchtime yet, she decided. But it was almost dark outside, she could see eddies of snow swirling around the car when she lifted her head to peer out the window, making it impossible to see where she was, and the wind was howling like a pack of marauding wolves.

Suddenly, the rear door flew open and a bulky figure tugged at her ankles, dragging her across the floor and out into the freezing cold. She tried to scream, but only a muffled shout came out from behind the tape over her mouth. Then she was slung over the man's shoulder and the icy wind was like knives on her skin through her thin sweater.

Oh, God, were they going to dump her out in the snow? It wouldn't take long for hypothermia to set in, and she'd freeze to death. But instead, the man—she thought it was the younger one from the back of the van—carried her around the side and placed her on the back seat of the car, shutting the door behind her. The relief to be out of the freezing gale was immediate. By the time she'd struggled to a sitting position, he'd come around to the other side and got in next to her, bringing in a blast of icy air with him.

Shaking off snow from his clothes, he removed a pair of thick gloves and then pulled off a knit cap and balaclava. Rubbing his hands together, he turned to face her.

"It's fucking freezing out there," he said with a laugh. Why would anyone find it funny to be out in an ice storm? "Hi, I'm Rocky," he added, as if that was supposed to mean something to her.

She just stared at him, shivering.

The passenger side door opened and the man she'd dubbed the neighbor-from-next-door got into the front seat. He removed from his gloves and headgear, much the same as Rocky had done, then turned to look at her and smiled. It seemed impossible to imagine how she'd ever thought of him as a nice guy. He was a *bad* man. A very, very bad man. Who'd tried to trick her once, but he wouldn't trick her again.

"Take the tape off her face, dufus, she can't talk with that over her mouth," he said, not unkindly. "And get her a blanket, she must be freezing."

Rocky leaned over and ripped the tape from her mouth, and she cried out in pain.

"You idiot," the other man roared. "Do it slowly. Can't you do anything right?"

Rocky cowered slightly at the older man's tone and then simpered and smiled at her. "Sorry," he said, and she wondered if he was a little simple. There was something not quite right about this young man.

He lurched over the back seat and rummaged around, finally returning with a thick woolen blanket, which he draped over her. It was scratchy and rough, but she tried to snuggle into it as best she could.

"You may as well undo her hands and feet," the other man continued. "She's not going anywhere in this weather."

Rocky grinned at her again and produced a Swiss Army knife from his jacket pocket and began slicing at the duct tape on her feet. Aria glanced outside and knew his words to be true. It was almost a complete whiteout. They must be in a forest somewhere, because she could make out the dark shape of tall tree trunks nearby, but she could see nothing more, not even the trail she knew must be there because they'd driven up it.

Rocky waved a small key at her and gestured for her to turn so he could unlock the handcuffs.

"Are you going to kill me?" she asked bluntly, rubbing her wrists to get circulation back into her hands. Because if she was going to die, she wanted to know.

"That's not my intention," Neighbor-next-door replied, a subtle frown flickering across his forehead as if she'd hurt him with her accusing words. "Why don't we start at the beginning?" It was as if he'd schooled his face into a pleasant, but bland countenance. Like he was about to give a sermon or something.

He pushed his long hair back from his forehead, gray eyes fixed on her. "You clearly don't remember me. But that's okay, you were only young when your parents took you away. My name is Parker Gaudin, and this is my son, Rocky."

Aria blinked. The name rang a small bell somewhere inside her head.

Then she wondered, *when her father took her away from where*?

Parker turned, so his face was in profile, and that sudden familiarity returned, but this time with greater clarity. This man looked a little like…her father.

He was correct, she had no memory of him, but a recollection of Tango's words came back to her in a rush. "If you ever see that no-good brother of mine, you gals run like hell." He'd been talking to her and Iliana out in the backyard; she'd been around five or six. They'd been helping pick carrots for dinner. Back when her mother was still alive, the vegetable garden was always well tended, a necessity to help them put food on the table. Aria couldn't be sure what had sparked the conversation, but Tango had glared at her and Iliana with such intensity, his blue eyes sharp and fierce. "That man's a monster, you hear me? You don't believe a word he says. He tells lies. Terrible, awful lies." Then Tango had launched into another of his tirades about how they had to wash their souls clean from sin, and how he was the only one that could protect them. Aria and her sister had heard it many times before, and would hear it many times more throughout their lives. But had her father been correct?

"You're my uncle?" she asked. But she already knew the answer. "But you just said your last name was Gaudin." If he were related to her, then his name should be Cusack, shouldn't it?

"Yes, that's right. You're a smart girl, I see." He flipped a disparaging look toward Rocky, but the young man didn't seem to notice. "I changed my name after I rose to become leader."

That explanation made no sense to her. The leader of what? She wracked her mind for the answer. Was this something to do with the cult she'd discussed with Jude the other day? The name, InXium, that her father used to mutter over and over, was that what this was? She'd always disregarded any mention of a cult, because they didn't exist in this modern day, did they? It was just too far-fetched.

"Did my brother ever talk about me?" Parker asked, mouth suddenly twisting into a grimace of distaste.

"Did you kill him?" she asked bluntly, ignoring his question.

Parker's gray eyes hardened. "The stupid fool. He was never meant for this world. He took away something very precious to me. And so he had to pay."

That wasn't the answer Aria had been expecting and not one that she fully understood, but it was still an answer in the affirmative. She shivered, but this time it wasn't from the cold. This was from the knowledge that she was facing her father's killer. And he didn't seem to be showing one iota of remorse. What did that mean for her? It didn't bode well. She took a quick glance at Rocky from the corner of her eye. He was blowing on his hands and nodding along as if in complete agreement.

"But you're missing half the puzzle piece. Because Rocky here is your brother."

"What? I'm not... He's not..." Surely, he couldn't be. Because that'd mean her mother and this man... No, she couldn't bear to even consider it. Had her mother cheated on Tango? Conceived another child before she was married to him? Rocky looked to be slightly older than her. Older, too, than Iliana. Could her mother have given birth to an older half brother that she'd never told them about?

"Yes, you are. You have the same parents," he said in a slightly exasperated tone. "You're my daughter, and that's why I want to take you back to Colorado. It's where you belong. Back in the arms of my fellow brethren. Then we can give you holy communion, so you are pure and you can prepare for the end time." His face took on a slightly dreamy look.

What the fuck was this guy talking about? He wanted to take her back to Colorado? Because what? Because she was his daughter? But what he was suggesting now was completely preposterous. She and Iliana were Tango's daughters. End of story. This guy was full-on looney tunes. She wanted to dismiss the idea that Parker was her father out of hand. But now he'd slipped that dagger of poison into her heart, how could she ignore it?

And then there was the idea of some sort of maniacal cult group. Was that what he meant by taking her back to the brethren?

"For so many years, I wasn't sure if you were my daughter. I've watched you grow into a woman from afar. When I confronted Dimitra, she denied it. But I knew in my heart of hearts you were mine. She was mine, too. Even though she refused to admit it. Even if she was the one to convince Tango to take you away." He paused for a second. "I thought Iliana was mine, as well, but it turned out I was wrong."

"Iliana," she whispered. Her heart squeezed tight. "What did you do to Iliana?"

"Her blood wasn't true." Parker seemed to wave away the thought of Iliana like she was nothing but a bad smell. "I thought she might've been mine, too. But one look into her face and I knew. She was no child of mine."

"So you murdered my sister and Craig in cold blood, because... Because you didn't think she was your daughter?" Aria couldn't hide her utter revulsion and outrage at this man's sick fantasy.

"Well, I couldn't very well let her live. She was Tango's spawn. And she was a witness, she could identify me. Don't worry, the poison worked quickly. They hardly suffered at all. She is with *Him* now, and she will be taken care of."

Aria had no words. She had no way of articulating the rage and hate she felt right now.

"You know, it was most fortuitous that you appeared back in town when you did," Parker went on, speaking as if in a dream. "I hadn't planned on taking you on this mission, that was for a time in the future. But when I recognized your face, when you turned up at Tango's house that morning, I knew *He* must've had a hand in our fortune. It was the only possible explanation." Parker lapsed into silence and Aria was left to ponder fate, or whatever it was that'd brought her back to town at the same time as her murderous uncle had reappeared.

It sounded like he was hoping Iliana was his missing daughter, and perhaps if she had been, Parker might've been satisfied to leave Aria to continue on with her own life, unencumbered. Why or how Parker had decided that Iliana wasn't his daughter, Aria had no clue, but the way he'd callously killed her and then discarded her because she was of no use chilled her to the bone.

She stared out the window, anywhere but at a man who'd single-handedly destroyed her whole family.

What would Parker do if he found out she was pregnant? The thought was so terrifying, she dare not even think about it. Instinctively, she let her hands cover her belly beneath the blanket. Poor *little problem*. Her baby had been through so much in the first nine weeks of its existence. Thinking of her unborn baby made her even more resolute to find a way out of this situation.

She felt the stare of the younger man sitting beside her on the rear seat prickling the back of her neck, but she ignored him, too. Rocky had remained mute while her uncle—no, she would never call him her uncle, the monster, her father's term was a far better one—revealed the extent of his atrocities. What part had he played in all of this, she wondered vaguely? He was obviously complicit in the murders, knew all about them, and didn't seem in the slightest bit worried.

Staring out the window, she considered her options. She could just open the door and make a bolt for it. The door wasn't locked. It was still sleeting heavily outside, and she couldn't even imagine how cold it must be out there. Icicles were forming on the branches hanging from the trees nearby, and even the branches themselves were coated in a layer of ice. It looked like a scene out of a movie she'd watched as a child. The Snow Queen had turned everything she touched to ice. In the movie, it'd been almost pretty and awe-inspiring. Out there, it looked savage and impenetrable. Even in the car it felt like the temperature must be below zero, but out there, with the wind chill factor and the ice and rain, it could be as much as ten or even twenty below. Even if she took the blanket with her, managed to evade the two men who'd definitely chase her, and dodge and weave through the forest, she had no idea where she was. She'd be lost on the side of a mountain and she'd freeze to death in under an hour. And she'd just sworn to protect her baby, no matter what, so that wasn't even an option.

But she also wasn't giving up. She was going to escape from these crazy-ass people, but she needed to bide her time to get it just right. Aria shivered and wrapped the blanket tighter around herself. If she asked for another blanket, would Rocky give it to her? But she was determined not to ask him for anything. She'd rather sit here and freeze than do that.

Rocky shifted in his seat, as if trying to get comfortable. At last he broke the silence, saying, "It's pretty cold. Maybe we should start the car, Dad. Get the heater going."

"Could you be more of an imbecile?" Parker's voice was like an oiled snake slipping down her spine. God, she hated that man. "We can't start the engine because we'll use up all the gas. We've got a long way to drive tonight." Parker shot daggers at his son, as if he were personally affronted by his son's lack of knowledge. "And we don't want to draw any attention to ourselves. We need to stay hidden up here, until the worst of the storm is over." Parker glowered at his son for a few moments before adding, "But you did do a good job of covering our tire tracks earlier. So go ahead, get us all one of those spare blankets from out the back. That'll have to do." Aria cringed inwardly at the way Rocky smiled gleefully at Parker's backhanded compliment. Like a mistreated puppy who lapped up every tiny bit of praise.

Eagerly, Rocky launched over the rear seat and reappeared with a handful of blankets. It seemed that Rocky didn't do anything unless Parker first ordered it. Aria took hers, even though she didn't want to. It'd be stupid to freeze to death just to spite them.

Silence descended once more over the car. All the windows had iced over, and it was like looking through a crazy, cracked mirror. The world outside was all white. Aria turned even farther away from Rocky, curling into the doorframe, hiding her face so they couldn't see her thinking, planning, scheming. Parker had made religious references more than once now. She considered the very little information she knew about cults in general. They often had a charismatic leader who was good at manipulating members into believing whatever he said, doing his bidding, no matter what. Well, it seemed Parker ticked that particular box.

They also often lived in secretive or isolated communities. That could well be true, seeing as how she'd never even known Parker and Rocky—she was damn sure he wasn't her brother, no matter what Parker said—had existed till today.

They were also usually loosely based on religious beliefs, often skewed to suit their own morality, tricking those poor, desperate people who were looking for love or answers. Aria wasn't so sure about this one, but Parker had mentioned being purified and some kind of deity, so he obviously believed in some neurotic version of a higher being.

This was all pointing toward the one undeniable fact. Parker and Rocky belonged to some cult. And Parker believed that she was his daughter. She still wasn't sure what he hoped to achieve by bringing her back to his house, or compound, or wherever the hell a cult lived. This was all tied in with some personal vendetta against her parents. Had her mother perhaps had an affair with Parker? Had Parker been secretly in love with Dimitra, but she'd gone ahead and married Tango instead? Who really knew, and she could turn herself inside out trying to figure it out and never get the correct answer.

Was there some way she could turn this around? Perhaps get Rocky on her side long enough so that she could make a run for it?

Mulling over all the possibilities in her head, she hardly

noticed how much time had sped by. At least a couple of hours since they'd abducted her, maybe more. It was hard to tell in this freaky half-light the storm created. The two men seemed comfortable with this suffocating silence, which was a small mercy. Giving Parker a sidelong glance, she thought he might be praying. He had his head down and his lips were moving in unheard words.

Rocky was staring straight ahead, as if daydreaming.

She wondered what they'd do if she reached down and tried to open the door handle.

Suddenly, Parker's head came up. He swiveled his gaze around the interior of the car.

"Did you hear that?" he asked Rocky, who'd refocussed his gaze and was staring at his father like an eager hound.

"No." Rocky shook his head, and Aria silently agreed with him. She hadn't heard anything, either. Except the moan of the wind through the trees. Actually, now she thought about it, the wind did seem to be letting up some. The clouds were still low in the sky, but the sleeting rain had eased, too.

Parker's gray eyes stared through the ice-covered window, as if he could bore a hole right through it. "I definitely heard a noise. I think *He* might be trying to tell me something. *He's* sending me a warning."

Aria shook her head. Parker was free to believe what he wanted. If he was delusional enough to think some deity had granted him extrasensory hearing, then he was a greater fool than she'd thought.

"Go and check it out," Parker instructed.

What? Aria sat up a little straighter. There was nothing out there. Was there? Her heart rate picked up slightly. Had someone come to rescue her? No, it was impossible. No one could've figured out where these two had taken her. *She* didn't even know where she was.

"Yes, Father." Rocky donned his balaclava and gloves and

threw his blanket aside, seemingly not too bothered by the freezing conditions outside.

"Take the gun."

"Yes, Father."

They had a gun? Rocky reached beneath the front seat and came up with a weapon in his hand. Aria gasped. But why was she so shocked? Half of America owned a weapon, and these crazies probably weren't afraid to use it. He opened the door quietly, sending a searching gaze into the surrounding forest before quietly slipping out the door and closing it behind him softly. A blast of freezing air came in through the door; and then he was gone.

What should she do? She reached for the door handle.

"Don't even think about it." Parker's voice was low but menacing.

She turned to see him staring at her. He stretched over the front seat and tried to grab her by the wrist, but the blankets got in the way and she twisted easily out of his grip.

There was a sharp retort; the sound of a gunshot, and they both froze.

CHAPTER SIXTEEN

Jude crouched in the snow, gun at the ready, waiting, watching. Two seconds. Three seconds. Four. Five. Waiting for the roll of the dice to go again. Jude wished he'd been able to get closer to the four-by-four twenty feet farther up the trail. He wasn't sure what'd gone wrong. They couldn't possibly have heard him, he was practically silent walking on the ice and snow. And even though the wind had died, it was still blowing hard enough to be covering any small sound he might've made. What had tipped them off to his presence?

Ladley's truck was parked a few hundred feet down the trail, as he'd decided to proceed on foot, not wanting to tip-off the abductors by driving blindly up behind them. Not knowing for sure if there was anyone up ahead, he'd left it parked in a flat spot where he knew he could turn around. He decided if he walked a mile and didn't find anyone, then he'd go back and retrieve the car, and drive up farther. But after walking for ten minutes, he'd got lucky and spotted the truck around a hundred feet up the fire trail, near to the first concealed campsite Levi had found all those days ago. It was well camouflaged, tucked in behind the trunks of two large pine trees. But Jude knew what he was looking for. It was the same four-by-four that'd been parked at the rest stop. He'd studied the car for many minutes until his feet had started to ache with the cold.

The man-shaped lump lying on the ice ten feet away still hadn't moved. Jude hadn't wanted to shoot him. The guy had suddenly appeared around the side of the car and spotted Jude almost immediately, charging at him on silent feet, not uttering a sound, his face hidden by a black balaclava. Jude had been so taken by surprise, he hadn't noticed the weapon until it was almost too late, until the man raised it while still running, and aimed it at him. Jude had fired a single shot, which'd hit the man center mass, dropping him to the ground immediately. There'd been no choice. Instinct and training had taken over, and Jude was glad he'd kept up a solid shooting regime at the range. He'd always been a good marksman, top of his class as a trainee. It all came down to this one split second.

If Jude didn't move soon, his hands were going to be too numb to pull the trigger, even inside his gloves. And his injured leg was aching; he hadn't considered how badly it'd be affected by this intense cold. But he couldn't keep waiting forever. The warm gloves, knit hat, and extra sweater he'd found in the police storage were a godsend, and his work-issued boots were made to handle these types of conditions. But it must be twenty below out here. Cold enough to freeze the balls off a brass monkey. At least the heavy sleet and snow had stopped falling, reduced to a light but freezing mist.

The drive out to the rest stop had been harrowing, the storm making it impossible to see more than a few feet ahead of the truck, and Jude had chafed at the slow pace. Keeping his impatience in check had been almost impossible; only the thought of him ending up in a ditch, or smashed headlong into a tree, and therefore of no use to Aria, helped him maintain a slow and steady pace. Ladley's truck was a godsend, the big fat tires sticking to the road even when it was icy and treacherous, the bright spotlights helping to light his way through the gloom. It'd taken him precious minutes to find a turnoff to the fire trail; everything looked so different covered in sheets of ice. He circled around twice before he found the opening, finally spotting the yellow police tape lying discarded by the edge of the trail. That yellow tape lying on the ground gave him hope that he was on the right track. Then he found the padlock on the gate had been cut and fresh tire tracks in the snow, and he knew his hunch had been right. And then Ladley's truck really came into its own, handling the fire trail like it was out for a Sunday afternoon stroll. Jude vaguely wondered how the police vehicles had fared on this road when they'd gone in to retrieve bodies.

He still needed to check the guy on the ground, make sure he was disarmed, and remove any weapon within his reach before he could continue. First rule of hostilities involving a deadly weapon, was to make sure your back was secure, and you weren't going to be taken by surprise when someone you thought you'd immobilized came back to life.

Nothing moved inside the vehicle. Jude stepped stealthily toward the body. With the balaclava covering his face, Jude had no idea who this man might be. The gun was still clenched in his right fist, and Jude prodded the man's foot just to be sure. When there was no response, Jude carefully leaned down and pried the weapon from the lifeless fingers.

He'd just made sure the safety was off and placed the gun in his jacket pocket, when suddenly, the car began to rock, as if there was a struggle going on inside. A muffled scream emanated from the car, and Jude dropped any pretence at staying quiet, racing up the hill toward the vehicle.

Aria.

She was in trouble.

He was still ten feet away when something tumbled out of

the rear passenger door. A swathe of blankets landed on the ice. The blankets began to move and writhe, and Aria's head popped out from beneath the pile. Then two booted feet landed beside her head as a man dressed in a bulky winter jacket leaped from the car behind her. Jude skidded to a halt, bringing his gun up to aim at the intruder, but at the same time, his wounded leg twinged sharply, and he slipped on the ice. Crashing to his knees, he was barely able to save himself from going down completely.

By the time he recovered and looked up, the man had Aria held against his chest, using her like a human shield; a knife held to her throat.

"Put the gun down, Deputy," the man called in a clear, commanding voice.

Jude got slowly to his feet, but didn't lower his weapon. He recognized the man as the same one from the side of the road a day ago. He'd been right.

"Let her go," he said in an equally clear tone, keeping his gaze trained on the man's face, half-hidden beneath a knit hat. Not daring to look at Aria, because the fear in her eyes might just drive him to do something stupid.

"Not going to happen, son," the man replied lightly.

Aria began to shiver, whether from the cold or from fear, Jude wasn't sure. The blankets had dropped away when the man pulled her upright, and all she had on was a thin sweater and jeans, the same clothes she'd been wearing when she left the house this morning. She wasn't dressed to be out in this weather. He needed to end this standoff soon, before she got hypothermia. The man, on the other hand, was well prepared for the cold, with sturdy boots, a thick jacket, and knit hat; but no gloves, Jude noted.

"If you don't put the gun down, she won't be leaving this forest alive," the man intoned, almost politely, as if he'd be doing both of them a favor by ending her life. "She's my daughter, you see, and therefore she belongs to me. I don't want to have to kill her, but I would rather she was safe with *Him*, than back in your unholy company."

What was this man talking about? Aria was his daughter? That was ridiculous. Who was this guy? But it sounded like his suspicion about the kidnappers being related to a cult might be true.

"I mean what I say," the man intoned again, pressing the knife harder against Aria's throat, eliciting a squeak of fear.

Jude considered him for a few seconds, saw the zealous light in his eyes, and decided that the man was telling the truth.

Moving slowly, he placed the gun with great care on the ground at his feet, then stood up again. "Now what?" he asked, thinking about the second gun he still had stashed in his pocket.

"Now you tell me what happened to my son?"

The person he'd shot was this man's son? Uh oh, Jude didn't like where this was going. Would the news of his son's death make him do something unpredictable? The body was probably visible down the hill behind him, if the man cared to look properly. He needed a diversion, something—anything—to direct the man's attention away from the truth. For the first time, Jude looked deep into Aria's eyes. One wrong move and he might lose her. He couldn't let that happen.

"Ah ha, I see. He's dead, is he not?"

Jude remained frozen to the spot, unwilling to answer. The man didn't seem to be that perturbed by the prospect.

"That is a shame." He sighed deeply and looked heavenward. "But I always knew Rocky wasn't long for this world. *He* will carry the young in his arms into the absolute, and shelter them in *His* heart." It sounded like he was reciting a verse from the Bible. Although it didn't quite match anything Jude knew. The man continued to spout more modified verses of some kind of religious text, but Jude stopped listening. Instead, he focussed on Aria. On her face. Jude didn't know who this guy was, or what he wanted, all he knew was that he needed to be stopped.

The man was still staring skyward, and Jude took the opportunity to try and communicate silently with Aria. She was shaking almost uncontrollably now. She must be freezing. But if she could do just this one thing, he might be able to save her. Reaching a hand slowly for his pocket, he raised an eyebrow. Would Aria understand what he was trying to convey? Jude opened his mouth slightly and mimed biting down on an object. Aria's dark eyes went wide as she stared at him, uncomprehending. He mimed the action again while continuing to move his hand until it closed over the gun in his pocket. *Please, try and understand.* If she could only do this, they might have a chance. It was a small chance, and Aria had to be prepared to take it for this to work. She'd be putting herself at risk, but no more risk than she was currently in, if they didn't do something soon.

Suddenly, the man stopped his chanting and Jude froze, scared that his slight movements had been observed. At the same time, comprehension finally dawned on Aria's face.

She opened her mouth wide and bit down hard on the man's exposed hand.

He roared with pain.

It was enough to make the man loosen his hold on her, and she twisted away and then dropped to the ground. And Jude fired.

The bullet went wide, pinging off the side of the car, near the man's shoulder, and Jude cursed loudly. Trying to shoot a gun through the pocket of his jacket had skewed his aim. But now Aria was no longer a shield, and the man knew he had a second weapon. The two of them stared at each other for unmeasured seconds, until suddenly, the other man took off like a startled rabbit, darting around the front of the car. Jude fired off another shot, but it, too, pinged off the metal of the vehicle.

Tugging the gun out of his pocket as he ran, Jude fired two more shots after the retreating figure, but the man kept running and soon disappeared into the trees.

A voice drifted through the forest. "I'll be back to get you one day, Aria. You are mine. *He* will show me the way. And *He* will protect me so that I may fight again another day."

Jude was about to keep pursuing the felon, when Aria's call brought him up short.

"Jude." There was a slight hitch to her voice that made a trickle of fear run down his spine.

When he looked down to where she lay on the icy ground, he saw her hand draw back from her neck. It was covered in blood.

CHAPTER SEVENTEEN

Aria was so cold she could barely feel her fingers. And barely register the fact she had blood on her hand. But Jude's look of pure terror made her own stomach quake with fear as she pressed her hand back to her neck to stem the blood. Oh, God, was she about to bleed to death? The thought was enough to kick-start her almost numb brain.

She hadn't been quick enough to twist out of his grasp, and Parker's knife had sliced her throat as she'd slipped from his under his arm. She'd felt it cut her skin like a burning brand, but there was nothing she could do. Everything had happened so quickly after she dropped underneath his arm. But at the same time, it felt like it was all going in slow motion. There'd been a gunshot, which must've gone wide, because she heard it ricochet off the car, then Parker had looked at her, knife still held high in the air, and for a spilt second she thought he might reach down and finish what he'd started. Instead, he'd turned and run, Jude firing more shots as Parker rounded the car and disappeared into the forest.

Jude went to follow Parker, clearly intent on hunting him down, but Aria's cry stopped him in his tracks. He couldn't go off and leave her. Not when she was bleeding to death.

"Fuck!" Jude was by her side in an instant. "Put as much pressure on it as you can," he commanded, pushing down hard on her hand. Then he surprised her by picking her up and bundling her into the car, shoving the blankets in after her, then climbing in himself and shutting the door, swearing constantly under his breath as he did so. It was such a blessed relief to get off the freezing ground that she sucked in a deep draft of air.

"Sorry," he apologized. "But I needed to get you off the ice." His voice was both contrite and soothing, as if he were talking to a skittish horse, and he grabbed her by the arms to steady her, like she may well bolt at any second.

"He got me, Jude. I wasn't quick enough," she sobbed, the tears starting to come now. "You have to help me. Am I going to die?" She knew what happened to people who had their throats cut. They bled out in minutes, their life force draining from their body, and there was nothing anybody could do to stop it. "The baby. What about the baby?"

"You're not going to die. Not if I can help it. And neither is your baby," Jude growled, and the fierceness with which he said the words calmed her a little. "Let me look," he said, tugging his gloves off with his teeth and gently prizing her hand away from the wound. His fingers were cold, but not as cold as hers. She stared up his face, couldn't tear her gaze from his beautiful hazel eyes, watching for her death warrant to be signed by his reaction. But astonishingly, mystifyingly, his mouth shaped into a huge grin, white teeth flashing, almost as blinding as the snow outside. What was he smiling about? She was going to die right here in this car and he was happy about it?

"The knife missed your carotid," he said, the stupid grin not leaving his lips. "It's a nasty cut, and it'll need stitches, but you're not going to die," he proclaimed.

"Really?" She could barely believe it.

"Really," he replied, sobering now. He laid his forehead against hers and closed his eyes. "Jesus, Aria. You scared the shit out of me." Then his arms came around her and he hugged her with such ferocity she thought he might crush her. "If you had died..." He didn't finish his sentence, and Aria's breath hitched in her chest. He cared about her. He really cared. He wouldn't have come looking for her if he didn't, but this sentiment went much, much deeper.

Then he became all efficiency. "Keep an even pressure on the wound," he commanded, taking the corner of one of the blankets and folding it to use as a pad to cover her wound and then helping her put her hand back over it. He shook out the other blankets and covered her with them, tucking them in around her body like she was a child. "I'm not leaving you," he declared, and she sat up straighter, worried that he was about to do just that. "I'm going to see if they have a first aid kit in the back." He glanced over into the rear compartment, which Aria already knew contained all kinds of camping paraphernalia, so perhaps he was right, there might also be a first aid kit.

"Okay," she replied, her voice coming out much stronger than she actually felt.

He slipped out the door; and then she heard the rear door open, letting in a stream of cold air. A few moments later, she heard a loud grunt of triumph and the door closed again. Aria expected Jude to climb straight back in beside her, but she watched his blurry form as he paced past the side windows, head lifted and eyes searching the surrounding forest, looking for Parker. Which was probably a sensible thing to do, but Aria just wanted him back by her side. Feeling in her feet and hands was beginning to return, and they burned like they were on fire. She was still shivering, and she burrowed deeper into the blankets as she waited for what felt like an eternity but was probably only a few minutes. Until the car door opened again and there he was, larger than life, solid, and real.

He clambered back in and retrieved the first aid kit from inside his jacket, pulling out gauze padding and bandages. "I think I hit him," Jude said, opening a packet of gauze with his teeth, then gingerly lifting her hand to take another look at her wound. "There's blood in the snow farther up the hill, but there's no sign of him."

Aria sat in silence as he worked on her, his fingers cold but gentle. *Good*, she thought savagely to herself. She hoped that horrible man died out there. It was such an uncharitable thought, and it hit her with such force that she was momentarily surprised. She'd never wished anyone dead before. But she wouldn't take it back. No, she wouldn't. That man had single-handedly destroyed her whole family.

Jude finished wrapping the bandage around her neck and said, "That should hold it for now."

"Thank you," she replied, her voice strangely small. "Hold me. Please." She stared at him, needing to feel the reliable presence of his body close to hers to help her believe this was truly over.

He grabbed another blanket, the one Parker had been using in the front seat, and draped it over the both of them, pulling her lightly in beneath his shoulder. She laid her head on his chest and just breathed. He stroked her hair, his lips resting on the top of her head, careful to treat her gingerly to make sure he didn't touch her bandaged neck. Emotion swelled within, and she found tears running down her cheeks.

"It's okay, baby, I've got you. Cry as much you like." His tender words were like a catalyst and the dam burst, her tears overflowing, sobs breaking out, so loud she could hardly hear him say, "I've got you. I've got you," over and over. And she started shaking, big convulsions, as she dragged air in and out, trying to breathe through her bawling.

She knew it was all the stress, the shock of the past few hours, the height of emotions strung so tight while she'd been in fear for her life, perhaps mixed with pregnancy hormones, but she couldn't seem to stop. Like she was crying for everything that'd happened over her life. For the loss of her mother when she was so young. For her shitty childhood spent with a distant, half-crazy father. For the way Beau had treated her so callously and wanted nothing to do with the child they'd created together. For the death of a father who she'd never get to know better, and then the death of her sister. Who knew what she and her sister could've become if they'd been able to repair the bridges they'd burnt? A family, perhaps? For the little person growing inside her and all the possibilities that represented. She cried for everything that'd gone wrong in her life up until now.

She knew they couldn't stay like this forever, but she needed this time with him to recover, to reconnect, both with Jude and with herself. Should she be concerned that Parker might come back for them? Probably, but with an armed deputy by her side, she decided to let him worry about that.

Finally, her weeping subsided and she sat up straight, wincing a little when the movement tugged at her injury. Using the other corner of the blanket as a handkerchief, she wiped her streaming eyes and nose, trying to get herself back under control.

"I can't believe you came to get me," she said, leaning back so she could look into his face, not bothered that he saw her red eyes and blotchy face. "And how did you know where I was? I didn't even know where I was," she laughed. It was a feeble attempt, but it felt good. A different form of release to the tears.

"Yeah, well, I'm sorry it wasn't the whole squad, but I couldn't convince Brady about my hunch, so you ended up with just me."

"And you were enough. Thank the Lord that you came." That was her intrepid and courageous deputy, single-handedly braving an ice storm, putting his own life on the line to come and rescue her.

Jude went on to briefly fill her in on how he'd come to the deduction that the kidnappers would most likely stopover somewhere to weather the storm. He told her about the fortuitous call from Levi, and how he'd spotted the van from the other day, when Parker had first tried to abduct her, in a nearby rest stop. How he borrowed a truck from the lawyer who was supposed to be there to defend her and then driven the treacherous roads until he found the fire trail and the small clues Parker had left behind that only Jude might understand. No one in their right mind was out there driving in that storm, and yet Jude had done it for her.

"But I need to know. How did you just disappear from a fully guarded police station?"

"One of the sergeants, he took me out in handcuffs to the rear parking lot, and just handed me over." Aria could still hardly believe she'd been betrayed by a corrupt cop. "He said something like, now his debt was paid. Then he mentioned a woman's name. Stacy, I think." At the time, she hadn't really thought about it, but perhaps Parker was holding something over the sergeant to get him to do his dirty work. Not that Aria much cared. The guy was a police officer, he'd made a vow to serve and protect, and he'd broken that vow and put her in danger.

"Ha, I knew it. I knew it had to be an inside job." Jude slapped his knee angrily. "Did you recognize him? Or can you describe him?"

"Yes, he was one of the sergeants who raided my house today. I think his name was McMurdo."

Jude nodded as if he knew the name, then his gaze turned

thoughtful, and he stared out the window for many long moments. "Don't worry, he'll be on the other side of that jail cell door by tonight. I'll make sure of it," he ground out from between gritted teeth. Then he added, almost in a mutter, "You hear about these fucking dishonest cops, but I can't believe we had one in our midst." The look of revulsion and disquiet on Jude's face was unmistakable, and her heart went out to him. In the short time she'd known him, she'd discovered Jude was a stickler for the rules, and expected everyone else to abide by them, as well. Jude would hate to be tarred with the same brush, but it was almost impossible not to. One corrupt cop was all it took to paint everyone in law enforcement in a bad light.

Jude's face softened as he looked at her. "Can I ask about the men who kidnapped you? Do you know why they did it?" he asked, his eyes crinkling at the corners with concern. Jude would've heard Parker say that she was his daughter and he would be wondering. Yes, Parker had told her things, but she still wasn't sure if she even believed half of them.

She guessed she owed Jude the truth; she was going to have to tell all this to the police soon enough, anyway. "His name is Parker Gaudin," she replied slowly. "And he's my uncle." The words were hard to say, her tongue almost refusing to form the words. "He said some things that confused me, that I don't believe are true. He tried to make out that he was my biological father, and that Tango had somehow stolen my mother away from him." She shuddered at the memory. "He also said the man out there, the one that you shot dead, was my brother. Not just my half brother, but my full brother. But there's no way he could…" She stopped speaking, overcome by rage, mixed with a hint of doubt. There was no way Rocky was related to her. She was determined to prove it, too. She would ask for a DNA test, because she had to know for sure. She had to know where her heritage lay, as much for her unborn baby as for herself. And if, by some unimaginable act, it turned out she was related to him, then she'd bear the weight of that knowledge. But she was sure the results would be negative.

"I agree," Jude said, stroking her hand beneath the blanket. "There's no way you could be related to either of those two people. Parker was obviously as delusional as your father. I didn't get a chance to delve into that cult we discussed, InXium, but I'm sure when we do, we'll find an interesting story of two brothers mixed up in something from an early age."

She nodded in agreement. "I think you're right. I think my parents were deeply involved in that cult way before Iliana or I were born. And perhaps they left to keep me and Iliana safe." She shrugged. If only her mother or Tango had been more forthcoming with information, all of this might've been prevented. "I do believe one thing Parker said, however. That he is my uncle, my father's brother." There must be a story woven into those three people's lives, perhaps one of intrigue and passion, affairs and betrayals. One that she may never truly know. "I don't really understand what Parker wanted with me, but he murdered three people to get to me, so it must have been important to him, at least."

"Hmm," Jude mused, still stroking her hand absentmindedly. His touch sent tingles up her arm, and her body came alive as much from him being near as from the thick blankets keeping her warm. "Hopefully, we can get to the bottom of all of this. Brady will definitely have to send a team down to Colorado to check it all out."

"He's not going to be happy that he was wrong," Aria said, a cynical twist to her mouth.

"No, but that man needed to be taken down a peg or two," Jude replied.

"Do you think he's still out there?" Parker's last words still echoed through her head. *I'll be back to get you one day.* Was she still at risk? Would she be looking over her shoulder for the rest of her life?

"If he is, we'll catch him." Jude sounded so sure of himself. He pulled her closer, and she laid her head on his chest again, enjoying the feel of his muscular pecs beneath her cheek.

"I don't know how I can ever thank you." Aria tilted her chin to look up into his eyes. His gorgeous eyes, scattered with tiny flecks of gold. Something stirred in her chest at the sight of him. Something wholesome and yearning and a little scary. She couldn't stop staring, trying to etch his features into her mind forever. The straight line of his nose, the small cleft in his chin, those firm, full lips—such kissable lips—high cheekbones, and dark, arched brows, one of which was cocked in her direction, observing her speculatively.

They watched each other for many long seconds.

Finally, he kissed her.

Slow and gentle, at first, as if she was made of spun glass. This kiss was quiet and unhurried, full of so many unspoken sentiments. She returned his generous tenderness, kiss for kiss. Each time their lips met, he seemed to claim a part of her soul.

He was the first to break away. "I almost lost you today, Aria. Do you know how that made me feel?"

Her heart skipped a beat at the intensity in his voice.

Before she could answer, he went on, "Honestly, the sense of despair was so great it nearly crushed me." He stroked a finger softly down her cheek. "I know we've barely had any time together. But the thought of losing you without telling you how I feel was soul destroying." He stopped, and she sucked in a breath. What was he going to say? "The logical side of me knows I can't possibly be in love, it's too soon, it's too early, the relationship is too new."

His words were an echo of her own thoughts, her own

explanations. Love didn't happen this quick. It was too much. Five days. That was how long they'd known each other. They'd been five very intense days, so much had happened. But how could something that was built on adrenaline and peril be real? Jude had been there for her because she needed someone. Because she'd been in trouble, and he was the only person who could help. Maybe they had formed an attachment on the way, but it wouldn't last. It couldn't last.

"That logical voice is very loud," he admitted. "But my heart is telling me a different story. All I know is that I care deeply for you, Aria."

She stilled, then lifted her head to look directly in his eyes. What was he saying?

"I think I might be falling in love with you."

Aria hesitated, biting her lip hard to stop her gasp of surprise. Because she was falling hard for this man, too. This brave, strong, and true man. But she couldn't return his sentiments. Not yet. On account that there was an elephant in the room—or should she say, *little problem*—that was the crux of everything. That meant everything to her. Perhaps even more than the possibility of love with this man, and she dare not explore her feelings for him until she knew where he stood on that matter.

As if he could read her mind, he said, "And if loving you means loving your baby, then so be it. I don't want to lose you. I want to be with you. I want to be part of this baby's life, too. Together, we could raise a happy and healthy child. But only if you'll have me." Uncertainty flared in his eyes. "I'll understand if you don't want to me in your baby's life. You haven't even mentioned the father...and I don't know what your intentions are with him. But I'd like to be your fallback guy, if you need one."

Hope flared in her heart. He was offering her a lifeline. Much more than a lifeline, a *life*. He was offering himself body, and soul. Stuff like this didn't happen to her. She always lurched through life from one calamity to the next, reacting, never really making conscious decisions. Was she finally going to make the right decision? For her and for her baby?

It was the thought of her baby that gave her pause. She wanted to give her child the best possible start to life, give them the opposite of her own childhood. And there was no doubt Jude could help her achieve that. He was a kind, generous, giving man, with a heart the size of Africa. But at what cost to himself? Even though he said he was prepared to take on another man's baby, did he really understand what would be involved? Aria needed time. She needed some space to think about this. And perhaps, he did, too.

The next few weeks would be full of sadness and a grief. She had two funerals to organize, and she had to come to terms with the enormity of everything that'd happened to her. Now wasn't the time to be making a lifelong commitment, not even to a wonderful man who meant the world to her.

"I think I might be falling for you, too," she admitted, biting her bottom lip as she watched his eyes light up. "And you can't know how much your offer means to me. I am truly grateful, and I think you would make a great father." She held up her hand and rushed on before he got his hopes up too high. She saw it in his face then, the growing understanding that there was a *but* coming. She hated this. Her heart was screaming at her to say yes to this man. To accept what he was giving. But her mind was urging caution, and for the sake of her baby, she was going to listen to that voice today.

"But I don't know what the future holds. I know now that I want to stay here in Stevensville, and I want to build a life here. But so much has happened in the past week. I need time to think about what that life is going to look like. I hope you understand." Stupidly, her eyes filled with tears again. She couldn't believe she was saying this. It was something her former self would never have dreamed of doing, taking it slow, thinking before she jumped in feet first. Perhaps she was finally growing up.

"I can live with that," he said at last, and she could see the effort it took for him to school his features into equanimity. "Let's just take it day by day, for now." He was so respectful of her, even when she couldn't give him the answers he needed. Answers that he deserved. "You can stay in the cottage for as long as you need, I want you to know that," he added.

"Thank you, Jude. You're a good man," she said, her throat choking with emotion. "And I do want you in my life. I do… it's just that…"

"You don't need to explain," he said, pulling her in close.

They stayed like that for many minutes, and Aria accepted the warmth and reassurance he offered, drawing on his strength to bolster her own. She snuggled in close, her hand sliding inside the zipper of his jacket, finding the warm skin above his collarbone, tracing the muscular cords of his neck, drawing in the smell of him, fresh, and piney, and the slightly damp wool of his black knit hat. Aria looked up.

"Where did you get that hat from?" she asked, suddenly realizing what the logo meant. It had the word Mickey scrawled across the front in white. It was a Disney hat. Jude didn't strike her as the type of man to wear a Disney hat.

"I stole it from lost and found at the police station." His deep voice rumbled through the cabin, the sound reverberating in her chest. "It was all they had."

He looked down at her, and she lifted her face to his and kissed him, long and deep and slow.

When she finally came up for air, he asked her, "Are you

feeling up to walking back to my truck? I need to call this in, and there's no reception up here. We'll need to drive back to the highway."

"Yes, of course," Aria agreed, squaring her shoulders. It was time to face the rest of the day, she may as well get it over with.

"I'm going to call Hank and Susan to come and secure the site. Brady won't like it, but I don't know who to trust at the Missoula station right now." Jude glowered at the thought of how Aria had been betrayed so easily, and she agreed with his decision. "We'll need to get a search party going to try and track down Gaudin, too. But I'll let Hank handle that."

They emerged from the vehicle blinking and dazed, like they were survivors of war emerging from a bunker. The world was a white winter wonderland, but with menacing overtones; dangerous as well as beautiful. The cold was shocking and bone chilling, and she walked as quickly as she could on the slippery ice while wrapped in swathes of blankets, holding Jude's hand for support. Absolutely everything was covered in ice. She'd never seen anything like it before in her life. Ice storms were a rare occurrence. Jude had wanted to give her his warm jacket, but she wouldn't hear of it. It would do neither of them any good if he froze out there; she was relying on him to get her safely back down the mountain.

"I can see why locals call it a silver storm," she said. "It's like everything has been draped in silver tinsel. Like Jack Frost has waved his magic wand, but only on steroids."

She kept her eyes averted from the dark lump lying on the frozen ground. Jude had assured her that Rocky was dead. But it was one thing knowing it and another thing completely to have to walk past his body. A very small part of her felt the tiniest bit sorry for Rocky. All he'd been was a pawn in Parker's game. He'd been manipulated into obeying his father's every command, and Aria briefly wondered what sort of life the man had lived. Probably not a free or happy one. Another life ruined by Parker.

The big, black truck was a shock, even though Jude had already explained it was borrowed. But when Jude helped her up into the enormous cabin, tuned on the engine, and cranked up the heat, she decided she was in absolute heaven. She was not leaving this truck cabin again, unless it was for a warm room in a secure building. She'd had enough of this cold to last her a lifetime.

CHAPTER EIGHTEEN

Aria looked up from the desk, catching the brilliant blue of the sky through the office window. She rested her chin on her hands for a second and soaked up the view of the mountains in the background. It was midmorning on Tuesday, a little over two weeks since her kidnapping. Naomi had just slipped out to get them some pastries from the kitchen for morning tea. Aria's stomach rumbled at the thought. She was always hungry now, it seemed. She stretched and stood, then winced as the scar on her throat pulled a little. It was still covered by a thick bandage. The doctor said it was healing well, but there would always be a scar, low down on the left side of her neck, an indelible reminder of her deadly run-in with her so- called uncle.

Wandering over to the window, she peered out, noting there was no sign of the ice storm now. No sign of the havoc that it'd wreaked. The ice had all melted, and apart from a few trees that'd toppled under the weight of the ice, which'd all since been cleared away, nothing looked out of place down below in Naomi's garden. The cold snap had been an aberration, and now the county was experiencing normal fall weather again. Cool days, and cold, clear nights.

Aria *had* bought herself a winter jacket in preparation for the next winter storm, however.

She'd been back at work for a week now, and it was beginning to feel like she'd been here forever. Everyone had welcomed her back with open arms, but Naomi had been particularly solicitous and continued to hover around her like a mother hen. Especially after she told her about the pregnancy.

Aria knew she could no longer keep it a secret, but it'd been a hard conversation to have, nonetheless. She'd been half expecting Naomi's face to freeze over as the words tumbled out of her mouth, aware that Aria had duped her by omitting the fact she was due to have a baby in the interview.

But Naomi's reaction had been the opposite of what Aria was expecting, one of joyful delight. "A baby," she'd crowed. "We're going to have a baby in our house? I can't wait. To have a child running around the lodge would be a blessing indeed." It seemed that Naomi was just as eager for a grandchild as any grandmother might be. But with no children of her own, she had to rely on the people around her to bring her the joy of a child. Now, Naomi was constantly feeding Aria, making sure she was comfortable, making sure she wasn't experiencing any morning sickness, and shooting happy smiles at her when she didn't think Aria was looking. Much to Aria's surprise, she was hardly affected by morning sickness. In fact, almost the opposite, she was ravenous all the time. People told her not to get too complacent, that it might still kick in. Aria patted her stomach with affection, deciding that her baby was too well-mannered to give her terrible nausea.

Aria had never contemplated how her pregnancy might affect others, and it was heartening to discover that people truly meant it when they offered her their congratulations. Penny, too, had been over the moon when she found out. And immediately, she'd become nearly as clucky as Naomi. Aria decided that Clayton had better watch out, as it was becoming clearer by the day that Penny wanted a baby soon, too.

Aria covered her belly with her hands. It'd become a habit over the past few weeks, an instinctive need to protect the little human being growing inside. At least she'd stopped calling it her *little problem*. Now that she'd fully come to accept she was having this baby, she'd become very maternal indeed. Even going as far as to decide it was a girl, and so she'd nicknamed it Bunny. Which was what her mother had used to call her back when she was very young.

"Aria, love." Naomi burst into the room, out of breath, a plate of pastries in one hand.

"What?" Aria turned in time to see Dean, hot on her heels.

The apprehensive look on Naomi's face said more than words ever could, and Aria wobbled a few steps and reached for the edge of the desk to steady herself as her knees threatened to buckle. Her mind immediately began whirling with different scenarios, all of them calamitous. Not more bad news. Please, no more. She'd had enough of that to last her a lifetime.

Jude. Oh, crap. Was Jude okay? She couldn't lose Jude, not now. She still hadn't told him how she felt about him. That she loved him. He'd been so good to her over the past two weeks, but she'd wanted to take things slow. Wanted to make sure she was making the right choice. But she knew her choice was inevitable. She searched Naomi's eyes for the answer.

"It's okay, Aria," Dean said, shooting his wife a quelling glance. Aria remembered that Naomi did have an inclination to make dramas out of nothing. "We've just had some news. But I think it may be good news. At least I think you'll find it interesting."

"Oh, thank God." She edged around the desk and sank

into the large chair, clutching a hand to her heart.

"Sorry, I didn't mean to scare you," Naomi apologized. "It's just a bit of a shock, that's all." She lifted her eyes to her husband. "But Dean can fill you in on the details." She came and stood next to Aria, perhaps to lend her moral support as Dean began to speak.

"You've met Tom, haven't you?" Dean asked, leaning his hands on the edge of the large desk. He didn't seem to mind that his wife and Aria had taken over his office. Naomi was his wife, and as such, could have whatever she wanted, as long as it made her happy. Because when she was happy, he was happy.

"Yes, of course," Aria answered. The man with the friendly face who towered over everyone else—and was affectionately known as Big Tom, but only when he wasn't within earshot—was one of the horse wranglers. She'd met him a few times when she and Naomi had been up to the stables to check a fact or get a measurement.

"He was leading a small contingent of riders out to Selway's Pasture today. We don't often go in that direction, not since we moved the cattle in closer for protection right before the big storm." Dean stopped to make sure Aria was following him.

She nodded because he seemed to expect it.

"Well, he saw something huddled next to the fence line, the one that divides Stargazer from the state forest at the bottom of Canyon Peak."

Naomi laid a hand on Aria's shoulder, and she tensed.

"It was a man. Well, actually a dead body. It looked like he'd been there at least a week."

Aria sucked in a breath and waited.

"Tom said he can't be sure, but it's most likely that man who abducted you. Jude showed us all a photo of him and asked us to be on the lookout, just in case."

Aria expelled her breath. The sheriff's office had asked everyone in the area to be on their guard after no sign of Parker had been found up on the mountainside. It was like he'd vanished into thin air. A police search party had combed the area, and they'd found signs of a blood trail. But that'd disappeared and even though they'd scoured the area for days, no trace of Parker could be found, until eventually the sheriff had called off the hunt. If this body was Parker, it meant he'd survived for quite a long time up there, wounded and alone on that peak. Aria shuddered, and Naomi's hand tightened on her shoulder.

"Tom's putting a call through to Sheriff Buchanan as we speak, but we're pretty sure it's the same guy," Dean continued. Aria tuned him out. The relief flowing through her veins was indescribable. Parker was a thorn in her side no longer. She was free. Completely free.

"Are you okay, honey?" Naomi was leaning down, peering into Aria's face with a concerned frown.

"Oh, what..." She refocused her gaze, and pursed her lips. "Yes, I'm fine. You're right, Dean, this is good news. I'm glad he's dead. And I'm glad you finally found his body." She nodded. It was true. She didn't feel the slightest bit of remorse or conflict about that man's death. Even if he was her uncle.

"It means you can move on with your life now. Right?" Naomi said softly.

"Exactly." Aria straightened her spine, letting a smile play over her lips as the realization hit her. She no longer had to look over her shoulder. She couldn't wait to tell Jude. He might be more ecstatic than her, because she knew he'd been worried about Parker coming back more than he liked to admit. Worrying that he'd been the one to let him get away.

"I thought you might feel that way. You're made of tough stuff, Aria Cusack," Dean said, smiling proudly, almost as if she might be his own daughter. "It means my cattle will be safe out in that pasture again," Dean added with a wink.

Aria had almost forgotten that was how this whole saga had started, with a few missing cows. After much investigation, and using Levi's superior tracking skills, it seemed that Parker and Rocky had been camping in the hills for weeks, using the time to scout out the town, and to plot and plan their horrific scheme to kill Tango and abduct Iliana. All while living off the land so as not to arouse suspicion, using Dean's cattle as a fresh meat supply.

Not for the first time, Aria wondered how things might've turned out if she hadn't stumbled back into town three weeks ago, just as Parker and Rocky were preparing to put their murderous plans into action. Would the two of them have gotten away with their killing spree? Then disappeared back to Colorado, leaving an unsolvable trail of crime and confusion behind them? Because if Jude hadn't become personally involved with Aria, and been so determined to find her, this may well have remained an unsolved case.

True to her word, she'd requested a DNA test. The results had come back to show that Rocky *wasn't* her brother. Even though she knew that'd be the result, a tiny part of her had been so relieved to have it confirmed. But then her hands had begun to shake when she thought about what Parker might've done to her if he'd had that same information at his fingertips. He'd decided she was his daughter entirely on her looks. The dark hair and dark eyes. While it wasn't completely clear why he'd decided Iliana wasn't his daughter, it probably had something to do with the fact she had blonde hair and a slightly Roman nose, instead of the ski-jump nose that ran in the Cusack family. He'd killed Iliana on the shallowest of whims, which was what hurt Aria the most.

Aria had asked for DNA tests to be done on Iliana, too, and she'd cried when her results showed she was the daughter of

Dimitra and Tango, even though she hadn't cried over her own results. It was so bittersweet. Parker had been right. Iliana hadn't been his daughter, after all. But then, neither had she.

There was a tap on the door, and Tom's face appeared around the edge. "The sheriff and Deputy Wilder are on their way out," he confirmed to Dean. Then he tipped his hat to Naomi and Aria. "Sorry, Aria, I know this must be another shock for you."

"Yes," she agreed. "And I must admit that I'm sick of all these surprises. If I live my whole life without one more surprise, I'll be a happy woman." She stood, her fingertips pressing on the desktop. "But I'm strong enough to handle one more. Shall we go and wait for the sheriff?"

"Ata girl," Dean said, patting her on the back as she walked past. "I always knew you were made of tough stuff."

* * *

Many hours later, Aria sank into the couch with a sigh, her mug of hot tea held tight between her palms. She was still living in the cottage in Jude's backyard, and it was beginning to feel a little like home. It'd been a long, cold afternoon, but she was home now and finally free of Parker Gaudin. Once Hank and Jude had arrived, Tom and Dean had escorted the whole group of them—Naomi and Aria had insisted on going, too—using the ranch's ATV's up to where the body lay near the fence. Aria needed to see him. Needed to make sure he was dead.

Tom had stationed one of the new ranch staff to guard the site, and the young man looked to be more than glad to hand over to the sheriff and his deputy. Jude had been wary about Aria wanting to see the scene with her own eyes, but when she'd declared that this was her right, he'd gently, but insistently, taken her hand to lead her over to the bundle of clothes lying this side of the fence. Then he held her shoulders, letting her lean into him as the sheriff bent down and, with latex-glove-clad hands, gingerly lifted the hair away from the man's face.

It was Gaudin. His features were unmistakable, even through his gaunt death mask. She gasped and pulled back, suddenly grateful for Jude's steadying presence behind her. Thankfully, the wild animals hadn't found him yet. Or perhaps it was the pervasive aura of evil that'd kept the animals away. But the body was intact, and it was definitely Parker. Vaguely, Aria wondered what had eventually killed him. The cold? Or his wound? Not that it really mattered. He was dead.

Once she'd seen the body and confirmed that the bane of her life was gone forever, she'd turned away.

"Are you okay?" Jude had asked softly.

"Yes." She'd nodded at him, but then been surprised when he'd wiped a stray tear from her face. "I'm not crying for him," she'd exclaimed. Because she wasn't, she really wasn't. "I think they're tears of relief," she added.

"Maybe they are," Jude said, the concerned look not leaving his face. "But it might be better if you went back to the lodge with Naomi now, while Hank and I sort this out." He smiled, bending his knees so he could look directly into her face.

He was so good to her, sometimes she thought he was her miracle. She wanted to kiss him right there, to let him know how much he meant to her. But the fact that the sheriff, plus Tom, the young ranch hand, and Dean and Naomi were watching put a brake on her emotions. Later. There'd be time for that later.

So she'd gone back to the lodge and waited for Jude. But he'd been caught up with waiting for homicide to come out to the body, and eventually she'd driven home by herself with Jude assuring her that he'd be there as soon as was humanly possible.

Now, she took a sip of the warming liquid and laid her head on the backrest. It was nice to have time to just think. The last two weeks had been a whirlwind. True to her word, Naomi had helped her plan Tango's funeral, which'd been a small affair, just her, Jude, Dean and Naomi, Penny and Clayton, Levi and Cat, and a few other Stargazer staff, there to support Aria, as no one from the town even bothered to come. But that was oaky, Aria understood their reasons.

Iliana's funeral had been another thing altogether, as so many people wanted to farewell her sister, the church had been overflowing. It'd been a shock to discover that Iliana was well-liked in town, but really it shouldn't have been. Aria had been gone for eight years and had lost all touch with what was going on in town, but Iliana had stayed and formed a network of friends around her. By all accounts, she'd married a good man in Craig and had become an integral part of the small community. Aria was strangely proud of Iliana. Craig's parents had been in town for Iliana's funeral; they'd come to collect their son's body and take him home for a service surrounded by all their family. They'd been absolutely devastated by their son's senseless death, but also devastated by the loss of what could've been; the potential of a young family growing up on the farm, grandchildren for them to visit. It was all terribly sad. Aria and Jude had spent many hours trying to explain the reasons behind Iliana's and Craig's deaths, but the parents were beyond logical thought at that moment and couldn't really understand why they'd lost their son. Perhaps Aria would fly out and visit them later, when they were ready to hear the whole story.

The most surprising thing was that part of Skyridge Farm had been left to Aria in Iliana's will. Seeing as how the couple had no children, Aria was listed as her next of kin. But even so, Aria was shocked and a little awed. It showed her sister was still thinking about her. Even if Aria had felt their connection was broken, it hadn't been completely severed, like she'd first thought. The rest of the farm belonged to Craig's parents, and they'd already mentioned they'd consider selling the place, which was fine by Aria. For about ten seconds, she'd contemplated perhaps buying out the farm from the Doncasters; the house had been so beautiful and it'd called to something inside her when she'd visited that day. But then she decided she knew nothing about farming, and had no wish to live on a ranch all by herself. But with the money from the farm, and the money from Tango's place— she was selling the family house too, the memories were just too strong for her to think she could ever live there—then she'd have enough to buy just about any house her heart desired. Which was an interesting concept.

But for now, she was quite happy where she was. Especially because Jude was here with her.

The conversation they'd had on the day of the ice storm still bounced around in Aria's head like a ping-pong ball. Back then, she hadn't been able to commit to him, had told him she needed time. And he'd given her that time, as well as the space she needed. He was always there for her, quietly supporting her through the funerals, helping her negotiate all the paperwork that went along with wills and estates and deaths and taxes. He'd been her rock. Never once asking her what her plans were for the two of them, letting her come to the decision on her own. He'd asked all the right questions about her pregnancy and the baby, but never pushing if she didn't want to answer, and so she'd told him all about Beau and his despicable behavior. The way she'd run from Portland and found herself back in her hometown.

They hadn't slept together since her abduction. Jude had been the perfect gentleman, not once overstepping the mark, even though she knew he wanted her. Not that she hadn't wanted to have sex with him, because she did. And his reaction every time he held her close was completely obvious, from the tender way he stroked her face right down to the bulge in his trousers. But she wanted to make sure her reasons for sleeping with him were the right ones.

He deserved an answer from her. And an answer was what he was going to get.

She wanted Jude Wilder. Wanted him with all her heart and soul. Now she just had to find the right time to tell him. Maybe even tonight.

Speak of the devil, she thought as the door opened, letting in a cold blast of air, followed by the man himself. "Hi," he said as he noticed her on the couch, giving her a special smile that was for her alone.

"Hi, yourself," she replied, tilting her head back so she could watch him walk toward her.

"How are you coping?" She knew he meant how was she coping with the knowledge that Parker Gaudin was dead. Like he did every night when he came in, he removed his jacket and gun belt and slung them over the back of the armchair.

"I'm really good," she told him, meaning it. She *was* really good. This chapter of her life could finally come to a close. It was time to start a new chapter. "You must be starving, I've got some dinner ready for you."

He sat down next to her on the couch. "Thank you." There were small lines around his eyes, and she could tell he was tired. It'd been a long day, but from her point of view, a good day, too.

She went to stand, to get his dinner, but he put a hand on her arm. "I can do it," he said with the lift of his eyebrow. That was another thing she loved about him, the fact he didn't mind doing his fair share around the house. "But first of all, I have some information I think you'd like to hear." He tugged her toward him on the couch, where they sat facing each other, knees touching, her hands held lightly in his. She looked deep into his eyes, not exactly dreading what he might say, but wary of any more surprises. "We've had a call from the medical examiner regarding your mother's autopsy."

Oh. That was interesting. Aria held her breath. She hadn't expected the results for a few weeks yet. Brady had grudgingly agreed to exhume Dimitra's body. They were looking specifically for arsenic poisoning, traces of which could be found in a person's hair or fingernails, even long after their death.

"And," she prompted.

Jude exhaled sharply. "They found it. They found traces of arsenic in her hair."

"Oh, God." It was the news she'd been dreading. And also the very thing she'd been wanting to hear. It answered the question as to why her mother had taken her own life.

And the answer was that she hadn't. Someone else had murdered her and made it look like suicide by placing a rope around her neck and hanging her from the rafters in the barn very soon after she was dead. Or perhaps even while she was still alive but dying from the poison. No one had thought to question the premise that Dimitra's death hadn't been anything but a simple suicide. But now Aria finally had closure. Now she could truly cry for her mother, taken from her by a vicious murderer.

They could never prove one-hundred percent that it'd been Parker who'd killed her, but everything pointed in his direction. They'd also never know the entire truth of what happened back in the early days of Tango and Dmitri's marriage while they'd been members of the cult. But Jude was helping her to piece it together, bit by bit.

Brady had allowed Jude to accompany him on a raid of the

InXium compound. Normally, a county deputy wouldn't be allowed on a police investigation, especially outside his county jurisdiction, but Brady owed Jude big time. It wasn't necessarily the detective's fault that a corrupt member of his team had played a part in Aria's kidnapping. But he'd certainly ended up with egg on his face, and there was now an ongoing investigation into the rest of the squad. It turned out that Camden McMurdo's sister, Stacy, was caught up in the InXium cult, and Parker had threatened her life if Camden didn't comply. Camden was remorseful and repentant, apologizing to Aria via a handwritten letter. But she wasn't ready to forgive him yet, and he'd still ended up in jail, which was where he belonged.

So Jude had called in the favor. That raid had uncovered a group of around thirty people all living in an isolated community on a block of land that was privately owned in the foothills near the Rocky Mountains National Park. Brady had interviewed each group member but there wasn't a lot else he could do. The law wouldn't allow him to order them to disband, because technically, they weren't breaking the law. So they went back to their little commune to continue their religious beliefs. But without their divine leader, perhaps they'd now become a toothless tiger.

Jude suspected there were many more members of the cult scattered throughout the country and they might never track them all down. He believed they might also reconnect at a later date and restart the group back in the shadows. But that wasn't his problem for now. Stacy had been among the members, and she'd been absolutely clueless as to the threats Parker had made to her life to keep her brother in line. She'd agreed to come home and visit her family, visit her brother, who'd gone to jail to keep her safe.

So far, they'd found out some fascinating tidbits of information. Back in the late eighties and early nineties,

InXium had been a fledgling religious movement, led by a man called Nelson Gaudin, who was the son of a Pentecostal minister. Nelson decided that mainstream churches were too limiting, and he'd developed his own scriptures where disciples lived as simply as possible, wandering across the state, gypsy-like, to find what they needed to survive. Which was probably why Parker and Rocky were so good at living for weeks on end in the Bitterroot Mountains.

Jude pieced together the stories and rumors some of the members had given Brady from what Parker had told them later. It seemed the two brothers, Tango and Parker, had joined the movement sometime in the very late eighties, becoming completely indoctrinated by the charismatic leader, pledging never to leave. Then a young, impressionable and very beautiful Dimitra had joined the group, and the two brothers had both instantly fallen in love with her. She eventually chose Tango, but Aria was left to wonder if Parker's accusations had been true, and she still held a candle for the older brother. It was soon after Dimitra had given birth to Iliana that she began to question Nelson's doctrines, deciding that the commune was no place to bring up a child. But by that stage, Nelson had become insecure and narcissistic, guarding his members jealously, and not allowing them to leave of their own free will. Three years later, Aria had been born, and Dimitra had become desperate to get out. She finally convinced Tango that they needed to leave, but as they were escaping through the forest, Parker had caught up to them, intent on stopping them. He and Tango had fought, both of them were injured, but finally Parker had struck Tango over the head with a large branch, knocking him unconscious.

The stories became a little unclear after that. All that the cult members knew was that Parker returned empty-handed, and Tango and his family disappeared. How Dimitra had managed to get her injured husband and two young children out of there on her own was anybody's guess. Parker had risen through the ranks, and on Nelson's deathbed a year ago, he'd been named supreme leader. It was probably then that Parker's long-held hatred had resurfaced. Now he had the power to do whatever he wished. He believed that at least one, or perhaps both of the Cusack sisters, were his biological children. And he'd come to claim what was his, believing that his version of God would grant him immortality, if only he could be reunited with his true progeny.

After that, it was more conjecture than anything else that filled in the blanks of the remaining years of the Cusack family. Word around the cult was that Tango had always been a little on the paranoid side, it was one of the ways Nelson gained his followers, by appealing to that absence of self-confidence in certain people, giving them something they believed they lacked in return. Jude surmised that perhaps Tango had received a brain injury when he'd been knocked unconscious, exacerbating his paranoia and ruining any presence of mind.

But one thing they both agreed on was that Tango's warnings that Parker would come back one day had held true. In his own mixed-up way, Tango had been trying to protect her. Even that day a few weeks ago, when she'd turned up on his front veranda and he'd told her to scram, he'd been trying to scare her away from the imminent danger he knew was lurking around him. She felt great sorrow at how his life had deteriorated until he'd become too insular and scared to venture out into the world. It was a sad legacy to leave behind. Jude had finally revealed the extent of Tango's stabbing injuries, and the only explanation he could come up with was that Parker hated his brother so much, that even after he died from the poison, he couldn't bear to leave his body intact. A crime of passion and loathing indeed.

No one knew exactly why Parker had come to Stevensville to murder Dimitra all those years ago. Perhaps he'd been trying to force a confession out of her. Or perhaps he'd been trying to convince her to come back to Colorado with him and flown into a jealous rage when she refused. The reasons would forever remain as conjecture and nothing more.

"I'm glad we finally have an answer," she said, leaning into Jude, resting her head on his shoulder. He smelled like the outdoors, woodsy and earthy and fresh, like the wind. His lips rested in her hair, and a buzz of electricity flowed through her at his soft, unassuming touch.

Sitting up, she gave him a sideways glance, arching her eyebrow coyly. She liked what she saw, the way his broad shoulders filled out his brown shirt and a sudden urge to touch him ran through her. So strong she couldn't resist. She ran her hands up the length of his arms and over his bulging biceps. Oh, my. Those biceps. They were to die for.

Thinking about starting a new chapter in her life, she decided that tonight was the night this self-imposed celibacy was going to come to an end. Tonight was definitely time to start again. With Jude.

She leaned in to capture his lips with hers, letting her desire funnel through her lips, letting him know how much she wanted him. Hadn't stopped wanting him. But now she was ready to share her body with him wholly and freely once more, with no guilt about secrets or lies to hold her back. He'd said over and over how much he wanted her, and wanted to be a father to her baby.

Now was the time to finally let him in. Let him know how much she loved him, and how she wanted to spend the rest of her life with him. To have a family with him. To grow old with him.

"Are you sure?" he asked, raising an eyebrow as her fingers found the buttons on his shirt.

"Oh, yes, Mr. Wilder," she breathed. "I've never been surer of anything in my whole life."

CHAPTER NINETEEN

Jude held his breath. He'd been too scared to even dream about this moment. Aria unbuttoned his shirt, slowly, seductively. The second she shoved his shirt down over his shoulders and raked her fingernails down his chest, he was hard. He'd been holding back his feelings, his urges, for weeks now, and it felt like he might actually burst out of his trousers.

Aria had needed time. And he'd been happy to give it to her. Hell, he'd give her as much time as she needed, because he knew she was the woman for him. And he knew she was worth waiting for. But did this mean she'd come to some sort of decision? God, he hoped so, because this not knowing was just about killing him.

She must've seen the hesitation in his eyes, because she took his hands and helped him draw the hem of her sweatshirt over her head, revealing acres of creamy skin. And breasts. Oh, Lord, she had beautiful breasts. He leaned in to suck on each one lightly in turn, eliciting a moan from deep in her chest.

"You are so beautiful," he whispered.

She gave him one of her winning smiles in return. The one where her nose wrinkled up, and he thought a balloon was expanding in his chest. She was so beautiful. The perfect woman for him. Drawing her hand up to his mouth, he kissed each of her fingertips, then took his time, tracing the delicate veins that lined the back of her hand, up the inside of her arm until she twitched and giggled at his touch.

He pulled her in close and caught the hint of roses as he buried his face in her hair. Then his lips trailed down the soft skin of her neck, and his blood pounded in his veins at the feel of her beneath his fingertips. He wanted her, wanted to make love to her, here and now.

Suddenly, she moved to stand before him, looking down with her dark, sultry gaze. With one practiced move, she removed her jeans and underwear, and now she was naked. A growl came from somewhere deep inside at the sight of her.

He began to unbuckle his trousers, but she pushed him back onto the couch. "Let me do it," she commanded. She tugged at his trousers and jocks until they were a puddle of material on the floor, and she was once more standing in front of him. It was too much, all that pale skin and lush curves, and he had to reach up and touch. To run his fingers gently over the curve of her hip, lay his palm over the flat planes of her stomach, then lower to cover her sex. She gasped as his fingers slid in between her legs and launched herself at him, so that she straddled him where he sat on the couch, her knees on either side of his thighs. Hovering above his lap, she looked down into his face.

"Wait," he managed to croak from between gritted teeth. "Is this okay? I mean…" he said, wanting to make sure that whatever they were about to do wasn't going to harm the baby in any way. Because this wasn't going to be slow and easy. This was going to be fast and fiery, and he didn't want to hurt her.

"Of course it is. The doctor said it's fine. I believe his exact words were, *you can have as much vigorous sex as you like.*" Aria rolled her eyes and grimaced. "How to make a patient feel uncomfortable," she added, which would've made Jude laugh if he hadn't been thinking about how good it would feel to be inside Aria. She'd finally gone to see a doctor about her pregnancy—which was progressing normally—and he'd set up an antenatal plan for her and scheduled regular visits to keep a check on her. But all he cared about right now were the words *vigorous sex*.

She reached down and put a hand over his heart. He could feel his own heartbeat inside his chest, strong and fast beneath her palm. "I want this as much as you do," she said huskily. The feeling as she grazed her teeth over the muscle of his shoulder made him just about lose his mind. If Aria said the baby would be fine, then he believed her.

But then another thought entered his head. "Condom," he moaned. "I don't have—"

"We don't need one," she whispered. "The doctor gave me a clean bill of health, and, well...I can't get any more pregnant at the moment."

His hands cupped her bottom as she lifted up on her knees and then settled over him, easing him inside her. Slow at first, so slow it stole his breath.

He couldn't help it, he began to thrust harder, and she moved with him, kissing him in a hungry tangle of tongues.

This. He'd never had *this* before with any other woman. This purely visceral response she drew from him every single time.

Waves of pleasure began to roll over him, his muscles spasming with growing force until he knew he could no longer hold it in.

"Aria," he cried out, suddenly scared he was going too fast, too hard, that he'd reached the crescendo without her.

"Jude," she answered with a moan, head thrown back in ecstasy, long neck exposed. Then she met his gaze, her eyes so dark they were liquid pools of desire, and he crashed over the edge as she followed him down.

It took him seconds, minutes, hours before he came back to himself, his breath still hitching in his throat. She was still straddling his lap, and he held her tight against him, never wanting to let her go, joined together in this blissful contentment forever. She rested her forehead in the crook of his neck, breasts pressed into his chest, her hands grasping his shoulders.

When at last he could control his breathing, he whispered in her ear, "I want to spend the rest of my life right here."

"I think that's a marvelous idea," she murmured back. "Because I want to spend the rest of my life with you." She drew backward a little so she could look him in the eye. "I love you."

His heart squeezed with painful intensity. Those words were from his deepest, darkest dreams. Words he'd been waiting to hear. She'd hinted them back on the day of the ice storm, but they'd both skirted around the emotion ever since. But he knew what he felt. Had known it for what felt like forever.

He'd been holding his own words of love back until she was ready to hear them. And now, it seemed, she finally was.

"I love you, too," he told her, holding her beautiful brown gaze tight within his own. "I want to marry you one day. We fit together perfectly, like we were always meant to be. Every time I look at you, I feel joy. I want this joy to last forever. And when Bunny is born, you and me and the baby will be our own special family." His heart felt like it was fit to burst as he stared up at her.

"I can't believe I was lucky enough to find you," she said, not taking her gaze from his face.

"Me, either," he agreed.

She lifted herself off him and he covered them with a

throw rug as they lay together on the couch, snuggling easily together.

"And I can't believe how far we've come in such a short time," she said, her head resting lightly on his chest.

"Perhaps not such a short time," he mused. "If you count our high school days, we've known each other for over fifteen years."

She lifted her chin and considered him from below lowered lashes for a few moments. "I never told anyone this, but I had the biggest crush on you back in high school."

"See, that proves my point," he exclaimed triumphantly. "We were fated to be together right from the start."

"Maybe," she consented. Then a small grin stole over her lips. "I was so in love with you back then, I even wrote a poem to you on the back of the girls' toilet door. An ode to Jude Wilder."

"You did?" He was genuinely surprised. "That's high praise indeed," he added. "I don't think any other girl ever did that for me." He squeezed the soft roundness of her buttock suggestively. "Do you remember what it said?" he asked, unable to keep the teasing note out of his voice.

"No, I do not," she said, pretending to be prim. "And even if I did, I wouldn't give away my teenage fantasies." She giggled, then hesitated, sucking in a breath. "Back then, I was so young and naïve, merely a girl with a stupid crush. But now… This is real, and big, and important. You know what I mean?"

He studied her for a second. "You're right," he agreed. "This is so much more than I could ever have dreamed of. I can't wait to start our life together. And I can't wait to meet Bunny," he added.

She laid a protective hand across her belly. She'd been doing that more and more lately; a completely maternal action that she probably wasn't even aware of. "Thank you,

Jude. For being you. For coming to find me in an ice storm. For loving me like you do."

"I'd do it all over again," he said, laying his lips alongside her ear.

"I know you would. But let's hope you never have to."

"Amen," he agreed.

CHAPTER TWENTY

One Year Later

Aria sat at the table, watching all the people mill around inside the large dining area, Thea nestled safely in her lap, chewing on a spoon. She could hardly believe all these people were here for her. Well, for her baby, but at her bequest. Thea was three months old today, and it was also the day of her christening.

Naomi swooped in and plucked the baby right out of Aria's arms. "My turn to hold the little munchkin." Thea gurgled with glee in Naomi's arms as she swung her up in the air and then brought the baby's face in close to kiss her cherub cheek. Thea loved Naomi, and Naomi loved Thea back, fiercely and unreservedly. No baby could ask for a better grandmother. Aria felt a twinge of regret that her own mother hadn't lived to see this day. She missed Iliana, too. Missed the possibilities they could've had, the shared families they might've brought up together. She was still sad that Iliana had lost all this when she'd been so young, with her whole life ahead of her. But Aria was learning to accept the good things in life and not dwell on things she couldn't change. And this day was just about as good as it got.

Thea Iliana Cusack was a sight to behold. She smiled so beatifically at Naomi, it brought joy to Aria's heart just to see it. Thea was a bright, bubbly baby, the life of the party, whom everyone wanted to cuddle.

When she and Jude eventually get married next year, they'd already decided to hyphenate Thea's last name to Cusack-Wilder. Aria wanted her daughter to continue the Cusack legacy. Some people might think that perhaps Aria would want to hide the terrible things that'd happened in her life, but Aria wanted to embrace them. What didn't kill you, made you stronger, and so she wanted her daughter to understand the hardships her family had gone through to bring her safely into the world. Aria also wanted Thea to take Jude's name. He was her father in every way that mattered. One day, she'd tell her daughter the truth about her biological father, but she hoped by then, Jude would always be the one she called Dad. And after they were married, Jude would legally adopt Thea as his own daughter. The idea made Aria's heart expand like a balloon.

Penny came over and sat down next to Aria. "Thea's dress is gorgeous," she gushed. "She looked so cute up there in your arms."

"Yes, until she decided she didn't like the minister." Aria frowned, remembering how Thea had screwed up her face and threatened to cry when the minister came near.

"I don't blame her." Penny jumped to Thea's defense. "That man had scary, bushy eyebrows. I didn't much care for him either." Penny made a face and waggled her eyebrows, much like the minister had done, which made Aria laugh. Penny had become a steadfast friend, and it'd been a no-brainer to ask her to become Thea's godmother. Penny had jumped at the chance, squealing in delight when Aria had posed the question. And while Clayton had been taken by surprise when she and Jude had asked him to become Thea's godfather, he'd also graciously accepted. Penny and Clayton were planning a wedding for next year, as well, but Penny had let it slip that they were already trying for a baby, because she couldn't wait that long. And seeing Thea with Aria and Jude, seeing how they were such a happy family together, made her desperate to start a family, too.

The christening had been held at Stargazer, of course. Naomi had insisted and how could Aria argue when Dean and Naomi offered their beautiful lodge, as well as Stella's magic French cooking skills. The christening had been held in the main atrium, with the high ceilings and enormous glass windows soaring above them. Then they'd moved to the restaurant, where everyone was relaxing with a glass of champagne and some of Stella's amazing hors d'oeuvres. The pile of pink-wrapped presents on a table in the corner was making Aria nervous. She'd never seen so many presents in all her life; it was a little embarrassing. But also uplifting to know so many people cared about Thea.

Stella whizzed past with a tray full of little stuffed mushrooms, looking a little frazzled. "I might go and see if I can help," Penny said, catching Stella's eye. She took off in Stella's wake, leaving Aria alone at the table.

"Hello, love of my life." Jude leaned in and kissed her cheek, then took a seat next to her. "Where is the other love of my life?" he asked, taking her hand under the table.

"Naomi has her," she said, squeezing his hand. "I think we should anoint Naomi with granny status. What do you think?" Aria had been considering the notion for a few weeks now. Thea had no natural grandparents of her own, but she was still surrounded by a family of people who loved her. This parenting thing was hard, but there was nothing to say Aria couldn't make up the rules as she went along. And Naomi and Dean fit the bill perfectly to fill the roles of grandparents.

"She's everything a real granny should be, and more," Jude agreed. "I think she'd be over the moon." Good. She was glad Jude agreed with her, because he had a say in every decision she made about Aria's future.

"Which would make Dean a grandad," Aria added with a mischievous wink. Dean had taken to Thea almost as quickly as Naomi, but was he ready to be called a grandad? She was sure Naomi would talk him around, even if he wasn't.

"It was a good day," Jude said, his eyes drifting around the room, watching all the people they cared about enjoying their time together.

"Yes, it was," Aria replied with a tired sigh. The long day was beginning to take its toll. While she couldn't have asked for anything more special and filled with fun and laughter, she needed a bit of alone time with just her and Jude and the baby.

"You ready to go home?" he asked, catching her mood immediately.

"Yes, please," she replied, shifting a lock of her long hair over her shoulder. She'd kept her hair long because Jude liked it so much. But there were days when she wished to cut it all off, especially when Thea caught a handful of it and pulled. Perhaps it was time to get a more grown-up haircut, something more manageable. Aria shrugged lightly. One more thing she was moving on with in her life.

"I'll go find our daughter," Jude said. "You wait here, I'll be back in a sec." He kissed her on the lips before he departed, leaving her with the taste of his love on her tongue, and a promise of what they might get up to once Thea was safely tucked in bed at home.

Home. It was funny that she'd had to come full circle, back to her hometown where she'd sworn she would never return, to find the place where she wanted to stay. Aria had moved into Jude's house only a few weeks after her abduction. Once they'd decided to be together, it'd been a no-brainer for them to move in together.

Jude still visited his mother almost every day. One more thing that made Aria crazy about him. Such a caring, thoughtful man. Edith came for a visit now and then, but it was getting harder to bring her home, as she often forgot where she was, or even who Jude was, which tore her heart open when she saw how it hurt Jude. But the one thing that often brought a little of the old Edith out from behind the hazy curtain of dementia was when they took her into the garden. She'd point out the tomato plants and herb garden with glee, and put the basil leaves Aria picked for her to her nose and inhale the scent deeply. The other thing that brought Edith alive was Thea. The baby fascinated her, and Thea would sit quietly on Edith's knee for long periods of time, just staring up into her face. Those visits were bittersweet. Edith would come home for Christmas this year, but after that, who knew…

They were now renting out the cottage at a very low rate to a young woman who'd recently escaped an abusive marriage. Jude had answered a call about a domestic violence episode a few weeks ago, and the woman had moved in a few days after that. Jude couldn't help himself, he was still bringing his wounded ducks home and he probably always would. Another thing Aria loved about him.

Jude returned, Thea balanced in his arms. She smiled up at them. The man who'd saved her, who'd shown her what true love was, holding their child, who'd shown her that family was what you made it, and the sins of the father didn't have to be revisited on their daughters. She was free to live a full and happy life with the man of her dreams. There was even talk of more children to come. Later. They had plenty of time. The rest of their lives to love each other.

**Want to know more about Stargazer Ranch?
Get your FREE and EXCLUSIVE Prequel Novella
STARDUST**
Read Dean and Naomi's story.

GO TO THIS LINK FOR FREE COPY
dl.bookfunnel.com/mw5jp7zmaf

Stay in touch via my website
www.suzannecass.com

Facebook: www.facebook.com/suzannecassauthor/
Instagram: www.instagram.com/suzanne.cass/
Pintrest: www.pinterest.com.au/suzanne_cass/

If you liked Silverstorm, then you might like the other books in the Stargazer Ranch Series.

Books can be read as stand-alone

Combustion - Prequel Novella

Wildfire - Book 1

Firelight - Book 2

Snowbound: A Christmas Novella Book 3

Snowfall - Book 4

Cloudburst - Book 5

Also by Suzanne Cass
NEW
Stormcloud Station Series
(A Stargazer Spinoff Series)
Small Town Romantic Suspense

Clear Skies
Starlit Skies
Crystal Skies
Dawn Skies
Tangled Skies
Outback Skies

Stargazer Ranch Romance Series
Small Town Romantic Suspense
Combustion: Prequel Novella
Wildfire
Firelight
Snowbound: A Christmas Novella
Snowfall
Cloudburst
Silverstorm

Island Bound Series
Mystery Romance (on an Island)
Books can be read as stand-alone
Bound by Truth
Bound by Silence
Bound by the Stars

Colors of the Earth Series
Small Town Romantic Suspense
Books can be read as stand-alone
Shadows in the Dust
Shadows in Deep Blue

Shadows of Red Earth

Romantic Suspense
Single Title
Island Redemption
Glass Clouds
Chasing Bullets

Love in the Mountains Novella Series
Small Town Short Romance
Novellas can be read as stand-alone
Rain on a Tin Roof
Lost and Found
Rescue his Heart

Please Leave a Review

The greatest gift you could ever give an author is to leave a review. You will be helping other people to discover this book and making a difference to me as an Independently Published Author. If you liked this book and want other people to read it to, please leave a review.

About the Author

Suzanne Cass is an Australian author who writes rural romance and romantic suspense abounding with passion and danger.

Her debut novel, Island Redemption, won the Romance Writers of Australia Emerald Award in 2016. Suzanne was also a finalist in the 2019 Romance Writers of Australia RUBY award.

She had always had a fascination with the tough resilience of people who live in our amazing red-dirt outback country. When not writing about the characters that inhabit her head, Suzanne can be found roaming the Perth beaches with her border collie, or encouraging from the sidelines as her two sons play sport.

Visit her website www.suzannecass.com or subscribe to her newsletter via: www.suzannecass.com/contact

Acknowledgements

I had to revisit Stargazer Ranch one more time as it has become so much a part of me, I wish it were real some days. I also had to tell Jude's story, he wouldn't leave me alone until I did.

Silverstorm is the 6th novel in this series. I enjoyed writing Jude so much, he is such a sweet, generous guy, but he's not afraid to take on the villains to save the people he loves. There is a new term that has been coined recently, a cinnamon roll hero. I think Jude might be one of those, tough, capable, but also agreeable and lovable heroes.

And Aria is such a complex character, determined to go through with her pregnancy against the odds and survive as a single mother, if she has to. (Which, thanks to Jude, she doesn't) I'm so glad these two found each other.

I'd never heard of a silver storm before, but when I started researching ice storms that name came up and I instantly fell in love, hence the title. I do not envy anyone who has to live through an ice storm, that is some seriously dangerous weather.

There is a team of people who I couldn't do this without, beta readers (big thanks to Rebecca, Jennifer, and Ceara for their amazing feedback) and my ARC team, who are essential to an Indie Author like me, for their wonderful reviews. Big thanks to my editor, Nicole at Evermore Editing

To Gary, who doesn't understand this romance gig, but encourages me anyway, and my two sons who are the light of my life.

And to you, the readers, I love to get your feedback and hear how much you enjoy reading about Stargazer Ranch and the different, interconnected characters and their friendships, families and growing love affairs. Thank you for reading my books.